CAPTIVE JUSTICE

Rayven T. Hill

Ray of Joy Publishing
Toronto

Books by Rayven T. Hill
Blood and Justice
Cold Justice
Justice for Hire
Captive Justice
Justice Overdue
Justice Returns
Personal Justice
Silent Justice
Web of Justice
Fugitive Justice

Visit rayventhill.com for more information
on these and future releases.

Published by Ray of Joy Publishing
Toronto

ISBN-13: 978-0-9938625-3-3

CAPTIVE JUSTICE

CHAPTER 1

Tuesday, August 30th, 5:12 p.m.

LINDA GOULD JUGGLED her purse in one hand and a stack of papers in the other as she pushed open the door to the underground parking garage. Another weary workday had ended and she wished only to get home for some much-needed rest.

She stumbled through the doorway and peered across the large space. The light near her vehicle was out again. It always took them days to replace a blown bulb and it was difficult enough to see in this dungeon, even with a full regiment of the low-watt bulbs they insisted on using.

As she trudged across the concrete floor, she fumbled in her purse and removed a ring of keys. She pressed the unlock button on the key fob and heard a distinct click from the direction of her vehicle.

A car thundered past, barely missing her as its horn filled the vast area with an echoing scream. She cursed the driver as she stepped back between two vehicles and watched him go out of sight.

She managed to open the driver-side door of her car and climb behind the wheel without dropping the paperwork. She deposited her burden on the passenger seat and pulled the door closed.

But it didn't close.

It swung back open.

She turned her head and gasped, her eyes frozen on the muzzle of a pistol pointed at her face.

"Get out of the vehicle," a man's voice said.

Her eyes drifted upward, away from the pistol and onto the shrouded face of the gunman. He wore a ski mask, so she couldn't see his face, but his dark eyes were unmoving, fixed impatiently on her, waiting for her to comply with his demand.

The keys slipped from her right hand and jangled to the floor of the vehicle. "What ... what do you want?" she managed to ask, her voice barely a whisper.

A gloved hand gripped her shoulder and, impatiently this time, the voice repeated, "Get out of the vehicle."

She reached for her purse.

"Leave the bag."

She hesitated, and then obeyed, and the man stepped back, allowing her to exit the car. He seized her and spun her around, her arm wrenched behind her back.

She smelled old leather and tasted the pungent flavor of cowhide in her mouth as a gloved hand cut short her attempt to scream. She struggled against her attacker in vain as she was prodded forward and shoved into the back of a windowless van.

Her abductor leaped in behind and forced her to the floor as the vehicle backed from the parking spot.

He rolled her over and pulled her arms behind her back, her face nuzzled against the cold steel of the van floor, stifling her attempt to scream for help. She felt the vibration of the vehicle as it pulled ahead and heard the zip of a cable tie as it tightened about her wrists.

2

His knee dug into her back and held her down as a cloth was tied around her mouth. It felt, and smelled, like fresh linen. At least it was clean and she could breathe. She struggled as a sudden panic swept through her, her hysterical screams becoming an unheard whisper, muffled by the rag around her face.

They traveled for several minutes, the van jostling over manholes and potholes, and then came a screech of brakes as the vehicle ground to a stop and the motor died.

The front door slammed, the side door squealed, and then a voice said, "Grab her feet."

"I can walk," she tried to say, but she couldn't be heard as strong hands seized her legs. Her face scraped against the rough steel as she was dragged halfway out of the van. Other hands gripped her shoulders and lifted her free.

They carried her into a building. She counted the steps, one, two, three, and then across the floor and down a flight of stairs. A musty smell was in her nose, stale, like old oil and rotting concrete.

They set her on her feet, twisted her around, and pushed her into a chair. She looked up at her captors. The second one, the driver, was a little shorter than the first and also wore a black ski mask.

They stood back and watched her a moment as she whimpered and begged with her eyes to be set free.

They ignored her silent pleas and she dropped her eyes a moment and allowed the tears to come. They ran down her face and soaked the cloth she clenched between her shivering teeth.

She raised her head and focused her eyes past her tormentors. She was in a basement somewhere, an old forgotten basement. Piles of rotting junk lined the walls. The floor was of pitted and worn concrete, dead, damp, and decaying. The walls were of a similar state, made of outdated cinder blocks, remnants of another age.

Forgotten habitats of long-dead spiders smothered the overhead beams, with new webs taking their place, expertly woven to the walls and ceiling.

A single naked bulb cast a glare from overhead, the lone ray of light in the windowless room.

The stairs were made of heavy wooden planks, probably repaired sometime in the recent past, the only way to freedom and beyond.

She focused her eyes back on her captors as the tall one pointed and said, "Tie her legs."

The shorter man pulled a pair of cable ties from his pocket and leaned down. She kicked at him but powerful hands held her. The plastic ties bit into her bare ankles and caused her to wince in pain as they held her to the chair.

"Get the rope."

He swept up a yellow nylon rope from the floor and wrapped it several times around her chest and the back of the chair. He tied a knot behind, tested it and grunted. "That should hold her long enough."

The tall man removed a cell phone from his shirt pocket and held it up. "Smile for the camera." She heard a click and then he tucked the phone away.

"Let's go. We have work to do."

She watched as they turned and climbed the steps out of sight. She shivered in the cool, stale atmosphere as a door slammed somewhere above, and then all was quiet except for the thumping of her heart and her frantic breathing.

CHAPTER 2

Tuesday, August 30th, 7:35 p.m.

ANNIE WAS SUNKEN into a comfortable armchair, her feet tucked under her, studying a book on family law. She looked briefly at Jake stretched out on the couch, his head supported by the padded armrest as he watched television. At six feet four inches long he barely fit on the full-sized sofa.

She glanced toward the picture window. A few dark clouds had gathered and a slight wind caused the branches of the large oak out front to dance in the gathering dusk.

"Looks like it's going to rain," she said.

Jake paid no attention.

Matty lay on the floor, a pillow under his head, reading a comic book. He turned and looked outside and then buried himself back in his reading.

She yawned. "You guys are boring."

Matty spoke up. "Mom, you can't be catching bad guys all day long. You need to rest sometime."

Her eight-year-old son was right, of course. They'd had so much excitement recently, much more than they'd ever expected as rookie investigators.

When Jake had lost his job as a construction engineer at

one of Canada's largest land developers due to downsizing, they'd decided to expand Annie's part-time research business into something more lucrative. Her experience was a natural progression into their current enterprise and the couple became Lincoln Investigations.

However, unlike most private investigators, whose job usually involves little more than research and the occasional surveillance job or background check, they'd had more than their fair share of frightening experiences.

And so, she was glad to have some rest, and as much as Jake loved their new vocation, she knew he needed a little downtime as well. Even though they often had to work at odd hours, and sometimes in the evening, she wouldn't trade their line of business for anything. She was pleased to be able to work alongside her husband and was now thankful for the day he'd lost his job.

Jake flicked off the TV, sat up, and looked at his wife. "Did you say something?"

She shrugged one shoulder. "I don't remember."

Jake grunted, stood, and wandered from the room toward the kitchen.

She dropped her book on the stand beside her and went into the office off the front room. She sat in the swivel chair and pulled it a little closer to the desk. Her iMac came to life when she touched the keyboard and she settled in to do some online banking.

Annie was confident in the future of their agency and though money wasn't as tight as it had been, thanks to some recent work they'd done for clients, they still needed to be careful.

The contents of the small office weren't much more than a used desk, a couple of chairs, a bookcase bulging with research materials, and the odd picture on the wall. A filing cabinet, rescued from somewhere, sat beside the desk, a printer perched on top.

Jake wandered in, a chicken drumstick in one hand and a Coke in the other. The guest chair groaned under his two hundred and ten pounds of muscle and bone but held as he settled into place.

Annie leafed through a small stack of papers, slipped out one page, and handed it to him. "Possible insurance fraud. A typical case where a guy claims to have a bad back from a car accident and can't move. The insurance company isn't so sure and wants us to look into it." She pointed to the report. "It's all there."

Jake set his drink down, held the paper with his free hand, and studied it briefly. "It shouldn't be a problem. These guys always mess up, every time. They think they have a new scam nobody has ever heard of before. I should be able to look into it tomorrow." He folded the paper and tucked it into his pocket. "What else do we have on our plate?"

Annie waved toward the stack. "I have enough here to keep me going awhile. Nothing pressing, mainly research."

"No killers to catch?"

Annie laughed. "Not right now."

CHAPTER 3

Wednesday, August 31st, 9:40 a.m.

ARTHUR GOULD HAD been up most of the night. His wife, Linda, hadn't come home and he'd spent the evening and into the wee hours of the morning distraught and calling everyone they knew.

No one had seen her or heard from her.

He was dead tired and though he'd been able to get a couple of hours sleep earlier camped out on the living room couch, he didn't feel rested.

This was unlike Linda. In fact, he'd never known a night in their twelve years of marriage when he hadn't known where she was at just about any given time. The only occasion she'd ever been out all night without him was a few years ago when she'd gone to Montreal for a friend's funeral and had to stay at a hotel.

He picked up the phone once more and called her work. She still hadn't shown and no one at the office had heard from her.

He was overcome with dread; something was definitely wrong. He wanted to call the police but knew they couldn't help until she'd been missing for forty-eight hours.

He felt helpless.

He'd called the clinic and told them he couldn't make it in. A family emergency had come up and they would need to get one of the other doctors to cover walk-in patients and reschedule the ones with appointments.

Though he'd missed dinner the evening before and hadn't wanted any breakfast, he didn't feel especially hungry. He drifted into the kitchen, started a fresh pot of coffee and made a slice of toast. That was all he wanted.

He sat at the kitchen table, the steaming cup in front of him, and nibbled at his snack. *Where is she? Something is terribly wrong.*

When the phone rang, it startled him, and he sprang from his chair and swept up the receiver. He expected to hear Linda's sweet voice on the line explaining what had happened and that she was okay.

He knew something dreadful was taking place the moment he heard his name spoken through a voice changer.

"Dr. Arthur Gould?" the freakish voice asked in a deep, disguised tone.

"Yes, this is Dr. Gould."

"I have your wife."

His nightmare was coming true. "Where is she? Is she all right?" He spoke in a frenzied tone.

"Relax, doctor. Your wife is fine."

"Why do you have her? What do you want?"

"Well, Dr. Gould, I'm glad you asked." The manufactured voice chuckled. "I want money, of course."

"You mean, like ransom?"

"Now you're catching on. Exactly like ransom."

"How ... how much?"

"How much do you have? Doctor." He emphasized the last word.

Arthur Gould was silent. What kind of game was this guy playing?

The voice continued, "How much is your wife worth?"

What was he supposed to say? How could he answer a question like that?

"You're hesitating, doctor. Is she of no value to you?"

"No, no, of course she is," Dr. Gould said. "I just don't know what to say."

The weird voice laughed and then said, "I'm not greedy."

Dr. Gould was silent.

The unnatural voice became more ominous, more serious. "I want one hundred thousand dollars. Is your wife worth that much, doctor?"

"Yes, yes, of course she is."

"Then we don't have a problem, am I right?"

"No problem," the doctor said carefully. "We don't have a problem."

"Wonderful. I knew you'd see it my way."

Dr. Gould waited.

"Now, I have some simple instructions for you."

"Yes?"

"Obviously I want cash. And you have until this afternoon to get it. Is that a problem?"

Arthur Gould paced back and forth in the kitchen. He knew he could arrange it easily. He said, "It's not a problem."

"Good. Good." Breathing rasped over the line and then the voice continued, "Do you love your wife, doctor?"

"Yes, yes, of course I do."

"Then you won't call the police, am I right?"

The doctor's mind was whirling. He had to get his wife

home safely and wasn't sure what he would do, but right now he couldn't afford to disagree with the kidnapper. He said, "I won't call the police."

"Excellent. Then everything should go smoothly."

"How can I be sure my wife is okay?"

"I thought you might ask. I'll send you a picture of her. Give me your cell phone number."

Dr. Gould gave him the number and then ran to his office for his cell. In a minute, a picture appeared on the screen. His wife was tied to a chair, a gag in her mouth, and her frightened eyes seemed to be pleading to him. He fought back his anger and tried to remain calm. He couldn't afford for anything to go wrong.

"Are you still there, doctor?"

"I'm here."

"So, you can see your wife is fine?"

"Yes, yes. Please, don't hurt her."

"I have no plans to hurt her. However, her ultimate fate is in your hands. If you follow my instructions perfectly, then your wife will be fine. Otherwise ..."

"I'll do exactly what you say."

Another strange laugh. "Now, this is where it gets interesting."

"Yes?"

"I want someone else to deliver the money."

"Someone else," the doctor repeated. "Who?"

"Jake Lincoln."

"Jake Lincoln? I don't know him."

"He's a private investigator."

"How will I find him?"

"Look in the phone book, doctor."

"Why him?"

"I have my reasons. Now, are you going to do as I ask?"

Dr. Gould didn't hesitate. He had no choice. "Yes of course. I'll find him."

"Good, good. You'll contact him and then I'll call him with my instructions later."

"What if he refuses?"

Another maniacal laugh sounded. "He won't refuse."

The doctor thought a moment. "How can I contact you if—?"

"There'll be no more contact between us, doctor. From now on I deal with Jake Lincoln. Your instructions are simple. Contact Lincoln, get the money to him, and then it's out of your hands."

Arthur Gould hesitated.

"Do you understand?"

He had no choice. "Yes, I understand."

"There's one more thing, doctor."

"Yes?"

"If anything goes wrong, your wife will die."

The line went dead as Arthur Gould sank into a chair and trembled, helpless and afraid.

CHAPTER 4

Wednesday, August 31st, 9:56 a.m.

ALL THAT COULD BE seen of Jake was his feet sticking out from underneath his pride and joy, a 1986 Pontiac Firebird.

He had heard a light rattle from underneath the engine, a sound not one in a hundred people would notice, but Jake had, and it needed to be fixed.

He turned his head and saw Annie's running shoes step inside the garage and move in his direction.

"Phone call for you," she said.

He pushed with his feet and the creeper rolled him out from under the vehicle. He stood, wiped his hands on a rag, and asked, "Who is it?"

"He wouldn't say. He only wants to speak to you, and he called on the house line," Annie said as she handed him the cordless phone.

"Hello?" Jake said into the phone.

"Is this Jake Lincoln?"

"Yes."

"Are you a private investigator?"

"Yes, who is this?"

The man spoke in a feverish tone. "My name is Gould, Dr. Arthur Gould, and my wife … she's been kidnapped."

Jake looked at Annie, touched the speaker button and whispered to her, "His wife's been kidnapped." He spoke into the phone, "Have you called the police, Dr. Gould?"

"No, I'm not sure what to do. He … the kidnapper said not to call the police."

Jake hesitated and then said, "The police should always be notified. They've had experience in this and they know exactly how to proceed without letting the kidnapper know they're involved."

Silence on the line.

Jake continued, "Perhaps you should let the police handle it, but we're happy to do what we can to help if they're unable to catch the kidnapper."

"There's more to it than that, Mr. Lincoln."

Jake waited.

"He's holding her for ransom and he told me to contact you. He wants you to deliver the ransom money."

Jake looked at Annie. She looked back at him and cocked her head. Jake frowned and said, "That's an unusual request."

"I realize that," the doctor said. "But he was insistent."

Jake thought a moment, trying to gauge Annie's thoughts. Dr. Gould was impatient. "Will you do it?"

Jake watched Annie nod and he spoke into the phone. "I'll do it."

The doctor sighed in relief. "Thank you, Mr. Lincoln."

Annie whispered to Jake, "How much?"

"How much money is he demanding?" Jake asked the doctor.

"One hundred thousand dollars."

14

Jake raised a brow and asked, "Can you get the money today?"

"Yes, I'd thought it might be more but I can get it immediately."

"Did you get any instructions yet as to when or where the exchange should take place?"

"He said I must get the money and get it to you by this afternoon and he'll call you."

Jake looked at his watch. "Then we'd better hurry," he said. "Perhaps my wife and I should come and see you right away."

"Your wife?"

"My wife and I are partners and it's best if we both come to interview you."

"Very well, then."

"We'll come over now."

Jake found a pencil and an envelope on the workbench, scribbled down Dr. Gould's address and phone number, and hung up the phone.

The couple looked at each other and Jake frowned. "We'd better get there right away."

CHAPTER 5

Wednesday, August 31st, 10:22 a.m.

DR. GOULD'S HOUSE was situated in what was once an old neighborhood, the houses built back when land was cheap and the lots were large. In recent years, the older houses had been torn down one by one, and the rich and the newly rich were coming in, tearing down the old, and building luxurious new dwellings.

Jake pulled the Firebird into the triple-width driveway and stopped beside a BMW. They climbed from the vehicle and went up the stone driveway, past the immaculately landscaped front lawn and onto a large verandah.

Annie clanked the knocker and the door was opened almost immediately.

Dr. Gould was in his midthirties, but the stress evident on his face made him appear a decade older, and as he invited them in, he sighed deeply and pointed through an archway toward the front room.

Jake sat carefully on a couch in front of a large bay window. Annie sat beside him, leaned forward, and waited until the doctor settled into a matching armchair.

Annie spoke first. "Dr. Gould, I want to say how deeply

we feel for you in this situation. I'm aware how hard this is for you and I assure you, our top priority is to get your wife back. Apprehending the kidnapper is secondary and we'll in no way endanger your wife."

Dr. Gould nodded slowly. "The money is no problem to me. The kidnapper said if anything goes wrong my wife will die. When I weigh the value of money against the value of my wife's life, there's absolutely no comparison."

"Our concern," Jake said, "is that your wife be returned safely. The problem is, we have no way of guaranteeing the kidnapper will keep his word and let your wife go free once he receives the payment."

Annie said, "All kidnapping is serious, but he's made a threat on your wife's life, and I'm afraid he might be willing to carry it out."

The doctor drew a sharp breath. "So, what do you suggest?"

"The question is this," Annie said. "Should we call the police and endanger her life, or is her life in more danger if we don't call them? That's something you have to decide."

"What's your opinion?"

Jake glanced at Annie and then addressed the doctor. "I believe the best plan is to bring the police in on this. They're well trained to handle these situations."

Dr. Gould gave a small nod and stared out the front window. Annie could almost see his mind weighing his options, knowing his wife's life was at stake.

"I ... I can't make that decision right now," the doctor said. "I'll need awhile."

"Of course," Annie said.

Jake asked, "Doctor, did the kidnapper say why he wanted me to deliver the ransom?"

Dr. Gould shook his head. "He said he had his reasons."

Annie's brow wrinkled in thought. "Perhaps he wanted someone emotionally unattached to the situation."

"Then he picked the wrong guy," Jake said.

Dr. Gould looked worried.

Annie explained. "What Jake means is, he's already emotionally attached. We both are, but obviously not as much as you. I'm just speculating, but he's clearly aware of who we are and he might think that as professionals we'll do everything exactly as he wants."

The doctor nodded and Jake changed the subject. "Doctor, did you by any chance recognize the kidnapper's voice?"

"No, he used one of those voice-changing machines. It came through deep and unnatural."

"Did anything in his wording sound familiar perhaps?"

"I … I wasn't listening for that. I was in too much of a panic to pay any attention, but offhand I have to say no."

"It's unlikely he would give himself away like that, but you never know," Jake said.

The doctor sprang to his feet and dashed from the room. He returned a moment later with a cell phone. "I almost forgot; he sent me a picture of my wife." He swiped across the screen a couple of times, took a deep breath as he looked at a photo, and then handed the phone to Jake.

Annie leaned over and looked at the picture on the screen. A woman was tied securely to a chair, a gag in her mouth. Annie winced at how frightened the woman appeared.

"Can we take this phone?" she asked. "The picture was likely sent from a burner phone. It's unlikely he would use one that can be traced but just in case …"

"Yes, please take the phone. It's my private number, so if anyone calls, tell them I'm unavailable."

Annie took another look at the photo, shut the phone off, and tucked it into her handbag. "We have someone who can take a look at it. I'll get it back to you as soon as possible."

"Dr. Gould," Jake said. "We need to know when your wife was last seen, and where."

"She left work at the usual time last night, just after five o'clock, and hasn't been seen since. She always parks in the underground parking area but whether or not she'd driven away, I ... I don't know."

"Where does she work?"

"She's a paralegal for a small firm a few blocks away. I'll get the address." He went into the den off the front room and returned a moment later with an address book. He leafed through it and handed it to Annie.

She removed a pad and pen from her handbag and jotted the information down. The firm's name was "Williams & Thresh," and she recognized the office building where they were located.

"What kind of car does she drive?"

"It's a silver Toyota Corolla. Brand new."

"We'll check this out right away," Annie said as she scribbled in her pad. "Again, it's unlikely we'll find anything, but I want to see if her car is still in the underground parking."

"How'll that help?" Dr. Gould asked.

"It might not, but we have to check all possibilities. He might have slipped up somewhere."

"Of course."

"Do you have a house line as well? We might need to contact you."

"Yes," the doctor replied. He gave Annie the phone number and she jotted it down.

"There's not much else we can do until the kidnapper calls," Jake said.

"I'll contact my bank right away and get them to put together the cash," the doctor said. "It might take them some time to get that much but I'm sure there'll be no problem."

Jake looked at his watch. "You should do it right away."

The doctor nodded and then asked, "Mr. Lincoln, would you come to the bank with me later when I pick it up? I would feel safer with you there."

"I will if possible," Jake said. "However, I need to get back home and stay there until I hear from the kidnapper. We have three phones: the house line, the line for Lincoln Investigations, and my cell phone. We have no idea which number he's going to use."

"I'll give you a call before I go," the doctor said. "If not, I might be able to get a guard from the bank to accompany me."

Annie stood and said, "If there's nothing else you think we need to know, we'll get on this right now and let you know how things proceed."

Dr. Gould stood. "Please, please get my wife back safely."

Annie touched his arm. "We'll do everything possible, doctor."

CHAPTER 6

Wednesday, August 31st, 11:14 a.m.

WHEN JAKE AND ANNIE arrived home, Annie grabbed her keys from the house and jumped into her Ford Escort. Her destination was a few blocks away and after a couple of turns, she pulled in front of a row of townhouses, ran up the steps of number 633 and rang the doorbell.

Jeremiah Everest was known by his friends as Geekly, and when he answered the door the reason was obvious. With dirty-blond hair over his ears, his feeble goatee, a face that spelled "geek," and John Lennon glasses, he more than looked the part.

He and Jake had been unlikely friends since high school and his expertise had been useful to their investigations several times in the past.

He answered the door with a graceful flourish. "Hello, my dear lady. Come into my humble abode."

Annie followed him into what was supposed to be a living room but rather was a forest of all things electronic. Computer parts took up space on bowing shelves, with mice, keyboards, and equipment of all shapes and sizes littering every corner. DVDs, drives, and cables bulged from neatly labeled boxes.

A television sat on a small table and faced a well-used easy chair, the only indications this room was more than a geek's paradise.

"It's a good thing you called first," Geekly said as he kicked aside a carton of electronic stuff and dragged an extra chair over for Annie. "I was just about to head out."

"I won't take up much of your time," she said as she sat and pulled Dr. Gould's cell phone from her purse.

"It's no prob. It's nothing I can't do later." He held out his hand. "Let's see what you have there."

She brought the photo up on the screen and handed the phone to Geekly. "What can you tell me about this photo?"

Geekly frowned at the picture. "What's this, a kidnapping?"

Annie nodded. "Yes, it is."

"Well, let's get right on it."

He spun around and pulled a box from a shelf, dug inside, and came up with a data cable. "I'll just transfer this image to my computer, then we can take a look at the metadata," he said as he plugged one end of the cable into the phone and the other into the USB port of his Mac Pro.

He clicked the mouse a few times and the image appeared on the monitor.

A couple more clicks and a window popped up, filled with technical data. Annie had no idea what she was looking at, but knew it must contain information on the photo.

"This is the Exif metadata," Geekly explained. "It's

22

contained within the image file itself and has information that relates to the image."

Annie leaned forward for a better look.

Geekly touched the screen. "Phones contain a GPS system, but just as I was afraid, on this phone the GPS/Location setting appears to have been turned off." He glanced at Annie. "I can't tell you where this photo was taken, only when. There's a lot of other useless information pertaining to this image and the only other thing that might help is the unique ID number of the device."

"ID number?"

"Yeah, every phone has its own identification." He turned back to the keyboard, and in a moment a small application loaded. He glanced at her and grinned. "I have some special software I can use." He chuckled. "Not publicly available software, of course."

"That's why I came to you," Annie said with a smile.

Geekly copied a string of numbers and letters from the first window, pasted it into a box in the second, and sat back. In a moment, another window popped up. "Looks like a burner phone."

Annie's shoulders slumped. "I was afraid of that."

"With the ID number, this software helps me track down the phone number as well." He grabbed a pad and jotted down a number and then handed her the paper, crossed his arms, and leaned back. "The only other thing I have is the timestamp. The photo was taken yesterday at seventeen forty-four, so that's five forty-four in the afternoon."

Annie thought a moment. "So, it looks like she was abducted right after work." She stood. "I'd love to stay and chat a bit, but this is rather time-sensitive and I have to go."

Geekly stood. "Come back when you can stay longer. Bring that lunk of a husband with you, too."

Annie smiled, and said, "You've been a big help, Jeremiah." She turned toward the door and he let her out.

She climbed in her car, removed her cell phone from her handbag, and dialed the phone number Geekly had given her.

It rang three times and then she heard breathing on the line.

"Hello?" she said.

A voice asked, "Who's this?"

She thought quickly. "I'm taking a survey. Would you have a minute to answer a few questions?"

"What about?"

"About … the amount of time you spend on the phone on a daily basis."

She heard a laugh, then silence, and then, "Not very much. This ain't even my phone."

"Could I speak to the owner of the phone?"

"Dunno who it is. Well, maybe I'm the owner now. Somebody throwed it away and I found it."

Annie frowned. "Can you tell me where you found it?"

"You ain't gonna take it away from me, are you?"

"No, you may keep the phone. I just need to know where you got it."

"It were in a garbage bin."

"Where was the bin?"

"In the alley."

Annie rolled her eyes but spoke patiently. "What alleyway? Do you know the name of the street?"

"Yup, right off Benson."

"Downtown?"

"Yup."

That was in an older part of the city and several minutes' drive away from the area where Mrs. Gould worked.

"I gotta go now," the voice said. "And I'm gonna keep the phone."

"Thanks for your help." Annie hung up. The kidnapper had tossed the phone in a dumpster after using it, so that was a dead-end lead. She was disappointed, but not surprised.

CHAPTER 7

Wednesday, August 31st, 11:44 a.m.

AFTER ANNIE HAD LEFT, Jake parked the Firebird in the garage and went inside the house to wait for the kidnapper's call.

When the phone rang in the office, he hurried in, flicked a switch to activate a recorder, and snatched up the receiver.

"Lincoln Investigations," he said.

A deep synthetic voice spoke. "Jake Lincoln?"

It was him.

"This is Jake Lincoln."

"It's nice to hear your voice again."

Again? What did he mean by again? "Do I know you?" Jake asked.

A deep, rasping chuckle came over the line. "Now, that would be telling, wouldn't it?"

If this guy wanted to play some kind of game, Jake wasn't interested. "Can we get down to business?"

"Business? I'm happy to hear you're approaching this with the right attitude."

Jake sat in the swivel chair, leaned forward, and spoke. "You know what I mean."

"You're right to call this a business transaction. An exchange of valuable goods for a financial consideration. Wouldn't you call that business, Jake? I can call you Jake, can't I?"

"Call me what you want," Jake said. "And what should I call you?"

A weird laugh, and then the voice said, "You don't need to call me anything. All you need to do is listen."

"I'm listening."

"We must get down to business."

"It might be business for you, but for the victims it's much more than that. You're playing with their personal lives."

"Oh, but money and life are linked. You can't have life without money."

"How so?" Jake asked.

"Well, Jake, just for the purpose of illustration, let's say you need a doctor or you'll die. Perhaps you need a heart transplant. Can you get that without money? Of course not. The doctor holds you hostage and if you have no money, you die."

Jake was silent.

The kidnapper continued, "Or perhaps you're starving to death. You need food or you'll die. Can you walk into a grocery store and help yourself? Of course not. They hold you hostage because, without money, you die."

"It's not the same thing," Jake said. "It's not even close."

"Oh, but it is, Jake. Money is life. I could give you many more illustrations. Perhaps you need a lawyer to keep you out of prison, where you'd likely die. Can you get a lawyer without money?"

"You can always get government assistance."

"Sure you can, but that's still money. Money, wherever it comes from, buys life."

"You're crazy."

"The world is crazy, Jake." The caller took a deep, rasping breath. "Can you buy clothes, or shelter, without money? Of course not. Without them you die of exposure."

Jake interrupted, "I've heard enough. Dr. Gould is willing to meet your demands."

A deep sigh came over the line. "I'm sure the good doctor told you my price already. One hundred thousand dollars."

"Yes, he did."

"And did he mention to you, this would go much smoother if the police weren't involved?"

"No one has notified the police."

"Ah, excellent." There was a pause. "And, of course, I feel I must mention the obvious. The funds must be cash, small, unmarked bills and no trackers or bugs anywhere."

"Of course," Jake said. "Dr. Gould is prepared to do what you ask. He only wants to see his wife returned safely."

"I understand how he feels. It would be a shame for anything to happen to such a wonderful woman. I've actually grown rather attached to her myself." The kidnapper laughed, creepy and deep.

Jake gritted his teeth but didn't speak.

The kidnapper continued, "I need your cell phone number, Jake. I'll need to contact you later and it would be a shame if you were unavailable."

Jake gave him the number and then asked, "Where and when do you want me to deliver the money?"

"Does the good doctor have the funds ready yet?"

"He has arranged to pick it up this afternoon."

"Excellent." An eerie chuckle sounded and then the voice

28

continued, "I can almost picture the reunion of the Goulds now. They make a lovely couple, Jake. Just a lovely couple."

Jake clenched a fist and said nothing.

"Are you there, Jake?"

"I'm waiting for your delivery instructions."

"All in good time, my friend. All in good time. You'll get the information when I feel it's appropriate and not before. Nothing personal, Jake, but it's business. I'm sure you understand my position. We're very much alike, you know?"

"You're nothing but a criminal and a lowlife. We're not at all alike."

"Oh, but we are, Jake. And you needn't make this so personal. Name calling will never do." There was silence a moment. "You care what happens to dear Mrs. Gould, as I do. I would be amiss if I led you to believe otherwise. I shudder to think what might happen should anything go wrong with our ... business arrangement."

"Nothing will go wrong if you keep your end of the bargain, I assure you."

The unearthly voice took on an ominous tone. "I'm counting on it, Jake, and I'm counting on you. I'll call you back this afternoon. Shall we say, four o'clock?"

"I'll be waiting."

The deep, abnormal voice continued, "And now, we must say goodbye. I look forward to speaking with you again soon."

And then the line went dead.

CHAPTER 8

Wednesday, August 31st, 11:57 a.m.

WILLIAMS & THRESH was located on the second floor of a small plaza in the northern part of the city. The vehicle entrance to the underground parking was at one end of the plaza, but a key card was required to open a large metal door to gain access.

Annie parked in the customer parking area and waited a few minutes for a car to enter or exit the garage, but none did, so she went into the main entranceway, where a set of stairs led up to the second floor.

Off to her right was the pedestrian entrance to the garage. She opened the door and took a flight of stairs into the cool underground area.

The garage held two rows of cars, perhaps fifty slots in all, most in use. She glanced around for a silver Toyota Corolla.

She crossed the floor to a darkened area and wandered down the row of vehicles. Then she saw it.

When she peeked in the driver-side window, she saw a

stack of paperwork on the passenger seat, a woman's handbag weighing down the pile.

She pulled a pair of surgical gloves from her pocket, slipped them on, and tested the door handle. It was unlocked. She went to the passenger side, opened the door, and examined the stack of file folders containing what looked like legal forms.

Then she spied the ring of keys on the floor. She left them there.

She knew then that this was where the abduction had taken place.

She examined the bench and floor of the backseat and found nothing unusual. Taking out her cell phone, she snapped a few photos of the front seat, the keys, the papers, and the outside of the vehicle.

Even if the police weren't notified before payment was made and Mrs. Gould was released, they would be called in after, so she was careful not to disturb anything. It was evidence, and she thought it best to leave everything exactly as she found it, but she was a little worried about leaving the handbag in full view. If someone were to happen along, it wouldn't be safe and it might contain money or credit cards.

She locked the car doors, closed them, and hoped there would be a second set of keys at the Gould house.

She wandered around the garage and checked the corners, walls, and above the doors. She was looking for cameras, but there didn't appear to be any type of security at all.

For a vehicle to exit to the street, a key card was not required. All that was necessary was for the driver to stop a few feet from the door and press a red button, and the door would open. She pushed the button to test it and the door slid up. After about thirty seconds it closed automatically.

What she couldn't tell was whether or not the abductor's vehicle had been inside or waiting outside. If there were two kidnappers it would be possible to gain access to the area through the pedestrian door, and then open the garage door from inside to allow a vehicle to enter.

She assumed the kidnapper had used a vehicle. It seemed likely.

It was clear now that the abductor, or abductors, had known where Mrs. Gould worked and had lain in wait and then kidnapped her.

They also had to have known about the lack of security and how easy it was to get a vehicle in and out of the underground parking.

She made her way from the building back to her vehicle and drove toward home.

~*~

JAKE WAS STILL in the office when Annie arrived. She stepped inside the house and called his name.

"In here."

She went into the office and sat in the guest chair.

"The kidnapper called," Jake said.

Annie leaned forward. "And?"

"He's insane."

Annie waited.

"He never gave me any delivery instructions. He just talked on and on about how this was business."

"So then, he'll call back. What line did he call on?"

Jake pointed to the phone on the desk. "This one."

"Did you record it?"

"Yup," Jake said as he swung around. He poked a button on a digital recorder sitting on a shelf behind him.

Annie listened intently while the conversation was played back. When it was finished, she said, "You're right. He's insane."

"With an insane philosophy." Jake shut off the recorder and turned back. "How did your trip go?"

Annie repeated the information Geekly had given her and recounted how she'd called the burner phone.

Jake asked, "Do you think there's any point in trying to find that phone?"

Annie shook her head. "I don't think so. Firstly, if the kidnapper was careful enough to use a throwaway phone, as well as turn the GPS off, it's unlikely he would be careless enough to leave fingerprints all over it."

"I suppose you're right."

"Secondly, we don't have the time right now. Rounding up the guy who found it could be a time-consuming task."

"We'll leave that for the police. Once they're called in, assuming the kidnapper gets away with this thing, they'll want to follow every possible lead."

"All we have is the area where the phone was tossed away, but that doesn't necessarily mean Mrs. Gould is being held near there. He could've dumped it anywhere."

"Let's take another look at that photo. Can you download it to the computer?" Jake asked.

Annie pulled Dr. Gould's cell phone from her handbag. "I'll email it to myself. That's the easiest way."

In a couple of minutes she had the photo on the monitor, blown up full-sized. Jake leaned in. "Look at the age of the walls behind her, and the floor." He pointed to the screen. "And you can just barely see the ceiling beams, but enough to tell that's an old building, and it very well could be near Benson Avenue where the phone was found."

"Yes, but there are a lot of old buildings there. It could be any of hundreds."

Jake thought a moment, and then squinted at the monitor. "Look at the beams again. They aren't strong enough to support more than a two-story building. In anything over that, they would've used metal beams, or in a building that old, possibly much stronger wooden ones."

"That narrows it down a bit more," Annie said. "It's a start, anyway."

Jake nodded and sat back. "What about Mrs. Gould's car? Did you find it?"

"Yes. It was in the underground parking of the building where she works." She recounted what she'd found and ended with, "There's no indication of how the abduction took place, but because her papers, purse, and keys were inside the vehicle, I assume she was heading home when they kidnapped her."

"And with easy access to the parking area," Jake added, "it would be a simple task."

Annie stared at the ceiling and frowned. "I wonder why she was chosen."

"Because the Goulds have money."

"Yes, but why her specifically?"

Jake shrugged. "Probably just the luck of the draw."

Annie glanced at the phone and then back at Jake. "You're probably right. I didn't hear anything on the recording that might indicate she was targeted in any way."

"Now we have to wait for the kidnapper to call back, but first I'll call Dr. Gould," Jake said as he picked up the phone.

He explained their findings to the doctor and arranged to go to the bank with him later in the afternoon.

Annie looked at her watch. "And now, let's have some lunch."

CHAPTER 9

Wednesday, August 31st, 12:54 p.m.

DETECTIVE HANK CORNING was at his desk in the Richmond Hill Police Department when the call came in. It was transferred to him immediately.

The caller's name was Dr. Arthur Gould and he was reporting the abduction of his wife, Linda Gould.

Hank leaned forward, grabbed a pen, and scribbled down the address. He assured the doctor it was top priority, and a detail would be there immediately.

He hung up the phone, memorized the address, and then spun around. "Callaway, we have a kidnapping. I need your guys on this right away." He handed Callaway the address. "Get there ASAP."

"Right away, Hank."

Callaway was a whiz with all things technical. Whether it was computer related or involved installing a wire or other recording device, Callaway was the one everyone turned to to get the job done.

Hank sat back and contemplated the grim situation. He was always affected personally when people preyed on others, and this was no exception.

Though he usually worked alone, he would swallow his pride and get Simon King to help on this one. He'd teamed up once before with the greasy-haired cop. He didn't like him and didn't like being around him, but this was no time for personal feelings to get in the way.

He dialed King's cell.

"Detective King."

"King, it's Hank. We have a kidnapping. You busy right now?"

"Just talking to a CI. Nothing that can't wait."

Hank gave him Dr. Gould's address. "Get there right away. I'll meet you there."

King assured him he would, and Hank hung up the phone and strode from the precinct.

Being a modest-sized city, Richmond Hill had a small robbery/homicide division. Kidnapping fell under its jurisdiction, and Hank, as head of robbery/homicide, pretty much ran things the way he saw fit. As long as he got the job done, the captain gave him a lot of leeway.

King's car was already pulled up to the curb in front of the Gould home when Hank got there. King jumped from the vehicle and joined him.

Hank frowned at King's stringy, unkempt hair, the three days worth of beard on his face, and his sloppy clothes. "You better not sit on the sofa," he said.

King laughed. "When you work in narcotics, you have to fit in."

Hank grunted. "Well, at least tuck in your shirt." He stepped onto the pathway leading to the house. "I apologize for dragging you away from your friends, but this is urgent."

King shrugged. "It's all the same to me."

Hank rapped the doorknocker and stood back. The man

who answered the door a moment later looked curiously at King, then turned his gaze to Hank.

They introduced themselves, and the doctor ushered them into the foyer and said, "I was unsure about calling you at first. The kidnapper said not to call the police, but I'm concerned about my wife's safety." He motioned toward the living room.

King eyed the sofa, glanced at Hank, and then sat down carefully. Hank sat at the other end and leaned forward as Dr. Gould took a seat in a matching chair.

Hank slipped a notepad from his inner jacket pocket. "Now, tell us from the beginning everything you can."

Dr. Gould related how his wife hadn't come home the night before and how the kidnapper had called that morning.

"The technical experts are on their way," Hank said. "They'll tap into your phone line and record any conversations."

"Detective, the kidnapper said he won't call here anymore. From now on, all calls will be to a private investigator named Jake Lincoln."

Hank frowned, sat back, and twiddled with his pen. He and Jake had been friends for a long time, ever since high school, when they'd been teammates on the school football team.

After that, Hank had wanted to be a cop. Jake had toyed with the idea, but since he and Annie had been a couple at the time, and she would be going to the University of Toronto, that had clinched it for Jake. He had gone there as well.

"I've already contacted Mr. Lincoln," the doctor continued. "He called me back a few minutes ago. He'd heard from the kidnapper but he doesn't know I called you."

"I know the Lincolns well," Hank said. "I'll talk to Jake right away. He's capable and he'll do what he needs to."

Dr. Gould nodded. "Yes, that's the indication I got from talking to him."

The doorknocker sounded and the doctor went to the door. He returned a moment later with Callaway and another cop behind, lugging two boxes of equipment.

"Where's your phone?" Callaway asked.

The doctor showed them to the kitchen. After he'd returned and sat down, Hank said, "They'll set up the phone recorder in case he calls back. It'll start automatically when the phone rings."

King said, "Dr. Gould, we need to know where your wife works so we can find out when and where she was last seen, and what kind of car she drives."

"And we'll need a photo of her as well," Hank added.

Dr. Gould gave them the information and then went to a stand beside a massive stone fireplace. He returned a moment later and handed Hank a close-up shot of Mrs. Gould.

"That's perfect." Hank took the photo and tucked it into his notepad.

"Detective, the kidnapper also sent a shot of my wife to my cell phone. She was … tied to a chair."

"We'll need that phone," King said.

"I'm afraid Mr. Lincoln has it."

"We'll get it from him. It might be something that can help us."

Hank leaned forward, sat on the edge of the couch and handed Dr. Gould his card. "If you think of anything else you need to tell me, you can reach me here any time." He waved toward the kitchen. "An officer will stay here in case the kidnapper calls."

The doctor took the card and said, "Detective, the kidnapper said not to call you or my wife …"

"Don't worry, Dr. Gould. Our involvement in this is strictly confidential. We won't endanger your wife, and the kidnapper won't even see us until she's been safely returned."

Hank turned to King. "Find out what you can at Mrs. Gould's workplace and I'll go to the Lincolns." He stood and faced Dr. Gould. "We'll let you know how we proceed."

They left Dr. Gould with worry on his face as they went to the street. "Let me know what you find out, King," Hank said as he jumped into his Chevy and started the engine.

As the other cop climbed into his car and roared away, Hank hoped he'd done the right thing in calling on King to help.

CHAPTER 10

Wednesday, August 31st, 1:56 p.m.

ANNIE SWITCHED OFF the recorder and sat back. "I listened to that a few times and can't find anything to give us an idea who it is."

"I can't either," Hank said, sitting forward. "But if you give it to me, I'll take it to Callaway and see what he comes up with. He might be able to do something with the voice, depending on what was used to change the tone."

Annie swung around, pulled the flash drive from the recorder, and handed it to Hank. She'd already made a copy of the recording for their own use, in case she wanted to refer to it later.

Hank took the drive and dropped it into his shirt pocket.

"And then there's this," Annie added. She removed Dr. Gould's phone from the top drawer of the desk and swiped the screen. She winced at the photo of Mrs. Gould, then flipped the phone around and handed it to Hank.

Hank took the phone. "The doctor said you had this. I need to get it looked at as well." His brow furrowed as he studied the photo of Mrs. Gould.

"We already had Geekly take a look at it," Jake said. "All he could tell us was the time it was taken."

Annie added, "And the number of the phone the photo was taken from, a burner phone." She copied down the number she'd gotten from Geekly and handed it to Hank. "I called this and got a bum who found it in a dumpster on Benson Avenue."

"The photo appears to have been taken in the basement of an old building," Jake said. "Probably a one-, or maybe a two-story." He pointed to the walls and the beams and explained his theory to Hank.

"I'll get King and Callaway to work on this," Hank said. "We'll see if they can track down the phone. If King calls the number, he may be able to find the guy. He knows his way around the streets and how to get what he wants out there."

Annie had had the displeasure of meeting King in the past and didn't think much of the crass detective. She frowned and asked, "Is Detective King working on this with you?"

Hank shrugged and slipped the phone into the pocket of his jacket. "Time is one thing we don't have a lot of right now and we need all the help we can get. I sent him to Mrs. Gould's workplace to see what he can find out."

"I've already been there and I found her car in the underground parking." Annie explained what she'd found. "But I locked the car and the keys are in it. I didn't want anything to be disturbed."

Hank laughed. "I'm sure King'll know how to get in." He looked at his watch. "We have to set up your phone to record the kidnapper's call."

"There's an app for that," Jake said. "It's set up and ready to go."

"Then let me get this phone to Callaway and give King a call," Hank said as he stood. "I'll be back before four o'clock."

~*~

HANK TAPPED ON Captain Alano Diego's open door. The captain looked up from his paperwork and motioned for Hank to come in.

Hank stepped inside Diego's office, swung a guest chair over to the desk, and settled into it. He leaned back and tucked his legs under the desk, crossed at the ankles.

He filled Diego in on the latest information regarding the kidnapping and then added, "Captain, this is an unusual situation. Jake Lincoln has agreed to deliver the ransom money as the kidnapper requested, but I need your permission for something."

Diego sat back, adjusted his navy-blue tie, and gave Hank his full attention.

"Captain, do you know the law regarding private investigators and firearms?"

"Is this a trick question? They're not allowed to carry them."

Hank shrugged one shoulder. "True, but there are special circumstances. If it's in the public interest, they might be able to."

"On rare occasions, Hank."

"I think this is one of those rare occasions." Hank sat forward and leaned his arms on the edge of the desk. "As you know, the registrar of firearms can authorize someone to carry a firearm on a one-shot basis if a senior member of the police service requests it."

Diego frowned. "And you're asking me to request it?"

"Yup."

"Listen, Hank, we have no official relationship with the Lincolns. They are citizens, and are not law enforcement. I have to admit, sometimes they're a help to us." Diego waved toward the precinct floor. "But there're some out there who feel antagonistic toward private investigators."

"I realize that, but PIs aren't competition, and as long as they don't get in our way, what's the harm?"

"When you put it that way, there's no harm. I know the Lincolns are friends of yours, but don't let them interfere." He pointed his index finger at Hank. "I expect you to keep them under control."

As head of Richmond Hill Police Department, Captain Diego had worked his way up through the ranks and Hank had a lot of respect for him, but sometimes the captain was just flat-out wrong.

"So far," Hank said, "they haven't gotten in anyone's way and I'll see to it they don't. But they aren't concerned with fame or glory. All they want is the same as us, to see justice done."

Diego seemed to consider that and gave a slow shrug.

Hank leaned back. "Now, what about a firearm?"

Diego sat back, dropped one elbow on the padded armrest and stroked his bristling mustache. "This takes time. It would first have to be shown he's fully qualified to obtain a permit. Background checks and things like that."

"He's a licensed private investigator. Background checks have already been done."

Diego picked up his pen and twirled it in his fingers. "What about training?"

Hank shrugged. "He's a fast learner. I'll show him the basics." Hank paused and watched as Diego considered it. "It's just for personal protection. It's unlikely he would even draw it. I don't think the kidnapper is foolish enough to take any chances."

Diego stared at Hank a moment before coming to a decision. He was a few pounds overweight and his jowls quivered as he nodded. "Let me make a couple of calls and see if I can get this fast-tracked, but there's no guarantee." He held up a finger. "But it's just this one time, you understand?"

Hank nodded. "Of course, and thanks, Captain." He stood and left the office as Diego picked up the phone receiver.

CHAPTER 11

JAKE PULLED THE Firebird into Dr. Gould's driveway, jumped out, and strode up the walkway to the front door. It swung open as Jake reached for the knocker.

"Come in a moment," Dr. Gould said. "I'll be right with you."

Jake stepped inside the large foyer and leaned against the wall. In a moment, the doctor came back with a briefcase and handed it to Jake.

"This is empty right now," the doctor said. "But I would feel better if you carried it."

Jake took the briefcase and stepped outside. Dr. Gould shut the door behind them, locked it, double-checked the lock, and then followed Jake to the Firebird.

Jake tossed the briefcase into the backseat and climbed into the driver's seat. He never fancied himself as a bodyguard before, but a job was a job. He watched as Dr. Gould stepped into the car. The man looked worried and stressed out, and his hands trembled as he fastened his seat belt.

Jake hit the ignition and fired up the V8. It purred like a

mountain lion as he backed from the driveway. He eased the shifter into gear, and Dr. Gould directed him to the local branch of the Commerce Bank. He parked under a No Parking sign and they stepped from the vehicle and went through the revolving doors.

The manager was waiting and greeted Dr. Gould the moment they stepped inside. He signaled to a teller and then led them into an office and motioned toward a pair of chairs pushed up to the desk. They sat as the manager went behind and perched on his puffy leather chair. The cushion gave a whoosh of air as he settled into it.

The banker talked on about the weather and the latest news as the doctor listened politely and Jake yawned.

In a few minutes, the teller came in and handed the manager a cloth money bag, fastened with a drawstring. The bag looked surprisingly small to contain that much cash.

"Just as you asked, Dr. Gould." The manager set the bag on the desk. "One hundred thousand dollars, in fifties." He pushed it toward the doctor. "Would you like to count it?"

"That won't be necessary."

Jake saw the doctor's mind was elsewhere; he was surely thinking of his wife. "Maybe we should," Jake said.

The manager nodded. "As you wish." He loosened the drawstring and bundles of fifty-dollar bills fell out as he tipped the bag, each wrapped in a paper band stamped by the Commerce Bank. "There're twenty packets here, each containing one hundred fifties." One bundle at a time, he removed the paper band and ran the stack through a mechanical bill counter.

The count was correct.

The manager slipped a paper from his top drawer and flipped it around. "I'll need you to sign for the cash." He handed the doctor an expensive-looking pen.

The doctor leaned forward, signed an illegible scrawl at the bottom of the page, and sat back again.

Jake tossed the bundles back into the money bag, flipped open the briefcase, dropped the bag inside, and snapped the case closed.

The manager seemed to be eyeing him suspiciously. "It's rather a large sum of cash to be carrying around," he said. It sounded more like a question.

Jake ignored the hint. "Yes, it is."

"Are you making a large purchase?"

"Something like that."

The manager persisted, addressing the doctor. "In the future, perhaps a cashier's check would do just as well as cash."

The doctor was in no condition emotionally to deal with nosey individuals, so Jake took the initiative to speak on his behalf. "Cash will do fine," he said.

The banker gave Jake another dubious look.

"Perhaps in the future," Jake added, "if this is too much of a problem for you, Dr. Gould would do better to take his accounts elsewhere."

The manager cleared his throat. "I was only trying to be helpful." He smiled at the doctor. "We're happy to serve you, Dr. Gould, and we're always ready to take care of your financial needs."

The doctor smiled weakly.

The banker smiled back. "Would you like an account balance, doctor?"

"That won't be necessary," Dr. Gould replied.

The banker stood and offered his hand. "Thanks for doing business with us."

Dr. Gould stood, shook hands, and thanked the banker. Jake grabbed the briefcase and followed the doctor from the office. They made their way back to the car, where Jake set the briefcase on the floor of the backseat, climbed in, and started the engine.

During the drive back to the Gould residence, Jake chanced a couple of glances toward the doctor, who seemed lost in thought as he stared out the windshield.

Finally the doctor spoke. "Mr. Lincoln, kidnappers usually ask for much larger sums of money. More like a million dollars or so. Why only one hundred thousand dollars?"

Jake shook his head. "I don't know. Perhaps he asked for what he assumed would be readily available. A larger amount might have taken more time to put together."

The doctor agreed.

Jake continued, "Or perhaps he assumed, with a smaller amount, you would be less likely to call the police."

"I'm still having second thoughts about involving them," Dr. Gould said.

Jake swung into the left lane and pulled onto the street where the Gould house was. "I'm sure they'll be careful not to put your wife in any danger."

The doctor turned to Jake. "Mr. Lincoln, I assume you know your job is to deliver the money and not to apprehend the kidnapper."

"That's my plan exactly." Jake pulled the vehicle into the driveway, got out, and retrieved the briefcase.

Inside the house, Dr. Gould locked the front door. "I have a safe in the office. I can put the bag in there for now, or would it be better if you took it with you?"

"I think it's best to keep it here until it's needed," Jake said. He didn't want to be responsible for it until it came time for the delivery.

Dr. Gould nodded and picked up the case. Jake waited in the foyer until the doctor returned.

"It'll be safe there," Dr. Gould said.

Jake looked at his watch. "I'm expecting the call at four. I'd better get back to the office, but I'll let you know what the kidnapper's instructions are."

CHAPTER 12

ANNIE LET HANK IN the front door and she motioned toward the office.

"Jake's waiting for the call," she said and looked at her watch. "It's almost four o'clock."

Hank followed Annie to the office and settled into one of the guest chairs.

Jake was behind the desk fiddling with his iPhone. He looked up as Annie slipped into the other empty chair. "I'm just checking the app to make sure it's working properly." He set the phone in front of him. "It seems to be ready to go."

"I'm sure it'll be fine," Annie said and then asked Hank, "Did Simon King find out anything?"

"He found Mrs. Gould's car in the underground parking where you said it was. He got a forensics crew there right away and they went over it. No surprise, they didn't find anything."

"Fingerprints?"

"Just the one set, presumably Mrs. Gould's. And no prints on the door handles except hers and they went over it thoroughly. It's been towed to the auto pound on Cherry Street."

"What about the people she works with?" Jake asked.

Hank slipped out his notepad and leafed through it. "Just three other people. Two of them were already gone for the day when Mrs. Gould left. The receptionist took the bus home, but one of the partners, Williams, also parks in the underground parking. He never saw anything suspicious when he left at approximately five o'clock."

"And the third person?"

Hank consulted his pad. "Whitney Thresh, the other partner. He said Mrs. Gould left just after five o'clock as usual. He was in his office at the time. She said goodbye to him and that's all he knew."

"So no leads there," Annie said. "What about the burner phone?"

"Between Callaway and King, they managed to track down the guy who had it. If the kidnapper's prints were ever on it, they were long gone by the time they got to it. The only prints were from the bum who found it."

"And inside the phone?"

"Three outgoing calls. One to here, the one to Dr. Gould's house line, and the one when he sent the picture to the doctor's cell."

"What about the dumpster where the phone was found?" Jake asked.

"They were able to track that down, but it'd been emptied in the meantime."

Annie said, "I doubt if there would've been anything else in there."

Hank shrugged. "Not likely, but they went over it anyway."

Jake said, "And what about—"

The phone rang.

Annie jumped. Hank leaned in.

Jake glanced at Hank and picked up his iPhone. He touched the screen and put the call on speaker. "This is Jake Lincoln."

A deep, synthetic voice spoke. "Jake Lincoln, it's nice to talk to you again."

"Unfortunately, I can't say the same."

"Now, Jake, there's no need to be rude."

Jake said nothing.

"Are you ready for my instructions?"

"I'm ready."

"There's no point in putting it off. We'll make the exchange this evening. Do you have my money?"

"I have your money. Just tell me when and where."

"You'll go to Richmond Valley Park at seven o'clock. I'll meet you there."

"Richmond Valley Park is a big place. How'll I find you?"

"Come in the north entrance and sit on the bench by the hot dog vendor. Just be there by seven and I'll find you, Jake."

"Anything else?"

The unnatural voice became ominous and even deeper. "I'm afraid I must repeat myself. As long as the police are not involved, everything will go off without a hitch, but ..."

"I'll be there," Jake said. "What about Mrs. Gould? Where'll we find her?"

"Mrs. Gould is safe, Jake. In fact, she and I were just having a lovely talk. She so longs to see her husband again, it almost brought me to tears to hear her."

Jake rolled his eyes and the voice continued, "I look forward to doing business with you, Jake."

There was a click on the line and then silence.

Jake touched the hang up icon, set the phone down, and looked at Hank, who was on his feet, talking on his cell.

Annie leaned back and waited for Hank to finish.

"No luck," Hank said as he dropped his cell back into its holder. "Callaway traced the call to somewhere in the downtown district, near Benson Avenue, but that's as close as he could get. The GPS was turned off, as expected. King is down there looking around, but with no exact location, he'll never find him."

"And the phone itself?" Annie asked.

"A burner phone."

"No surprise there," Annie said.

"So we have to carry out the money drop," Jake said.

Hank nodded. "That's our only option, but we'll get the park covered and we'll catch him."

Annie wasn't so sure. The kidnapper hadn't left a trace behind him thus far and she was sure he would have a foolproof plan in place.

"I talked to the captain," Hank said. "He made a phone call and was able to get an exception for you to carry a pistol."

Jake's head spun toward Hank. "A pistol?"

"Just for this one time. Just in case, you never know."

Jake shrugged. "I haven't had much experience with a gun, but I'll manage."

Hank looked at his watch. "We don't have a lot of time, so let me get the detail in place. They'll know exactly what to do, and then you and I'll go to the range and fire off a few shots."

"Sounds good to me," Jake said.

Just then Matty came charging into the office with a younger boy shadowing him. "Hey, Uncle Hank."

Hank grinned and tousled Matty's hair. "What's up, Matty?"

"Not much. I saw your car out front." Matty motioned toward the other boy. "Kyle and I are just messing around, probably practice a little soccer later."

Annie and Kyle's mother, Chrissy, were good friends. Chrissy lived next door, and her seven-year-old son seemed to trail Matty wherever he went.

"What're you guys up to?" Matty asked.

"We're doing a job for a client," his mother answered.

"All right. Call me if you need any help," Matty said as he zipped from the room, Kyle behind him.

Hank chuckled and turned back to Jake. "We'd better get going."

CHAPTER 13

Wednesday, August 31st, 4:39 p.m.

JAKE FOLLOWED HANK to the Richmond Hill Police Precinct, parking their vehicles behind the building. He jumped from the Firebird, looked at his watch, and joined the cop. "We don't have a lot of time to spare."

"This won't take long."

The pistol range was located in the basement of the precinct. Half the lower level contained holding cells, divided by a concrete wall from the range.

It wasn't an elaborate setup like the big cities had, nothing more than an area set aside for target practice, padded and soundproofed, with two stationary shooting positions a dozen yards from the targets.

A small shelf held a variety of protective equipment. Hank selected a pair of earmuffs along with safety glasses and handed them to Jake. "Put these on." He chose a similar pair for himself, settled the earmuffs in place, and donned the goggles.

Hank slipped his hand under his jacket and removed a pistol. "I got this for you. It's a Smith & Wesson forty-caliber. A semiautomatic and not too big." He hefted it in his hand, seemed satisfied, and moved to the shooting position. He flicked off the safety, went into a firing stance and fired. As the gun exploded, a hole appeared in the forehead of a human-shaped paper silhouette.

Hank pushed back his earmuffs. "Think you can do that?"

Jake shrugged. "Piece of cake."

Hank demonstrated how to pop the magazine in and out, and how to grip the weapon in his right hand and steady it with his left, before handing the gun to Jake.

Jake took the weapon and wrapped his hand around it. It felt natural and not too heavy. He snapped the magazine in.

"The first round has to be manually loaded into the chamber," Hank explained. "To load, pull back this slide and release it. After a round is fired, the spent casing will be ejected and a new round loaded into the chamber."

Jake fumbled with the pistol a moment, finally got it loaded, and aimed at the target.

Hank looked at Jake in amusement. "Make sure you're in the proper firing stance. Your feet should be shoulder-width apart, with your left foot about a step past the other. Lean forward slightly with your knees bent, keep your head up, and make sure you're balanced."

Jake did as he was told. It felt a little uncomfortable and not at all natural.

Hank chuckled. "You look like you're about to start the hundred-yard dash. Relax a bit and keep your thumb away from the hammer, or else when it pops back, you can get a nasty bite."

Jake frowned at Hank, adjusted his stance, and relaxed.

"Now, line up the front and rear sights and then take a breath, exhale, and pull the trigger at the bottom of your breath cycle. Jerking the trigger abruptly will throw off your aim, so you need to squeeze the trigger."

Jake aimed for a spot between the sightless eyes of the target and squeezed.

Nothing happened.

"The safety's on."

Jake grinned. "I knew that. I was just testing it." He flicked off the safety and lined up the sights again. This time, when he squeezed the trigger, a shot exploded and echoed off the bare walls behind.

"Not bad," Hank said. "You only missed the target by eight inches. Try again."

Jake frowned at the weapon and took another shot.

"That's better," Hank said. "You clipped his ear."

Jake took a few more shots, emptying the weapon, and finally managed to come close to where he was aiming.

Hank showed Jake how to reload and the next shots were more accurate.

"I got the hang of this," Jake said.

"Okay, that's enough for now. Click the safety back in place and reload the magazine," Hank said as he turned away.

As Jake reloaded, Hank returned with a shoulder holster and a bulletproof vest. "When you get home, wear a t-shirt, then put the vest on, then your shirt over top and then the holster. It might get a little warm under there, but you'll get used to it."

"I don't expect to get shot at," Jake said.

"Probably not, but at least you'll be safe."

CHAPTER 14

Wednesday, August 31st, 6:55 p.m.

JAKE PARKED THE Firebird on the side street nearest the north entrance to Richmond Valley Park and stepped out. He felt a little uncomfortable in the vest, especially when he was driving, and the weapon underneath his jacket felt bulky.

And to make matters worse, Hank had insisted Jake wear a wire, so Callaway had fitted him with a small microphone fastened inside the lapel of his jacket.

He reached into the backseat, removed the briefcase he'd picked up from Dr. Gould a few minutes ago, and strode across the road and onto the grass of the expansive park. It was a warm summer evening and all was quiet except for the tweet of a bird somewhere in the trees. A dog barked somewhere off in the distance and the occasional person, or couple out for an evening stroll, wandered past.

As he crossed the lawn near a hot dog vendor, he glanced at the man behind the counter. Jake recognized the apron-clad merchant as one of the officers he'd seen around the precinct. He suspected the cop had a weapon nearby, probably under his apron. He was busy chopping something up, but from where he worked, he would have a clear view of the bench where Jake was headed.

A lamppost fifty feet away supported the back of a wino, sitting on the grass, wearing tattered clothes and hat, his right hand holding a brown paper bag, his head bowed as if dozing or in a drunken stupor. From that position, the bum would still have a clear view of the entire area from the corner of his eye.

Jake approached the bench where he was to meet for the exchange, sat down, and laid the briefcase beside him. He leaned back and looked around.

Off to his right, on another bench, a couple of lovebirds were deep in conversation, not giving him a glance, seemingly intent only on each other. Between the two of them, they would have a clear view of anyone coming into the park from either direction.

He was surrounded by cops. Jake suspected there were more about, probably at all entrances to the area and perhaps even a hidden sniper. Hank would be around somewhere as well.

He looked at his watch. It was one minute after seven. He didn't know what to expect.

He watched a pair of squirrels run by, weaving and dodging as one chased the other across the grass and finally up a tree and out of sight. The leaves rustled and branches bowed as the furry animals leaped from tree to tree and continued their game elsewhere.

Jake felt under his jacket. The pistol was loaded, the safety on.

And then his phone rang.

Jake frowned. That wasn't his ring.

It rang again. The sound came from under the bench. Jake got down on one knee and peeked underneath. A cell phone was taped to the underside, held firmly in place by a piece of duct tape.

He carefully peeled back the tape and retrieved the phone. "Hello?"

"Jake?" It was a deep abnormal voice.

Jake examined the buttons on the front of the disposable phone. He touched the speaker button so the mike under his jacket could pick up the conversation.

"This is Jake."

"It seems we have a problem."

"What problem?" Jake asked. "I'm here and waiting for you."

"I said no police."

"I'm alone."

"I'm surprised at you, Jake. Who're you trying to fool? The place is surrounded. You don't think we can make a successful exchange under these circumstances, do you?"

Jake was silent.

"I was explicit in my instructions. Did you not understand?"

"I understood."

"Then why are there police around? I can see at least four from where I am."

Jake glanced around. Was the kidnapper nearby? There were a couple of cars parked on the street near Jake's vehicle, but they'd been empty when he'd arrived. If anyone was in the park and within sight, the police would already know about them.

He decided the kidnapper was bluffing. He wouldn't be careless enough to show himself if he knew the police had the area covered.

"Where are you?" Jake asked.

The caller gave a deep ominous laugh, and then asked, "You don't expect me to give myself away, do you?"

"I have the money and I'm here to make the exchange. That's what you asked for."

"Change of plans, Jake."

Jake wasn't surprised. He didn't expect things to be quite so easy. "What're your new plans?"

"Very simple. You want Mrs. Gould and I want the money. Under the current circumstances, that can't happen." There was the rasp of breathing on the line. "You'll take the money and get in your car."

Jake stood, grabbed the briefcase, and glanced at the pair of cops on the other bench. He had no choice but to do as he was told. The safety of Mrs. Gould was at stake.

He strode across the lawn, climbed into his car, and set the briefcase on the passenger seat.

"Are you ready to go?" the voice asked.

"All ready," Jake answered as he started the engine.

"I know the police are listening, so do exactly as I say and don't try to tell them where you are by making some obscure comment you think might give them a clue to where you're going. I'm not that stupid."

"I'll do exactly as you say."

"That's the spirit, Jake. You're being cooperative and that's the best thing for the sake of dear Mrs. Gould." There was a pause and rumbling on the line. "Drive straight ahead. Go slowly."

Jake dropped the gearshift into first, let out the clutch, and pulled onto the street.

"Excellent, my friend. Now, I'm going to let you make a choice. When you get to the next intersection, you may either go right or left, but don't tell me which way, just turn."

Jake eased up to the intersection and turned right. "Okay, I've turned."

"Keep going, slowly."

What was he up to? This made no sense. Jake continued to drive for a couple of minutes.

"Now, turn again at the next street, either way, left or right."

Jake spun the wheel to the left onto a narrow street. "I've turned."

"Perfect. Now, take a right at the next street."

Jake turned to the right.

"And now, a left turn."

Jake understood now. If the police tried to calculate the location he was heading, they would be confused, but somehow the kidnapper knew where Jake was going.

"Keep driving, Jake. You may go faster now, but keep to the speed limit please."

Jake drove for several minutes. He was heading out of the city. Soon, the buildings grew scarcer until he was on a two-lane road, heading north.

The voice on the phone interrupted him. "You'll take a left at the next road, at the traffic lights. Let me know when you have turned."

Jake knew the area. A narrow road intersected the one he was on a few hundred feet ahead. He eased up to the intersection. The light was green and he spun the steering wheel.

"I've turned left."

The road was rough and narrow and he drove carefully for a couple of minutes, dodging potholes and bulging pavement, as he eased up the tree-lined road.

"Stop. Pull over."

Jake pulled the Firebird to a stop.

"Get out of the vehicle with the briefcase and throw it over the fence to your right."

Jake dragged the case and stepped from the vehicle. He held the handle of the briefcase and swung. The case sailed through the air and landed in a patch of weeds over the fence.

"You may leave now."

Jake took a glance in all directions, struggling to see through the darkness of the trees on either side of the road. Nothing moved. If the kidnapper was around, he was well hidden.

"Jake, you're to leave now."

Jake knew he was being watched from somewhere. He took another quick glance and stepped back inside his car.

"Toss the phone into the ditch."

Jake did as he was told, dropped the shifter into gear, spun the car around, and headed back to the city.

He was disappointed they had no indication of who the kidnapper was, but he'd done his job and he prayed for the safe return of Mrs. Gould.

CHAPTER 15

Wednesday, August 31st, 8:11 p.m.

ANNIE WAS CURLED up in her favorite chair in the living room, stealing frequent glances through the front window while attempting to concentrate on her book.

Jake had called a few minutes ago to let her know he was okay and he would fill her in on the rest when he got home. Hank was on his way as well.

She'd been concerned about Jake, but knowing he was safe, her worries turned to Mrs. Gould and of course, Dr. Gould, who she imagined was pacing about anxiously waiting for his wife's homecoming.

A familiar roar sounded outside and Annie watched Jake pull the Firebird into the driveway. Hank parked by the curb and joined Jake, and together they strode up the path to the front door.

"We're here," Jake called, as he stepped inside. He peeked into the living room and grinned. Annie came to meet him and wrapped herself around him. "I'm okay," he said, giving her a quick kiss.

Annie greeted Hank and asked, "Any news about Mrs. Gould?"

Hank shook his head slowly. "She hasn't been heard from yet."

"I'm worried about that," Jake said. "I assumed he would let me know where she is once I dropped off the money."

"Unfortunately, we're at his mercy and there was no choice but to deliver the money," Hank said. "I have people on it right now. King was downtown in the area where the cell phone was found, knocking on doors, but I've sent him and several officers to the place where Jake tossed out the briefcase. If there's anything to find, they'll find it."

Hank dropped onto the couch as Annie returned to her chair. Jake undid the holster and removed his outer shirt and vest. He dropped them onto the floor beside the couch and sat at the other end. "That feels better."

"Make sure you lock that pistol up safely," Hank said.

Annie leaned forward and eyed the vest. "It doesn't look comfortable."

"It's not too bad," Jake said. "But as it turned out, I didn't need it."

"It's a good thing," Annie said. "It might stop a bullet, but the impact could still knock the wind out of you." She laughed at Hank's perplexed look and continued, "I do a lot of reading."

Jake turned to Hank and explained. "She's got a whole stack of books on police procedure, crime scene investigations, you name it, she's got it."

"You can never know too much," Hank said as he looked at his watch. "I'm waiting for Callaway. We suspect there was a tracer attached to your vehicle. He's on his way and he'll go over it thoroughly, but for now all we can do is wait until Mrs. Gould returns. Hopefully, she'll have something we can go on to track this guy down."

"I'm worried about Dr. Gould," Annie said.

Hank said, "I've been in contact with the doctor and needless to say, he's anxious. I've convinced him he has to wait, and there's an officer there with him, but he's almost out of his mind with worry."

"I can understand that."

Hank turned to Jake and slipped a notepad from his inner jacket pocket. He flipped it to a blank page and found a pen. "I have to get your statement, every detail."

Jake told him everything that had happened while Hank took notes. Finally, Hank folded up his pad and tucked his pen away. "We'll get your official statement later."

Annie leaned forward. "So, the original plan to do the exchange in the park was just a ruse?"

Hank nodded. "It seems that way. And his instructions had us confused as to which direction Jake was heading."

"But how did he know you had men covering the park?"

"I'm not sure," Hank replied. "I believe he just assumed we did."

"Is it possible there're more than one of them?" Jake asked. "If he truly was at the park, he wouldn't have had enough time to get to the drop-off point before I did."

"That might explain it," Hank said. "However, our officers were well hidden in plain sight. Anyone nearby couldn't have known for sure who they were."

"And this guy is careful," Jake added. "I don't think he would take that chance."

Annie turned as soft footsteps padded down the steps from upstairs and Matty wandered in.

"Hey, Uncle Hank," he said, greeting him with a fist bump and then perching on the couch between Hank and Jake. He looked at his father. "What's going on?"

"Just working on a case."

The doorbell rang and Matty jumped up. "I'll get it," he said, charging from the room.

In a moment, Callaway appeared in the doorway. He held up an evidence bag. "We found a tracker hidden under the rear bumper." He walked over and handed the bag to Hank.

Hank inspected the device, squinting thoughtfully. "I presumed we'd find this. We're not dealing with an amateur here. He had this well planned in advance." He turned the bag over. "It's magnetized." He thought a moment and then handed it back to Callaway. "Get this to the lab and see what they can find out about it."

Callaway took the bag and nodded. "Right away." He turned and was gone.

Matty found a seat on the floor and leaned back against the wall.

"I've seen those trackers at Techmart," Jake said.

"I'm surprised you haven't bought any yet," Hank said dryly. "To go along with your pen camera and your baseball cap video recorder."

Jake shrugged and gave a half grin. "Haven't needed one yet, but perhaps I will."

"I've been thinking," Annie said. "The kidnapper could have asked for much more money. It seems like a hundred thousand is a small amount compared to what one would expect a ransom to be."

"We've been over that before," Hank said.

Annie spoke slowly, her brows drawn together. "Yes, but I

think he's going to strike again unless we catch him first. He's not going to be satisfied with that amount, especially if he gets away with it this time."

"I'm afraid you might be right."

"What do we do now?"

Hank replied, "We can only wait and see what the officers turn up and wait for the return of Mrs. Gould."

CHAPTER 16

Thursday, September 1st, 7:15 a.m.

TRENTON SCOTT'S OLD pickup truck rattled and rocked as he hugged the steering wheel. He was leaned forward and squinting at the road ahead as he expertly dodged potholes and patches of loose gravel.

There wasn't much traffic on the road this time of day. In fact, this backroad didn't see much traffic at all anymore, with drivers now choosing the new and better roads to the north. Only old farmers like him were apt to be seen along this route.

He slowed and eased to the right to allow a white van to pass him, coming from the opposite direction. Trenton shook his head. It was traveling much too fast for this old road. Where on God's green earth could anyone be going in such a hurry?

He's liable to blow a wheel bearing, the stupid fool.

He eased back into the center of the narrow road and picked up a little speed. The missus would be expecting him back for lunch and he wanted to get those parts and have the tractor fixed up and running before noon.

He drove awhile, humming to himself, working out his plans for the rest of the day.

What in tarnation is that?

Trenton pumped the brakes and brought the vehicle to a stop. The gears ground as he worked it into reverse, and then he backed up twenty feet and stopped. He leaned sideways and peered through the dusty passenger-side window.

Looks like somebody lying in the ditch. Can't see too good from here, but it shore don't look natural to me.

He dropped the transmission into neutral, pulled back on the emergency brake and swung from the vehicle. He headed over to the edge of the road for a better look.

He stopped short and squinted again.

"Well, I'll be darned," he said out loud. "It's a woman, I think, and she shore 'nuff looks dead to me."

~*~

HANK GLANCED AT the clock above the stove. It was 7:37 a.m. He pushed aside his half-finished coffee and reached for his ringing cell phone. This couldn't be good news.

He listened intently a moment and then sighed deeply as he clicked off the phone. The body of a woman had been discovered earlier that morning along County Road 10.

He finished his coffee in one gulp, dropped the cup into the sink, grabbed his keys, checked his service weapon, and left his apartment.

He'd been in contact with Dr. Gould a little earlier. The doctor's wife hadn't shown up and there had been no word from her. And now the body of a woman had been found.

As he climbed into his Chevy, he felt a wave of anger

come over him. Anger mixed with helplessness. After almost twenty years on this job, he'd seen his fair share of victims. It never got any easier. Whether or not this latest victim was Mrs. Gould, it still incensed him when people preyed on others.

The body had been found several miles from town and in a few minutes, Hank turned onto County Road 10. In the distance he saw flashing lights as he approached the scene.

The already narrow road was constricted to one tight lane, with police cars parked on either side of the now busy thoroughfare. Hank pulled in behind a cruiser fifty feet from the center of activity and shut down the engine. In his rearview mirror he saw the forensics van pull in behind him and lead crime scene investigator, Rod Jameson, swing from the passenger seat.

Hank stepped out and greeted him. "Morning, Rod."

Jameson grunted. "You'd think these perps would at least wait until a decent hour."

"Yeah, well, you know how it is," Hank said. "Crime waits for no man."

Jameson took another sip of the take-out coffee he was holding. "I guess we best see what this is all about."

Hank approached the scene carefully and stopped at the edge of the path adjacent to the body. He pointed to the grass and weeds that lined the shoulder of the road and down into the ditch. "The body was rolled down the grade," he said. "The grass has been flattened."

Jameson nodded and made a note on the clipboard he was carrying.

A police photographer came over, adjusting the lens of his camera. He got it set up to his satisfaction and began taking shots along the edge of the road. Other investigators had stepped up, combing the ground and bagging potential evidence.

To avoid disturbing the scene, Hank stepped down the incline at one side, circled around behind the body and crouched down. It was a woman with dark, medium-length hair, dressed in a business suit. She was missing one shoe; it was halfway up the incline and he assumed it had fallen off as the body rolled down the grade. He couldn't see her face as it was turned partly downwards, but from the description, he was sure it was Mrs. Gould.

The photographer moved down the incline and approached the body from the side. His camera continued to click.

Hank leaned over, rolled the body back slightly, and examined the gray face. It was Mrs. Gould. No doubt about it.

Hank stood and looked up the incline. The medical examiner, Nancy Pietek had just arrived and was stepping gingerly down the bank. Hank gave her a grim nod.

"Hello, Hank," Nancy said as she approached, pulling on a pair of surgical gloves. She crouched down beside the body and made a preliminary examination.

"Livor mortis shows she wasn't likely killed here." She pointed to a purplish discoloration of the skin on the back of the body. "See how the blood has settled. The body is lying on its side, but the pooling is present on the back. That indicates she was killed elsewhere and then dropped here at a later time, or … if she was killed here, then the body was recently moved."

"I'm guessing she was killed elsewhere," Hank said.

"And rigor mortis has set in," Nancy continued. "I'd put

the approximate time of death at about ten to twelve hours ago."

Hank frowned. Twelve hours ago would mean she'd been killed shortly after Jake had delivered the ransom money.

Nancy pulled back the collar of Mrs. Gould's jacket, revealing strangulation marks dug into the flesh. "Looks like she was strangled with a garrote." She leaned in a little closer. "Probably wire."

"Any identification on her?" Hank asked.

"Not that I can find," Nancy said. "But there is this." She pulled the collar back a little more, exposing a thin gold necklace with a small diamond in a gold ball pendant.

Hank pulled out his cell phone and snapped a close-up photo of the pendant. If Dr. Gould recognized that, it would be an almost positive ID. The doctor would have to identify the body later of course, but that would do for now. He wasn't looking forward to the uncomfortable task of breaking the news.

Hank would get a full autopsy report as soon as Nancy could get it done, likely later today. He stood, went back up the bank and approached Jameson.

"Who called this in, do you know?"

Jameson consulted his clipboard. "A farmer on his way to town. Trenton Scott."

Hank glanced around. "Where is he now?"

"At home. He doesn't have a cell, so he went home to make the call." Jameson pointed up the road. "He lives that way with his wife. About three or four miles." He scribbled on a blank sheet of paper and handed it to Hank. "Here's his phone number, but I suspect his name'll be on the mailbox."

Hank took the paper, glanced at it, and then folded it and tucked it into his pocket. "Any other witnesses?"

"Nope. Not that we know of."

"I'd better go see him. Do you have anything else for me before I go?"

Jameson shook his head. "Doesn't look like it. I'll give you a call if we find anything that appears real important."

"All right," Hank said as he turned to leave. "And get that forensics report to me ASAP."

CHAPTER 17

Thursday, September 1st, 8:23 a.m.

JAKE SET HIS COFFEE cup down and picked up his ringing cell phone. The caller ID showed it was Hank.

"Jake here."

"Jake, I have some disturbing news." There was silence on the line a moment. "Mrs. Gould's body was found along County Road 10 early this morning."

Jake jumped to his feet and glanced at Annie. She was leaning with her back to the counter, watching him and frowning. "What is it?" she asked.

Jake put the phone on speaker. "It's Mrs. Gould. Dead."

Hank continued, "She was strangled with a garrote sometime last evening. A farmer discovered her body. I'm on my way to interview him now."

Annie sat and stared open-mouthed at the phone.

"Then I need to break the news to Dr. Gould," Hank said. "I'll call you later, but I wanted to fill you in."

Jake hung up the phone and sat at the table. He dropped his head into his hands, feeling physically sick, feeling responsible for her death. He'd recommended Dr. Gould call the police and now … He'd trusted the kidnapper, and he'd been certain Linda Gould would be set free as long as the money was delivered.

Matty clumped down the steps from upstairs and, in a moment, appeared in the kitchen. He stopped short and looked at his mother, then his father. "Is something wrong?"

Jake looked up and forced a grin.

"Just … a setback on a case we're working on," Annie said.

Matty frowned slightly and cocked his head. "You guys look upset."

Annie smiled tightly as she stood and retrieved a paper bag from the counter. "Here's your lunch. You'd better be getting to school."

Matty took his lunch and turned a cheek to receive his obligatory kiss. He took a worried look at his father before leaving the kitchen. "I hope everything turns out okay," he called back over his shoulder.

Annie sat back down and dropped her hand onto Jake's. "I know you're blaming yourself, but it's not your fault."

Jake sat back and sighed. "I know … but there was no reason to kill her. He got his money."

Annie nodded. "He didn't need a reason. He's a killer and that's what killers do."

~*~

HANK SQUINTED AT the mailbox, touched the brake, and swung the Chevy into the long drive leading to the farmhouse.

Split-rail fences lined either side of the drive, half a dozen cattle grazed contentedly off to his right, and as Hank drew closer, a rooster strutted his stuff behind a chicken wire enclosure.

Gravel crunched as he pulled his vehicle to a stop beside an old pickup truck. He climbed out, sniffed the faint scent of manure, and made his way to the back door of the ancient dwelling.

His knock was answered by a pleasant-looking woman, probably approaching seventy, but as robust as a middle-ager. Probably from fresh air and exercise, Hank thought. Something he could use a little more of.

The woman smiled, raised her brows, and waited for Hank to speak.

"I'm Detective Hank Corning," he said. "Is Trenton Scott available?"

"Sure is. Wipe your feet there and come on into the kitchen. He's waiting to see you."

Hank did as he was told and stepped inside. The aroma of something newly baked was in the air, mingling with the scent of freshly picked flowers.

"The police are here to see you," the woman said.

Hank glanced toward the focus of the woman's words. A solid kitchen table took up one end of the large room. A breeze from an open window fluttered the checkered tablecloth, held in place by an array of baked goods.

An elderly man rose from a chair at the table as Hank glanced his way. A tattered baseball cap was perched high on his head, his teeth arrayed in a welcoming smile. He pointed to a chair. "Have a seat, friend. Maggie'll rustle you up a cup of coffee and we can talk," he said as he extended his hand.

Hank introduced himself and shook the timeworn hand. It was unusually strong, made so by the years of hard work necessary to maintain a livelihood at this dying occupation.

Hank settled back in his chair and spoke. "Mr. Scott, I understand you were the one who discovered the body a little earlier."

The old man nodded. "Yup. It were a shock, I'll tell you that. Ain't never seen anything like that in all my years. Maggie and me been running this place nigh on fifty years now and ain't nothing like that ever sprung up. Least not as I can recall."

Hank smiled at the man's words. It brought back warm memories and reminded him of his own grandfather and of the many pleasant days he'd spent on a farm such as this.

He turned his head a moment as a kettle whistled on the stove. Maggie was fixing coffee.

"I just have a few questions for you, Mr. Scott. I know you're busy and I won't take up too much of your time."

"Ain't no worry. Things'll wait. I know this is mighty important and all. That poor girl. Did you find out who she is?"

"We believe we know who she is," Hank said. "However, we need to keep that quiet until we notify her husband."

The old farmer shook his head. "This'll be bound to rip a hole right through the man's heart. It ain't easy finding out your kin's met with something like that."

Maggie set two cups of coffee on the table along with cream and sugar. She bustled back to the counter and returned with two generous portions of some kind of loaf. Hank caught a whiff of the warm snack. Banana bread, covered with a slab of melting butter. "Try that," she said. "It's fresh baked. And you can fix up your own coffee and there's fresh cream, skimmed off the top."

Hank thanked her and fixed his coffee, lots of sugar and a generous portion of the thick cream.

"If you want more, just holler," Maggie said as she wiped her hands on her apron and turned away.

Hank assured her he would and spoke again to the old man. "Mr. Scott, when you discovered the body, did you disturb it in any way?"

The farmer shook his head firmly. "No sir, I surely didn't. I just raced for home and called you up right quick. I know enough to not touch nothing 'cause I didn't want to be mixing with the evidence. I know you investigators can find out a lot of stuff these days just by looking at how things are. Me and Maggie watch that *CSI* on the TV and sometimes they just has to take one quick look and they got the whole thing figured out, just like that."

Hank chuckled. "It's not usually that easy, but we've come a long way." He took a bite of the banana bread and turned to Mrs. Scott, who beamed as he said, "This is delicious."

"Mr. Scott," Hank continued. "Did you see anyone at all in the area?"

Scott shrugged. "Nope. Weren't nobody around. Only people you see out here that time of day is just old farmers like me."

"Would you happen to know an exact time when you saw the body?"

"Nope, but I calculate it weren't more'n five minutes afore I was on the phone to the police."

Hank took the final gulp of his coffee. "You've been a big help, Mr. Scott."

The old man looked at the ceiling, and frowned. "Come to think of it," he said as he faced Hank and leaned forward, "I did see a truck. It were coming at me mighty fast, maybe just a mile or so from where I seen the woman."

Hank was about to pop the last bite of banana bread into

his mouth. His hand stopped halfway and froze. "You saw the truck before you saw the body, or after?"

"Before."

"So, you passed the truck, then saw the body a minute or two later?"

"That's right."

Hank sat back and pulled his notepad and pencil from an inner pocket. "Can you describe the truck?"

"It was white. A white van and it had no windows in the side."

"And it was going fast?"

"Yup. Way too fast for this road."

Hank thought a moment. "Did you see the driver?"

"Not really. Like I said, it was going fast and I slowed a bit and moved to the side to be safe. I could tell there was a driver, but couldn't see no features or nothing like that."

"Was it a man?"

"Pretty darn sure it were a man."

"What about a passenger?"

"Couldn't say. Maybe, maybe not."

"Was there any markings on the side of the van? Writing, or anything unusual?"

The farmer shook his head slowly. "Nope. Just plain and white. Nothing unusual as I could remember."

"I suppose you didn't see the license plate?"

"Nope. Didn't suspect anything untoward was going on."

Hank nodded. "Of course, why would you?" He scribbled a note and drummed the head of his pencil against the notepad before finally looking back to the old farmer. "Can you think of anything else? Anything at all?"

"That's all I got, my friend. Wish I could help more, but I didn't see anything else that were suspicious."

"You've been a big help," Hank said as he shoved the rest of the banana bread into his mouth. He put his notepad and pencil away and stood, extending his hand. "Thank you very much, Mr. Scott."

The old man stood and gave Hank another firm handshake. "Don't mention it. But I sure would appreciate a favor."

"What's that?"

"Just let me and Maggie know if you find out what happened. It's been kinda weighing on us and we sure would like to know when you get this wrapped up."

"I will," Hank promised.

Maggie bustled over and handed Hank a paper bag. "Seeing as you like my banana bread so much, here's a portion you can take along with you."

Hank thanked her with a smile, took the bag, and tucked it under his arm.

Maggie gave him a bright look. "You're welcome to come see us any time, Detective."

Hank smiled again, bade them goodbye, and was let out. That was the easy one, now he had to see Dr. Gould—a task he was dreading.

CHAPTER 18

Thursday, September 1st, 10:33 a.m.

ANNIE AND JAKE WERE in the office when the doorbell rang. Jake jumped up and in a few long strides had left the room, returning a moment later with Hank following.

Annie swung her chair away from the monitor and greeted Hank with a weak smile as he entered the room. He looked peaked, no doubt a result of the emotional stress he'd been under—the same stress they'd all been under.

Jake resumed his position in the guest chair as Hank pushed the other one closer to the desk, settled into it, and dropped his arms on the table. Annie saw the strain on Hank's face as he spoke. "I just came from Dr. Gould. Needless to say, he's not doing very well."

Annie glanced at Jake. The pressure her husband was under, blaming himself for Mrs. Gould's death, had put a haggard look on his face. He was drained, mentally exhausted, and angry.

No one interrupted as Hank continued, "The doctor broke down and wept. The poor man is heartbroken and more distraught than I think I've ever seen anyone." The cop dropped his head, shaking it slowly. His voice quivered as he spoke. "And to make matters worse, though I doubt he had anything to do with his wife's death, we still have to rule him out as a suspect. That means he has to face some uncomfortable questions." He paused. "I have to catch this guy."

"We'll catch him," Annie said, not so certain her statement was true, but determined to do all she could to track down this vicious killer.

Jake spoke up, exasperation in his voice. "He got his money. Why'd he have to kill her?" He jumped to his feet and paced awhile. Suddenly he stopped, crossed his arms, and glared at Hank. "Annie and I are willing to do anything ... anything, to catch this scum."

Hank sat back and looked up at Jake. "The farmer who found the body gave me something that may be useful."

Annie leaned in eagerly.

"He met a white van on the road just a couple of minutes before he saw Mrs. Gould's body," Hank said. "It was traveling fast and heading away from the place the body was found. It may be nothing, but then again, we have to check it out."

"There have to be a million white vans out there. Did he get the plate number?" Jake asked.

"Nope." Hank shrugged. "It's all we have right now, but at least it's something. I talked to Callaway and he'll cross-check the records for any registered white vans. The only other thing we have is the area where the cell phone was found in the dumpster."

"That still doesn't narrow it down a lot," Jake said impatiently.

"It's a start," Annie said. "Jake, it's a start. We need to give it some time."

"It doesn't stop there," Hank added. "Once we get the list from Callaway, King has a detail ready to check each and every white van within a ten-mile radius of the city. Inside and out. There might be some dust on it from traveling the backroads, or perhaps something inside."

"I doubt if the kidnapper is stupid enough to leave anything lying around," Jake said. "Did the farmer have anything else?"

Hank shook his head. "That's all."

"What about the location where I dropped the money?" Jake asked. "Did King and the officers find anything there?"

Hank sighed. "No. Nothing at all."

"So we have an unknown white van from an unknown location." Jake raised his voice somewhat. "And a killer on the loose. And I think the only reason he killed her was because the police were involved. He warned the doctor and he warned me."

"You couldn't have known he would kill her, Jake," Hank said patiently.

Jake sat back down, leaned back, and took a deep breath. "Yeah, you're right. I just feel helpless at the moment."

Annie was drumming her fingers on the desktop. She stopped and sat back. "I wonder why Mrs. Gould's body was left in such a remote location. I mean, he could have left it anywhere. Why there?"

Hank said, "I was curious about that as well, especially if she was held somewhere in the downtown area, as we suspect."

"To draw attention away from that area," Jake said. "Remember, he doesn't know we found the cell phone, and even if we can determine the approximate location of the building from the picture he sent of Mrs. Gould, it doesn't exactly show what area she was in."

"Perhaps he's operating from a remote location," Annie said. "And he dropped the phone in the city to throw us off."

"Yeah," Hank said. "There is that possibility."

"But he's smart," Jake added. "And I don't think he would dump the body in the same area he's operating from."

"We only have two choices," Annie said. "In the city, or out of the city."

"My gut tells me it's somewhere downtown," Hank said. "But where?" He looked at his watch. "I'm anxious to see what Nancy comes up with in the autopsy report, but that'll take a while longer."

"What about that cloth stuffed in her mouth?" Jake asked.

"It had been removed, as had any ties from her arms and legs."

"Why was she killed with a garrote?" Annie asked. "What a horrible way to die." Annie's hand moved instinctively to her throat and she shuddered at the thought of a wire being tightened around her neck, cutting off her breath and then her life.

"It's quick and clean," Hank said. "But you're right, strangulation, especially in that manner, is a painful way to die."

"He's definitely a psychopath," Jake said.

"No doubt about that," Hank said. "And that might be his weakness."

"How so?"

"A psychopath has a low restraint and a demand for immediate gratification. That desire, combined with a low level of fear, makes him not only dangerous but, despite his intelligence, prone to mistakes."

Annie broke in, "And they have a need for a level of fame sometimes, considering they're generally narcissistic."

"So," Jake mused, "if that's the case, then we haven't heard the last of him."

"I believe he'll be back," Annie said. "Especially if he gets away with it this time."

Hank sighed. "I'm afraid you're right. I'm so afraid you're right."

CHAPTER 19

Thursday, September 1st, 11:00 a.m.

LISA KRUNK CONSIDERED herself a first-class reporter. Truth is, she wasn't all she supposed herself to be, but her sensational stories, sometimes faked and usually exaggerated, always put her on top of the ratings for Channel 7 Action News.

She'd been up late last night, chasing her latest spectacular piece, and slept in this morning. She was angry she'd missed the events that had taken place out on County Road 10 early this morning. By the time she'd gotten there with her cameraman in tow, there'd been nothing left to see but a few officers combing the nearby woods and, unfortunately, she couldn't nail any of them down for information on who the victim was.

She had left disappointed and now was aching for a lead. All she knew was someone was dead, this was a great story, and she wanted a piece of it.

She pushed aside her frustration to answer her ringing cell phone.

"This is Lisa Krunk."

"Ms. Krunk, I'm a great fan of yours."

Lisa rolled her eyes. She knew she had a lot of fans, but this guy was some kind of a nutcase. His voice was deep and unnatural. It sounded like it was filtered through something that made it that way.

"I don't have time for this," she said. "I appreciate your call." She touched the hang-up icon, tossed the phone onto the dashboard of the van, and turned to her cameraman, dutifully maneuvering through the city streets. "Just one of my many fans."

Don nodded knowingly.

The phone rang again.

Lisa shook her head and retrieved the ringing cell. She looked at the caller ID. Unknown number. "This is Lisa Krunk."

"I have a story for you." It was the same voice.

Lisa perked up.

"It's about the woman found dead this morning."

Lisa sat forward, now giving the caller her full attention. "I'm listening?"

The unearthly voice continued, "It's unfortunate, obviously, but certain people didn't play by the rules and now a woman is dead because of it."

"What rules? What woman? Who is she?" Lisa spat out the words.

"Her name is, or should I say was, Mrs. Linda Gould. Her husband, Dr. Arthur Gould, was given a simple task and yet ... he failed."

Lisa scrambled in the console beside her seat and found a pen and something to write on. "Failed how?" She furiously jotted down the names.

Don was frowning, casting frequent glances her way.

The voice said, "I offered him a fair trade. His wife, for one hundred thousand dollars. That's fair, wouldn't you agree, Ms. Krunk?"

"Yes … yes, I guess so."

"How can you put a value on a human life? Of course it's fair. More than fair."

Lisa had dug her digital audio recorder from her bag of tricks and switched it on. She put the phone on speaker and held it close to the microphone. "Can you tell me who you are?"

The caller gave a deep, eerie laugh. "You may call me the Merchant of Life."

"What does that mean?"

"I sell life, Ms. Krunk. May I call you Lisa?"

"Yes, and what do you mean, you sell life?"

"I enter into a fair verbal contract with the purchaser. If that contract is kept, the life is preserved. However …"

"Yes?"

"If the contract is broken, then I'm under no obligation to keep my end of the bargain."

Lisa was bewildered. "What bargain? Are you trying to tell me you're a kidnapper?"

"That's one way to describe me. But it's much more than that." There was a pause, then the voice continued, "I'll dumb it down for you, Lisa. Linda Gould was held to facilitate a trade—money for her life. Our contract stipulated the police were not to be involved. Alas, the good doctor failed to understand the seriousness of the situation, the police were notified of our bargain, and a change had to be made in the agreement."

Lisa arched a brow. "And so you killed the woman?"

"It was a necessary penalty. A forfeiture, you might say.

I'm a man of honor, Lisa, but I expect others to be honorable as well. I've expressed my regret to Dr. Gould. However, my regret only goes as far as being disappointed in the eventual outcome."

This guy was crazy, but she liked crazy. It made for a compelling story.

Don had pulled the van over to the side of the street. He was twisted sideways in his seat, leaning in, listening intently to the conversation.

Lisa spoke into the phone. "Did you not get the payment?"

"Oh, I got the payment. It was delivered by someone you know well. Jake Lincoln was kind enough to do the delivery."

Jake Lincoln. So, he was involved in this. She'd had occasion to run into him several times in the past. He and his ditzy wife were always sticking their noses in somewhere.

"I know the Lincolns," Lisa said. "But why are you calling me?"

"I like you, Lisa. You're my kind of woman. Another place, another time, who knows … ?"

A sneer twisted Lisa's already unattractive mouth. "I don't think so."

"You'd like me, Lisa. However, I'm calling you because I know you're always anxious to get the word out."

"What word?"

"That I'm serious, and next time, the rules must be obeyed."

"Next time?" Lisa was at an unusual loss for words.

"Yes, next time. If the people can be made aware a human life is nothing to be trifled with, then perhaps they won't be so quick to break a bargain, should they be in the same position as Dr. Gould and his late wife."

Lisa paused. She had some morals, albeit rarely put into practice.

"Can I count on you, Lisa?"

And now, she had to weigh the value of a good story against the value of doing the right thing. The good story invariably came out on top. This time would be no different. She had a duty to the public and, of course, to herself.

"You can count on me," she said.

CHAPTER 20

Thursday, September 1st, 11:21 a.m.

DETECTIVE KING WAS climbing from his vehicle when Hank pulled into the parking lot behind the precinct. Hank jumped out and hurried to join King, who looked like he hadn't changed his clothes since yesterday. He wore the same sloppy shirt and pants, and his unkempt hair and beard were a bit scruffier.

"Got anything?" Hank asked.

King slammed his car door and turned to face Hank. "Officers are canvassing the city checking the white vans," he said. "But there're a lot of them and it'll take some time."

"It's the best lead we have at this point," Hank said. "Let me know as soon as anything turns up."

They made their way in silence around to the front of the building, up the steps and into the precinct.

"Hank, King," Captain Diego called as they passed his office door. "Come in here a minute."

Hank followed King into the office, slumped into one of the guest chairs, and sat back, while King leaned against a filing cabinet and crossed his arms.

Diego peered at King and then addressed Hank. "Fill me in."

Hank cleared his throat. "There's not much to report, Captain. We're on every lead and we're hoping something will turn up."

Diego brushed aside a file folder, leaned forward, and dropped his arms on the desk. He frowned. "I have a dead woman on my hands, a distraught husband, and a killer on the loose. What happened?"

"I don't know. The doctor kept his end of the bargain and the money was delivered."

"Perhaps he wasn't happy we were involved," King put in.

Diego stared at King a moment. "How would he know?"

King shrugged and shook his head. "I don't know. There were no uniforms around and no police cars in sight. Perhaps he just took a good guess."

"Or perhaps your people weren't as undercover as you thought," Diego said.

"There might be something else going on here, sir," Hank said.

Diego waited for Hank to continue.

"I haven't ruled out Dr. Gould as a suspect. He has an alibi for the time of the kidnapping, but he was the only person outside of us who knew about our involvement."

"The Lincolns knew," King said.

Hank looked at King in disgust. "Are you actually insinuating they had something to do with this?"

"I'm just saying. They knew."

"Well, you can stop that line of thinking."

Diego asked, "Is it possible they let it slip to someone?"

Hank shook his head adamantly. "No way. Never."

King pulled back the other guest chair, sat down, and slouched back, tucking his feet under the desk. "Maybe the kidnapper was watching the doctor's house and saw us show up there."

"That's a more plausible theory," Hank said. "He does seem to have all the bases covered." He paused. "But right from the start, he might never have intended to let Mrs. Gould go free."

Diego said, "That way he gets his money and there're no witnesses."

Hank sighed. "That's what I'm thinking, Captain."

Diego twiddled his pen a moment before sitting back. He waved his hand toward the door. "Get out of here, guys. I need you to catch this maniac before he strikes again. And keep me posted."

~*~

JAKE KNEW WHO was calling the moment he answered his cell phone. The rasping breath on the line was the giveaway. He paused a moment before saying, "Jake here."

"Jake, my good friend. How are you this lovely morning?"

He didn't answer. He put the call on speaker and dashed into the office. Annie looked away from the monitor and leaned forward as he slid into the chair and held up the phone between them.

Jake spoke slowly, trying to hold back the anger he felt seeping into his voice. "Why'd you have to kill her?"

"Alas, I deeply regret that, and my sympathies are with the good doctor, but unfortunately it was necessary because the rules were broken."

"What rules? You got the money and you're free and clear?"

"My rules. The police were not to be involved." A pause and more breathing. "At any rate, you'll hear more about that on the news. Right now I have other things to discuss with you."

"It's over. Mrs. Gould is dead and you got paid. What else is there to discuss?"

"Jake, Jake, don't be so harsh. I only called to give you a warning. Please, for your sake and others', keep the police out of our affairs next time."

Jake's eyes narrowed and he took a sharp breath. "What do you mean, next time?" Jake and Annie exchanged a look. Annie frowned as she listened intently.

"Exactly what it sounds like. You didn't think this was a onetime arrangement, did you?"

Jake closed his eyes and inhaled deeply. This was just what they had feared. "You won't get away with this. The police are on top of it and already closing in. It's just a matter of time."

A deep laugh, eerie and ominous. "The police are running around in circles, Jake. They're not even getting close and they never will. They might as well try to shoot rabbits from a tree. That's about as much luck as they'll have in catching me."

"Don't be too sure of yourself."

"Oh, I'm sure of myself. I'm aware of my shortcomings, but I also know my strengths. I'm smart, my friend, and a businessman, and you can be sure you're a long way from hearing the last of me."

Jake gritted his teeth. His fist tightened around the phone, threatening to break it in two. "I'll see you dead if I have to kill you myself."

"You mustn't let your anger control you, Jake. I've seen many people get into a lot of trouble, simply because their emotions took over. If you want to catch me, you'll need to keep a cool head." A weird chuckle, then the killer continued, "You know what they say; cool heads prevail and all that."

"I don't need your advice." Jake raised his voice. "And I will catch you."

"Just trying to be helpful. I wish you luck in your endeavors, but in the meantime, be sure to watch the twelve o'clock news."

Jake frowned. "Why is that?"

Another chuckle. "Oh, I can't give that away. It would spoil all the fun."

Jake wanted to reach through the phone and tear the scumbag's heart out. His eyes narrowed as he held the cell up and glared at it. He knew the kidnapper was goading him, trying to get to him, and he was succeeding.

Annie reached out and placed a hand on Jake's arm. He saw her anger rising as well, but she was telling him to remain calm. And she was right.

He relaxed his grip and forced himself to speak in an even-tempered voice. "Is there anything else?"

"That's all for now, Jake. Take care of yourself and give my regards to your lovely wife. I'll be talking to you again real soon."

The line went dead.

CHAPTER 21

Thursday, September 1st, 12:00 p.m.

LISA KRUNK BARELY had time to put her story together for the twelve o'clock news. It had been a rush to get it to the editor, do the voice-overs, and get everything finalized and cued up for the lead story.

And now, it was the Channel 7 Action News at Noon. Viewers throughout the city saw the familiar station logo flash on the screen, and teasers for upcoming news stories ran.

The anchor took his cue, shuffled his papers, and looked at the camera.

"Our top story. The kidnapping of a woman ends in brutal murder. In an exclusive report, here's Lisa Krunk."

The scene flashed to a view of Lisa in front of a large building. To one side, a uniformed police officer could be seen climbing the set of concrete steps that led up to the precinct.

"I'm standing here in front of the Richmond Hill Police Station. Earlier this morning, officers responded to a frantic 9-1-1 call from an

98

unidentified caller. A body of a woman had been found in a ditch along a secluded road."

The view switched to a panorama along County Road 10, where a few officers could be seen combing the nearby woods. Police cars lined the seldom-used road, their lights flashing. The camera view continued to pan: across, then down, where the crumpled grass at the bottom of the ditch hinted that something alarming had taken place.

Lisa's voice-over continued.

"My sources have identified the victim as Mrs. Linda Gould. The body of Mrs. Gould was discovered here early this morning. It has since been removed and officers are in the midst of a manhunt for her killer. As of now, they haven't been able to name any one suspect."

A smiling photo of Linda Gould along with her husband came on the screen.

"Mrs. Gould was the wife of Dr. Gould, a family physician who has a practice at Richmond Medical Clinic, here in the heart of the city. She was the victim of a kidnapping gone terribly wrong.

"Mrs. Gould was abducted from her workplace late Tuesday afternoon. In a surprising turn of events, Jake Lincoln, of Lincoln Investigations, was named by the kidnapper to deliver the ransom. It was successfully delivered and though the police did everything possible, the killer was not apprehended."

A picture of Jake came on the screen.

"I've had occasion to cross paths with Jake Lincoln in the past and though Mr. Lincoln's involvement has been confirmed, I'm unable to determine if he's a suspect in this horrendous killing, but he's certainly a person of interest."

Lisa came back on the screen. She held the microphone close, her thin, sharp nose raking the mike, her tight lips almost twisted into a triumphant sneer. She gave a calculated pause, cleared her throat, and sighed.

"The audio I'm about to play is disturbing. It contains certain threats and I struggled with it before I made the choice to air it. I believe the public has a right to know what's going on and what you might be up against and therefore concluded you should be the ultimate judge of its meaning."

She paused again, glared at the camera for effect, and held up her cell phone.

"Earlier today, someone claiming to be the kidnapper called me. As he was privy to otherwise unrevealed information, I have reason to believe he is who he claims to be.

"For the record, I in no way condone his message. I've turned this recording over to the authorities and am working closely with them in their attempt to apprehend this vicious individual. For clarity, certain parts have been removed."

As scenes of the police combing the woods, photos of the Goulds, and the picture of Jake continued to roll in a never-ending loop, a sinister voice-over played. Lisa's voice was heard first.

"Can you tell me who you are?"
"You may call me the Merchant of Life."
"What does that mean?"
"I sell life, Ms. Krunk."
"What do you mean, you sell life?"
"Linda Gould was held to facilitate a trade—money for her life.

The police were notified of our bargain and a change had to be made in the agreement."

"And so you killed the woman."

"Dr. Arthur Gould was given a simple task and yet ... he failed. Our contract stipulated the police were not to be involved. Next time, the rules must be obeyed."

Lisa's face came back on the screen.

"In this disturbing exchange, the kidnapper revealed to me the abduction of Linda Gould was the first with more to come.

"Her subsequent murder was, according to him, the result of the police being involved, which was against his twisted rules. Apparently, she would have been set free if the terms of what he called his contract had been kept.

"Let me state however, our police force is among the best in the world and though I've played the message for you, I urge you to be sure to notify the police should you be an unfortunate victim of this madman.

"I believe this killer, who calls himself the 'Merchant of Life,' has made one fatal mistake in announcing his intentions to find more victims. You, the public, must be aware of your surroundings at all times and be careful until the police have captured this lunatic and the streets of Richmond Hill are safe again.

"I'll continue to pursue this story as it unfolds. It's my hope that with my help, the perpetrator of these shocking crimes will be brought to justice.

"I'll bring you more on this story as it breaks. For Channel 7 Action News, I'm Lisa Krunk."

The anchor announced another, less sensational story. Lisa, standing in the wings, smiled grimly to herself. Another scoop and another job well done.

101

CHAPTER 22

Thursday, September 1st, 12:04 p.m.

ANNIE SWITCHED OFF the television, sat back in her easy chair and glanced at Jake. He stood with his arms folded, glaring at the blackened TV screen, obviously upset by the broadcast.

"Lisa Krunk should know better than to air that rubbish," he said.

"Yes, she should, but it's not at all unlike her. You know she'll do just about anything for a sensational story."

"I'm sure that's why the kidnapper called her. He knows her nature and he knew she would air his message." Jake shook his head, his brow furrowed. "And she practically accused me of being in on this. She certainly seems to have it in for me."

Annie sighed. She didn't think it was personal, but Lisa's comments and near accusations were approaching inflammatory. She knew Jake's anger at this situation was aimed more at the kidnapper and less at Lisa.

"Lisa's just a pawn in this," Annie said. "She'll get what's coming to her one day, so for now, let's concentrate on catching the killer."

Jake rubbed his massive hands together, his eyes narrowed. "I'd love to get my mitts on him, but we have nothing to go on."

"We'll need to come up with a better strategy next time." Next time. Annie shuddered at the thought of another innocent person being a victim of this madman. "We're dealing with someone not only devious, but dangerous."

Jake sat on the edge of the couch and leaned forward. "But can he be trusted? I mean, if the police aren't called in next time, will he keep his word and let the victim go free?"

"If he's a psychopath like we suspect, he might find another excuse to kill. Another one of his rules broken and another person dies."

"Yes, but I think he's smart enough to know if he kills all the victims, he'll stop getting paid. He has to show some good faith to keep things going."

Annie frowned. "So, are you saying not to call the police next time?"

Jake shrugged. "I don't know. We'll have to wait until it happens, but I think we can be sure of one thing. If the police are involved and he knows about it, then it's not going to turn out well."

"We have to hope the police come up with something before then and stop him so it doesn't happen again."

Jake sat back and ran his hands through his hair. "As far as I know, all they have is that white van, which may or may not have anything to do with it."

Annie felt frustrated. She knew Jake was right; there was little to go on right now. It seems they had to wait until the kidnapper, the self-proclaimed "Merchant of Life," made his next move.

The doorbell rang and Annie looked toward the door. "I wonder who that could be."

Jake shook his head.

Annie stood, went to the door, and peeked through the small window.

It was her mother.

This was not a good time for her to show up.

Annie opened the door, forced a smile, and looked at the woman waiting impatiently on the step. "Hello, Mother."

Alma Roderick looked remarkably like Annie, but a generation older. Although she was not unattractive, her sour disposition made her appear that way on most occasions. This was one of those occasions. She smiled thinly and brushed her way past Annie, then spun around and stared at her daughter, her hands on her hips.

"I just caught the twelve o'clock news," Alma said in an accusing voice, a loaded question contained in her comment.

Annie gave a long-suffering sigh. She knew what was coming.

"How dare you let him get you involved in something so dangerous?" Alma pressed her lips together into a thin line, waiting for an answer.

Annie's body stiffened. "We're not in any danger, Mother. I've told you before, this is our job now and we're careful."

Jake appeared in the doorway. "Uh, I'll just be in the garage if you need me."

Alma whirled to face him, her arm raised and her finger pointed, and spoke in a sharp voice. "You're despicable, and you ought to be ashamed of yourself. Are you responsible for that poor woman's death?"

Jake jutted his chin. "I had nothing to do with that." He

raised his voice. "And we don't need to ..." His voice trailed off. He'd caught Annie's eye over her mother's shoulder. She was shaking her head gently and pleading with her eyes. "I'll be in the garage." He wheeled around and was gone.

Alma turned back. She opened her mouth to speak, but Annie interrupted, leaning in.

"I know you have a bizarre compulsion to hate my husband." Annie wagged her finger. "But let me tell you, Mother, he's a good husband and a great father and he's never put either one of us in any danger."

Alma raised her head. "I saw it on the news, darling. He was involved and I don't know why you're protecting him."

Annie shook her head in frustration. She loved her mother, but she loved her more when she wasn't around. Her mother and Jake had never gotten along and from the day he'd proposed to her, her mother had been obsessed with driving him away.

Alma continued, "I'd like to take my grandson to live with your father and me until this is cleared up."

Annie crossed her arms and glared. "Not a chance, Mother."

"Then at least let me stay here a few days so I can watch out for him."

Annie threw her head back and laughed. "Yes, that would work out really well." Then her eyes narrowed, she leaned close, and in a firm voice she said, "Never."

Alma feigned shock, her hand going to her mouth, her eyes wide. "I ... I only want to help."

"We don't need your help. Try to understand that."

Alma glared a moment, then stepped toward the door and put her hand on the doorknob. "I must go now. I have things to do." She leaned in and brushed Annie's cheek with hers, gave her an air kiss and pulled the door open. "Goodbye, darling."

Annie watched her mother leave, wishing she would move to the Arctic Circle. She sighed as she headed for the garage to tell Jake it was safe to come out of hiding now.

CHAPTER 23

Thursday, September 1st, 12:43 p.m.

JAKE AND ANNIE weren't the only ones angry at Lisa Krunk's news report. Hank was fuming.

He'd talked to Captain Diego and they'd decided the best way to approach the matter was to hold a press conference, with one stipulation. It was to be broadcast live, the intent being to eliminate any clever editing by the likes of Lisa Krunk.

He'd called Lisa right after he'd been made aware of the broadcast. He demanded she turn the recording over to him unless she wanted to get hit with a charge of obstruction of justice. She'd balked at first, claiming freedom of the press and a right to protect her sources. Hank had reminded her Jake could pursue a lawsuit against her for slander if he so desired. That seemed to have changed her mind and she'd promised to deliver the recording right away.

Hank stood as he saw Lisa enter the precinct and approach the duty desk. "Ms. Krunk," he called to her.

She spun in his direction. "Hello, Detective," she said, a wry smile on her face as he approached. She held up a small plastic item. "Here's the flash memory card from my recorder."

Hank smiled. "I'm happy to see you've decided to help us out, Lisa." He reached for the memory card but Lisa held on tight.

"Detective, you'll give me first crack at this story, won't you?"

"I can't promise you that. Besides, you seem to have a way of getting all the information you need."

Lisa sighed and let go of the card, forcing a smile. "At least consider it?"

"You're welcome to attend the press conference like anyone else. I can't promise you any special considerations." Hank paused. "But I'll keep it in mind."

"Thank you, Detective Corning." Lisa's smile appeared genuine now; Hank could never tell for sure. He watched her leave and wondered how any one reporter could cause him so many headaches.

He turned back to his desk, reached to his belt for his ringing phone, and sat in his swivel chair. "Detective Hank Corning."

It was the ME, Nancy Pietek.

"Hank, I've finished the external examination of Mrs. Gould's body. I'll get my complete report to you ASAP, but I wanted to give you a heads-up on what I found."

Hank sat forward and listened intently.

"I found a note inside the mouth, folded and placed under the tongue. I have someone bringing it over to you now."

"What does the note say?"

"It says, 'I said no police.' That's all that's written on it."

Hank frowned. "Anything else, Nancy?"

"Not at this point."

"Has the lab examined the note?"

"They have. They found nothing unusual. No fingerprints."

"Thanks, Nancy." Hank hung up the phone. The kidnapper was making his point about police involvement. But they were involved now and he was going to do everything he could to bring this maniac to justice.

Hank looked up as a young intern approached his desk and handed him an envelope. "This is from the Medical Examiner's Office."

Hank thanked him, took the envelope, and dumped its contents onto his desk as the intern left. The note was in a small plastic bag. He removed it, unfolded it carefully, and examined it. The message was handwritten in block letters on what appeared to be newsprint, probably the corner of a page of a newspaper.

The writing was stilted and unnatural, written in black ink.

"I SAID NO POLICE."

Hank examined it thoughtfully a moment, then dropped it back into the bag and tucked it into his pocket. He wasn't sure if it could lead him anywhere; it wasn't much.

~*~

WHEN HANK STEPPED from the precinct doors, flanked by the captain on his left and King on his right, he saw a crowd of expectant newspeople gathered.

Lisa Krunk's newscast had roused up the press from all over the province. Vans with familiar logos clogged the thoroughfare. Traffic was rerouted past the street, and curious onlookers were held back by a handful of police officers.

The reporters moved in, cameras and recorders poised and ready, as the entourage came down the steps and approached the podium. Lisa had claimed the spot front and center, Don at her side, and Hank caught her eye briefly as he stepped in front of the podium and scanned the crowd.

He leaned into the mike. The crowd hushed.

"Thank you all for coming. My name is Detective Hank Corning and I'm the lead detective on this case."

They waited.

"We've called this press conference in response to a news story, broadcast earlier today, and the subsequent deluge of questions by reporters." Hank looked at Lisa and a hint of a frown appeared on his face. "As this is an ongoing investigation, I'll keep this brief."

Hank paused and looked down at his notes before continuing.

"As you know by now, a woman was kidnapped on Tuesday and held for ransom. The ransom was paid as instructed; however, the victim's body was found early this morning.

"I want the public to know we have all available officers following leads and we expect to make an arrest shortly. This murderer will not go unpunished. We're not taking this threat lightly, and his proclamation will not deter us from tracking him down.

"I would also like to state for the record, Jake Lincoln is not a suspect in any way. He was merely chosen by the perpetrator to deliver the ransom, which he did, and neither he nor Lincoln Investigations has had further involvement in this case to date.

"I'll take any questions now."

The newspeople buzzed, their questions cued up and

waiting, and they all spoke at once. Hank pointed to a reporter in the second row.

"Detective, the murderer has stated specifically the police are not to be involved in the future. In fact, he has declared any future victims will be killed if you're involved. How do you intend to approach that, knowing your involvement could lead to the death of another innocent victim?"

Hank thought a moment. "I can't make any statement on possible future victims. At present, we have a dead woman and a distraught husband, and we're already involved, and he knows we're involved."

Hank avoided Lisa's upraised hand and pointed to another reporter.

"Detective, this killer called himself the Merchant of Life and he has stated there'll be more kidnappings. What're you doing to prevent that?"

Hank cleared his throat.

"This vicious killer would be more aptly named the Merchant of Death. He has promised to take life, not give it, and I object to the self-proclaimed title he has given himself." Hank paused a moment, then added, "As I said, we're tracking leads and we're going all out in a concerted effort to bring him to justice."

Another question. "Can you give us some information on what leads you're following?"

"Not at this point. We have a number of leads and certain valuable information that can't be disclosed at this time."

And again. "How can members of the public prevent themselves from being victims?"

"Please take precautions. Use common sense, be vigilant if in secluded places, lock your doors at night and don't open your door to anyone you don't know."

Someone in the back row spoke up. "And if anyone is kidnapped and becomes a victim, should the police be notified?"

Hank frowned. "Use precautions and that won't happen." He straightened up. "There'll be no more questions. Thank you." He turned away and then spun back and added, "I would like to ask you to give Dr. Gould his privacy until he's willing to speak to you." Hank motioned toward the captain. "Any and all future contact with the press regarding this case will be handled by me or Captain Diego until further notice."

Hank turned away again and he, King, and the captain headed up the steps to the precinct while the gathered crowd continued to shout questions—unanswerable questions that Hank himself wanted answers for.

CHAPTER 24

Thursday, September 1st, 3:15 p.m.

IT WAS A GORGEOUS summer afternoon, a bit warm to take a long jog, but Rosemary Coleman never went a day without a good afternoon run.

She'd finished up the invoicing, contacted a client or two and paid some bills online, and her work was done for the day. She would let the answering machine take care of any stray afternoon calls.

Walter would be home not long after five o'clock, so after a jog and then a quick shower, she would still have plenty of time to prepare the special dinner she had planned.

She enjoyed the freedom of being able to work at home, taking care of clients and overseeing the day-to-day operations of the successful landscaping business she and her husband had built. She saw it as the best of both worlds—a rewarding and undemanding job, along with the ability to take care of their home and her husband.

His recent infidelity was forgiven and forgotten, and to Rosemary, their five-year marriage was back on track. She planned to do everything she could to keep it that way.

She donned a t-shirt, jogging pants, and running shoes,

and slipped out the side door of their sprawling bungalow, located out where the suburbs led into the adjoining countryside.

Her route took her down a narrow sidewalk, past the last couple of houses, then a quick cut across a large vacant lot to a pathway leading into an overgrown forest.

It wasn't a large area; it covered maybe a few acres or so. Not enough to attract any wildlife other than squirrels and the continually chirping happy birds nestled in the overhead greenery, but it was pleasant, away from the city, and Rosemary loved it.

Leaves rustled beneath her feet as she ran. The air was refreshing and she breathed in the light pungent scent of decaying foliage mixed with the faint smell of pine sap.

She'd been through here almost every day and considered this path her own, and she was surprised when a figure cut in front of her less than twenty yards away. Even more surprising, the man was wearing a ski mask, his face completely covered, which was more than unusual at any time and especially on this warm summer day.

She stopped short, her breath caught in her throat, and her instincts warned her of danger.

She wasn't going to stick around and ask him what his plans were.

She spun around to head back the way she came but was halted in her path by a second man who stepped from behind a large maple, cutting off her retreat.

She froze a moment, now fearful something was dreadfully wrong. Her assailant stepped closer and as he was about to seize her, she dropped to the ground, rolled and managed to scramble to her feet and stumble from the path into the thick forest.

With her arms in front of her face for protection, spidery branches scratched at her as she ran. A fallen tree barred her way, but a leap brought her over. She held her footing and continued her frantic flight, panic beginning to overtake her.

A hand touched her shoulder. It gripped, but she managed to pull free and spun to her right.

Her freedom was short-lived as again she was grasped, this time with a firm hold on her shirt, wrenching her off balance. She fell backwards and landed heavily on one shoulder.

She looked up at the masked figure and cried out, "I have no money."

A muffled voice, "We don't want your money."

They were going to rape her. She wouldn't stand a chance against the two of them. Not a chance.

"Please ... please don't hurt me. I'll give you what you want."

She continued to struggle as he straddled her, her breathing coming fast, her heart beating even faster.

She pleaded again, "Please." Then a gloved hand was clamped to her mouth, cutting off her air.

"Be quiet."

She saw her other attacker approach from the side and stand over her, his arms crossed. "Keep her quiet," she heard him say.

"Are you going to shut up?"

She forced her head to nod, her eyes unblinking with fear.

The hand was removed and she was rolled over. A cable tie zipped as her wrists were bound behind her back. She lay on her stomach, the once pleasant smell of decaying greenery now tasting foul on her tongue. A rag was tied about her mouth and she lay still, unable to move, helpless and shaking with fear.

They dragged her to her feet and though she tried, she was unable to work free from the strong hand that gripped her arm. She stared back and forth at her captors. One was a little shorter than the other, but both were of average weight and she couldn't see any of their features.

She had no idea who they could possibly be or what they wanted. She only feared the worst. Were they going to kill her?

"Give me the bag."

The shorter man produced a black bag from his back pocket and tossed it to his partner. It was pulled over her head and a drawstring tightened, cutting off all light, but at least she could breathe.

Whoever they were, they didn't want her to be able to identify them. And wherever they were going, they didn't want her to know. That was the only thing that gave her some hope; they might not kill her after all.

With the grip still on her arm, she was prodded and pushed through the wooded area, occasionally tripping over fallen branches, half-stumbling. Her foot caught on something and she fell to her knees, was held by the grasp on her arm, then wrenched upright again.

She felt herself going down an incline, then gravel under her feet.

A vehicle door slid open, probably a van, and she was prodded inside and lay trembling.

The door screeched shut with a bang and in a moment, the front doors opened and slammed. She heard the engine start and the whine of the tires as they picked up speed.

They drove for what seemed like fifteen minutes, maybe more, and then the vehicle stopped and the motor died.

She was dragged from the van and again pushed forward,

up a set of steps, across a floor. A door squeaked open and she was led down a set of stairs and across a hard floor, then pushed into a chair.

She blinked at the blinding light when the bag was pulled away. She looked up at her captors, her eyes appealing to them. She tried to talk, but with the rag in her mouth, her words were muffled, unintelligible.

A musty smell hung in the air. She was in a basement somewhere, dirty and old, with the taste of mildew.

More cable ties were produced and her legs were fastened to the chair. Her hands were cut free and she rubbed her wrists and arms to increase the circulation. Her shoulders ached from having her hands tied behind her back. Her freedom didn't last long as more ties zipped and her wrists were again bound, this time fastened to the arms of the chair.

She struggled as a yellow nylon rope was wrapped around her chest and tied to the back of the chair. Her struggling soon stopped and she was helpless, unable to move.

"Smile for the camera."

She looked up as her picture was taken.

The tall man spoke. "You'll be okay. We'll be back."

Their footsteps died away as they climbed the stairs, then the door at the top slammed and she was alone. Alone and afraid, tears running down her face as she shivered under the bright overhead light.

CHAPTER 25

Thursday, September 1st, 5:16 p.m.

JAKE WAS EXHAUSTED. He'd spent the last hour in the basement, pushing his body to the max, working out his anger and frustration on the exercise equipment. He finished with the bench press, racked the weights, and lay still.

His stress had evaporated. His frustration with Annie's mother and his anger at the kidnapper was lessened. All he needed now was a long shower and he'd be good to go again.

He made his way upstairs, turned the shower on, and stepped into the hot downpour. As the water eased his aching muscles, he thought about how much he wanted to nail this guy. He was determined to do all he could but wasn't sure where to start. His role in this case seemed to be limited to serving as a pawn in the kidnapper's evil game.

He stepped from the shower and toweled off before making his way to the bedroom. He donned a t-shirt and track pants and went downstairs to the kitchen, where Annie was preparing dinner.

She turned from the counter as he entered. "Feel better?"

"Much." He peered through the window by the sink to the large backyard where Matty and Kyle tossed a baseball back and forth. "Have you heard from Hank?"

Annie shook her head. "Not since the press conference. I'm sure if they'd found anything substantial he would've let us know."

"The meatloaf smells good," Jake said as he popped the oven door open and peeked inside. As his cell phone rang, he turned and picked it from a wicker basket on the table.

"Jake Lincoln."

"Mr. Lincoln," he heard. "My name is Walter Coleman. My ... my wife has been kidnapped and I ... I was told to call you."

Jake sank into a chair and shook his head slowly. Another one. He put the phone on speaker and glanced at Annie. "Yes, Mr. Coleman," he said.

Annie sat and leaned forward, facing him, her brow lined with concern.

"I got home from work just after five o'clock. My wife wasn't here. I thought it was a bit unusual, but didn't think a lot of it until ... until he called. He said he's holding her and demands fifty thousand dollars for her return. And then he said to call you. He wants you to deliver the money."

"Try to relax, Mr. Coleman. I'll do everything I can to get your wife back safely."

"He said not to call the police or my wife would die. I ... I don't know what to do."

"We'll come and see you right away. Don't call the police until we talk to you."

Jake wrote down the Coleman address, hung up the phone, and leaned back. Annie was already on her feet.

"I guess we'll have to put dinner on hold for now," she said. "I'll just get Chrissy to watch Matty and then we'll go."

~*~

THE COLEMAN RESIDENCE was a few minutes away, out on the edge of town, and Jake pulled the Firebird to a stop in front of the double-width lot.

They climbed from the vehicle, walked up the wide driveway to the front door, and rang the bell. Mr. Coleman answered the door immediately, worry on his face.

"We're Jake and Annie Lincoln," Jake said.

He ushered them into an immaculate front room. A large fireplace took up much of one wall, the opposite being mostly windows, with an abundance of houseplants and greenery filling the air with a pleasant scent.

Coleman motioned toward a couch under the window. Jake sat at one end, while Annie chose the other and watched Coleman pace back and forth on the hardwood floor. His hands were clasped behind his back, his head down, his brow ridged in worry and thought.

Annie spoke first, choosing her words carefully. "Mr. Coleman, it's our duty to inform you to call the police. The final decision is up to you, of course, but we're concerned about getting your wife back safely."

Coleman stopped pacing and faced Annie. "So what do you suggest?"

Jake spoke. "We think it's best if you don't involve the police until after your wife has been returned."

"Why is that?"

Annie exchanged a look with Jake and said, "Have you

heard about the abduction of Linda Gould earlier this week?"

"Yes ... I did hear something about that."

"We believe it's the same kidnapper. Are you aware the police were involved and Mrs. Gould ... well, she wasn't released?"

Coleman frowned. "He told me in no uncertain terms not to call the police. But they always say that, don't they?"

"Of course," Jake said. "They always do, but this guy is deadly serious."

"Then we'll pay him. It's as simple as that." Coleman reached into his shirt pocket and produced a cell phone. He touched the screen a couple of times and handed the phone to Jake. "He sent a picture of her."

Annie leaned over and squinted at the phone. Mrs. Coleman appeared to be tied to the same chair Mrs. Gould had been tied to earlier. She had a cloth in her mouth and her frightened eyes stared at the camera, pleading for help.

Jake sent the picture to his own cell and handed the phone back. "Mr. Coleman, what do you do for a living?"

"I'm a landscaper."

Annie had taken a notepad from her handbag and took notes as Coleman continued, "And my wife takes care of the business end of things from home."

"What time did you get home today?" Annie asked.

"About five thirty or so."

"Was the house broken into, or did you see any signs of a struggle?"

"Not at all. The door was locked and the burglar alarm set. Wherever it happened, it wasn't here."

"Would your wife have been out somewhere, perhaps at the grocery store, or at a friend's place?"

Coleman shook his head slowly. "It's doubtful. I spoke to her on the phone about three o'clock or so and she rarely went out after that. She's always here when I get home."

"And yet, the burglar alarm was set," Jake said.

Coleman snapped his fingers. "She often goes for a run." He motioned vaguely to his right. "There's a wooded area just over there where she likes to jog, sometimes in the mornings, but she usually goes out in the afternoon."

Annie pursed her lips, her forehead puckered in thought. That had to be where she'd been abducted. The kidnapper must have known she usually went for a run and exactly where she went.

"Will you have any problem getting the money together?" Jake asked.

Coleman shook his head. "It's a much smaller amount than I would've expected and I can withdraw it from our savings account."

"I suggest you do that as soon as possible and let me know when you have it. I believe the kidnapper will be calling me shortly with instructions."

Coleman looked at his watch. "I'll have to get it in the morning. The banks are closed now."

Annie looked at Jake. "If there's nothing else, I'd like to take a look at the wooded area."

Jake stood and offered Coleman his hand. "We'll do what we can to get your wife back," he said.

Annie stood and followed Jake to the door. As Coleman let them out, she said, "We'll let you know when we hear from the kidnapper."

Coleman stepped onto the front porch behind them. "The

wooded area is just down there," he said, motioning with his hand.

They walked to the Firebird, climbed in, drove a couple hundred feet, and pulled to the curb where the road ended in a cul-de-sac. They stepped from the vehicle and looked at their surroundings. Annie could see the wooded area on the other side of a large vacant lot. They took a footpath leading from the street, crossed the lot, and approached the treed area.

The overhead greenery darkened the forest and shaded them from the early evening sun. All was quiet and peaceful, a sharp contrast to the events Annie was sure had taken place here earlier today.

"Watch for any signs of a struggle," Annie said.

They wandered down the path for several minutes, keeping watch on both sides.

Annie stopped short as she heard the sound of an engine—possibly a motorcycle—coming from their right.

Jake had stopped too and frowned as he pointed in the direction of the sound. "I think there's a road over there somewhere. The motorcycle is going too fast to be on a path."

Annie followed Jake as they turned off the trail and headed through the overgrown forest. They dodged fallen trees and shrubbery and finally came to a slope.

Annie pointed. "There's the road."

They continued to the tree line and then down the grass-covered slope to the edge of a dusty gravel road.

"This is where it happened," Annie said. "Somewhere along here. Unfortunately, there are no houses along this stretch of road. It might be difficult to find anyone who saw a vehicle in the area."

She closed her eyes and pictured the scene—Mrs. Coleman, out for an afternoon run, and then seized in the forest, dragged to this spot where the vehicle had waited and then carried off to who knows where.

They spent the next half hour examining the edge of the road for any signs of a disturbance, a struggle, or anything that just didn't seem right. They came up empty-handed, but Annie was confident they were on the right track.

CHAPTER 26

Thursday, September 1st, 6:12 p.m.

ROSEMARY COLEMAN struggled against her bonds for what seemed like hours. Her legs were cramped from being unable to move them and when she tried, the plastic ties bit into her legs. Her wrists were red and raw from tugging uselessly at the restraints.

She'd been left alone, her abductors probably certain she was securely bound. And they were right. Any attempts to free herself only resulted in more pain.

She looked up as the door at the top of the steps creaked open. A pair of legs appeared and then, except for the ski mask covering his head, one of her abductors was fully in view. He stepped to the floor, stood under the bright overhead light and watched her a moment.

"Do you want some water?" he finally asked.

Rosemary nodded. Her throat was parched, her head throbbing, and she was hungry. Water would be welcome.

The man stepped behind her chair. "If you promise not to scream I'll remove the cloth."

She nodded again and tried to say, "I promise."

He struggled with the knot and the cloth fell away. He pulled a plastic bottle of water from his back pocket and screwed the top off, and she drank greedily as he tipped the container, the warm liquid a balm on her dry lips.

He set the bottle on the floor beside her and stood back.

She stared up at her abductor. "Why ... why are you doing this?"

"You'll be set free if your husband pays our ransom." He paused and added ominously, "That is, as long as he doesn't call the police. If he does, well ... bad things could happen, but let's not think about that right now."

She caught her breath and felt panic rising inside. So that was it. A ransom. She was sure Walter would pay whatever they asked to get her back. But he would be sure to call the police and she hoped they would find her first. Otherwise, she feared for her life. She had no doubt the kidnapper would hold good on his unspoken threat and she knew what that would be.

She swallowed hard and implored with her eyes, now streaming with tears. "If you let me go, I ... I promise not to say anything." She dropped her head. "I just want to go home."

"That's not my decision."

She looked up and begged, "Please ... you can let me go."

He shook his head. "No, I can't," he said as he wrapped the cloth around her mouth again and tied it securely behind her head. "I can't let you go."

Then he hurried up the stairs, taking them two at a time, and the door banged shut behind him.

~*~

JAKE AND ANNIE HAD barely made it home and into the kitchen when Jake's cell phone rang. Caller ID showed an unknown number.

Annie sat at the table and leaned forward as Jake sat down,

set the phone on the table, and touched the screen to put the call on speaker. "This is Jake Lincoln."

"Good afternoon, Mr. Lincoln. It's a fine day to do business."

It was him.

Jake got straight to the point. "I talked to Walter Coleman. He's agreed to pay your ransom."

"And I assume our good friends down at the precinct are unaware of our impending arrangement?" the deep voice asked.

"I advised him not to call the police. I can't assure you he won't."

"Excellent work, my friend."

"He'll get the money from the bank in the morning."

"Wonderful."

"How can we be sure Mrs. Coleman will be returned once the ransom is paid?"

"You need to be more trusting, Jake. I've given my word. Isn't that enough?"

"Frankly, no. Your word means nothing."

A sigh came over the line. "I realize it takes time to build trust, but you shall see, I'm a man of my word. Keep your end of the contract and I'll keep mine. After a few transactions, I expect we can build that bond between us."

Jake gritted his teeth. "There'll never be a bond between us." He dearly wanted to catch this scumbag before more innocent people were harmed, but he feared going to the police. He couldn't even tell his best friend, Hank. Hank would be bound to report it and get involved. Jake's hands were tied and he was torn between doing what he was legally obliged to do and what was best for the victim.

"There's one small change in our contract," the kidnapper said.

Jake frowned. "What's that?"

"I want your loving wife, Annie, to deliver the funds this time."

Jake looked at Annie and shook his head vigorously. "Never."

"Just this once."

Jake raised his voice. "I will not endanger my wife. I'll deliver the funds or nobody does. There's no bargaining with that. Take it or leave it."

Silence on the line and then, "Very well, Jake, we'll do it your way. I just wanted to make things more interesting for all of us and I assumed Annie would like to be involved in our little escapade."

"She wouldn't," Jake said flatly.

"Then I'll call you tomorrow morning with delivery instructions," the strange voice said. "In the meantime, I wish you and your wife a pleasant evening and we'll talk tomorrow."

The line went dead.

Jake hung up the phone and leaned back in his chair. "I wasn't about to get you involved in this."

"I'm already involved."

"You know what I mean. I don't think I'm in any real danger in delivering the money, but you never know. I don't trust this character and we need to be careful."

Annie leaned her elbows on the table and cupped her hands under her chin. "We need to come up with a better plan this time. This is not going to stop until we, or the police, catch them."

"Them? You're sure there're more than one?"

"I think there're two. The leader, who makes the calls and arranges everything, and I believe he has someone to help him. Someone to drive for him and likely to guard the prisoner. I might be wrong, but I'm not sure one person could handle everything."

Jake nodded. "I think you're right, so let's hope Hank's guys come up with something before it's too late for Rosemary Coleman."

CHAPTER 27

Thursday, September 1st, 8:45 p.m.

ROSEMARY WAS PRETTY sure of one thing: if she didn't escape from this dungeon and soon, she would be dead.

By her best estimate, it had been a couple of hours since her tormentor had brought her the water she so desperately needed, and now her throat was dry again, and her stomach was aching for food.

Occasionally, through the overhead floorboards, she heard the faint sounds of someone moving about, probably one of the kidnappers stationed there to guard her.

She had thought long and hard about how to free herself—first from the chair, and then from the house. It seemed like an impossible task, but Rosemary was determined.

Her bonds were secure and the wooden chair she was fastened to was solid, but she had an idea.

She rocked back and forth and then sideways. The chair slid an inch or two but held solid. She continued to rock, forcing her weight back and then forward as much as the ropes would allow. She set up a rhythm. Back and forth. Back and forth.

Every few minutes she stopped for a break to catch her breath and relax her tiring muscles. But she wasn't dreaming; the legs were beginning to loosen, ever so slightly, and if she kept it up, something would snap.

And it did.

The right front chair leg was ready to give out. Just a few more careful heaves and then, crash …

Rosemary's shoulder hit the concrete as the chair leg came free and sent her tumbling forward. With a little more effort she was able to kick her right leg free, slipping it over the end of the now useless chair leg. And then she twisted about and managed to loosen the other leg and it, too, slid free.

Now what? She was in an awkward position, still fastened to the back of the chair, but at least her legs were free.

The cumbersome chair forced her to bend at the waist, making it hard to keep her balance, but she managed to stumble to her feet and stand precariously. Then leaning sideways, the left rear chair leg on the floor at an angle, she forced her entire weight to bear on it, and the already weakened leg snapped free and she went down again.

But she was making headway.

She rolled over and pushed to her feet. The remains of the chair still clung to her back, and her wrists were still tied to the arms, but now she knew she would succeed.

She waddled over to the stairs and was able to wedge the left arm of the chair between the third step and the floor. Then, using that as leverage, she threw her weight the other way. The arm came loose and she slipped her hand free. Then the other arm of the chair got the same treatment and both hands were free. She slipped the gag from her mouth and took a deep breath of the stale air.

After that, it was just a matter of twisting the ropes that

bound her chest to the back of the chair until she was able to reach the knot. In a few minutes, she worked it loose, the ropes fell to the floor, and she was free.

Well, not exactly free. She was still a prisoner in the basement.

She had two options. Bring him to her and subdue him somehow, or go up the stairs and try to get through the door. She was pretty sure she'd heard him lock it when he left, so trying to break through a locked door would be futile.

She only had one logical choice and she hoped there was only one person she had to deal with. Then at least she would stand a chance.

She picked up one of the chair legs and hefted it. It was solid and would make a good weapon. Good enough, she hoped.

Then taking a few deep breaths to calm her nerves, then a final one to fill her lungs, she screamed, over and over. "Help. Help."

There was the sound of running footsteps on the floor above. He had heard her. She slipped behind the stairs, out of sight, and raised her weapon.

The door at the top rattled and then creaked open, and through the space between the steps a pair of legs descended one step at a time.

Her grip tightened on the chair leg. She poised herself, and when he reached the final step and touched the floor, she stepped out and swung with all her might. The solid wooden weapon connected with her abductor's forehead. The makeshift club flew from her grasp, rattling across the floor and into the wall.

He went down, stunned and groaning, and lay still at the foot of the stairs.

His eyelids fluttered and he looked up with vacant eyes as she stepped carefully around him and scrambled up the steps.

She chanced a look over her shoulder as she neared the top. He wobbled as he rose to his feet and glared at her.

"Stop," he shouted.

Rosemary paid no mind. She clambered up the final step, tripped, and fell through the doorway. As she struggled to her feet, she heard him behind her, coming up the stairs, slowly, but getting closer.

She looked around her for a doorway to freedom. What was this place? It wasn't a house. It seemed more like a small warehouse, or perhaps an empty store. To the right was a door, framed by a large window on either side, but the door and both windows were boarded up securely. To her left, at the rear of the room, was another door, a smaller one, made of metal.

"Stop." Much closer this time, almost behind her.

She slammed the door to the basement and as she wrestled with the lock, he rammed into the door from the other side. It burst open.

Her heart pounded. She was out of time. She dashed to the rear of the room toward the metal door. It was locked and bolted from the inside. She struggled with the lock on the knob first and then slid back the bolt and turned the knob.

In her peripheral vision she saw him stumble over a loose board. He sprawled across the floor.

She pulled at the door, metal squealing against metal, then felt a hand grip her heel. She wrenched loose and half-ran, half-fell through the doorway. Weak and tired from her exertion, she scrambled to her feet and looked frantically around.

She was in a narrow alleyway. In front of her loomed tall

buildings, old and run-down, much like the one she'd escaped from. She dove to the left, screaming, her attacker panting behind her. A hand touched her shoulder, his labored breath almost in her ear.

In desperation she mustered up a little more endurance, but it was futile. Her shirt was gripped from behind and she stumbled and hit the ground, her assailant on top of her.

He growled at her, his voice raspy and angry. "Thought you could get away, did you?"

She didn't answer. She couldn't. A hand over her mouth cut off her screams and her breath as his other arm wrapped around her neck.

"Stand up," he said as he held his grip, heaved her to her feet, and then half-carried, half-dragged her back to her musty cell.

CHAPTER 28

Friday, September 2nd, 10:15 a.m.

THE MAN SHIFTED HIS position on the uncomfortable street bench, slid forward, leaned back, and yawned. He dropped one arm across the armrest and stretched out his legs, crossing them at the ankles.

From where he sat, he had a clear view of the bank across the street. He knew what his job was. There was a small element of danger, but still, everything should go off without a hitch. After all, he was an expert and he had no fear of getting caught as long as he stuck to the plan.

The fake beard he was wearing was itching him something awful, but he resisted the desire to scratch and kept his eyes on the bank.

He'd been waiting for more than an hour, ever since the bank opened. To kill time, he'd read the morning newspaper almost all the way through, where news of the murder of Mrs. Gould still commanded the front page. Today, it was a story on Dr. Gould. The whole thing was a shame, but it had to be done that way. His boss knew what he was doing, and as long as he got paid, who was he to argue with the methods used?

The boss had given him an earful the night before, after

the Coleman woman had almost escaped, and he counted his blessings he'd been able to capture her again and the boss hadn't fired him. But that was then and this was now, and he wasn't going to allow anything to go wrong this time.

He was pleased the boss took care of most of the dirty work. The final disposal of Mrs. Coleman's body would be up to him, but at least he wasn't the one who had to perform the unpleasant task of taking her life. It made him a bit squeamish and he had to draw the line somewhere.

He straightened up and leaned forward when he saw his target round the corner and enter the bank, carrying a briefcase in one hand. He would give it a few minutes. He assumed Coleman had called ahead to arrange for the money to be ready, so it wouldn't take him long to get the funds and leave.

He waited five minutes and then sauntered up the sidewalk to the corner, waited for the walk signal to appear, and then crossed the street behind a couple of old ladies who took their sweet time about it.

He walked a dozen yards and leaned against the wall at the corner of the bank, lit a smoke, slipped on a pair of thin leather gloves and waited. Before long, he butted his half-finished cigarette on the sidewalk as Walter Coleman stepped from the bank and turned his way, a briefcase dangling from one hand.

Now.

He slipped his hand into his jacket pocket and tightened his fist around the grip of his trusty pistol, his finger poised on the trigger. This was gonna be easy.

He withdrew the pistol, took two steps forward, and stopped as Coleman approached. He held the weapon at arm's length, pointed straight at the heart of his target.

"Give me the briefcase."

He heard a muffled scream and glanced toward the sound. Through the window of the bank he saw a wide-eyed woman looking his way, rising from her chair behind a desk. It was one of the loan officers, her office conveniently located with a view of the street.

The robber turned back to Coleman. "I said, give me the briefcase."

Coleman swung the case forward and handed it to the thief. "Don't shoot, please."

"I won't shoot you." The robber took the case with his gun hand, dangling it from two fingers, careful to keep the weapon trained on Coleman. Then with his other hand, he reached into his jacket pocket and removed a folded paper. He handed it to Coleman. "This is for you."

He chanced a look through the bank window as Coleman took the note from his hand. He could see through the office to the main area of the bank. It was a chaotic scene. He'd better get out of here and fast.

"Don't try to follow me," he said and switched the briefcase to his other hand, then spun around and pounded up the sidewalk in the opposite direction.

He glanced over his shoulder. Coleman was still standing there, looking stunned, the note clutched in his hand. A security guard had exited the bank and was yelling at the robber to stop. Fat chance. He couldn't figure out why they always wasted their breath that way—as if a robber is ever going to stop just because some dummy tells him to.

He chuckled as he ran. This job was well planned, the boss had taken care of all the details and he was going to make a nice fat five grand to do a simple job. Along with what he was already getting paid, he would be living on easy street.

A couple of passersby heard the security guard yell and were about to interfere, but soon changed their minds and stepped back when he brandished the gun in their direction. He knew from prior experience, nobody was fool enough to interfere when they could intercept a bullet. That just wasn't human nature and nobody cared that much about someone else's money.

But the security guard—that was a different story. He was overweight, but he was coming up the sidewalk as fast as his pudgy legs could carry him, still yelling.

The mugger rounded a corner, down a narrow street—a lane, tucked between two towering buildings. A shot cracked behind him. The stupid security guard was shooting at him. The bullet missed by a mile, but the robber stopped quick, spun around, and returned a shot, aiming high. He probably could've nailed him easy as pie, but didn't see the need to kill the dumb twit.

The shot did its job. The guard stopped and ducked behind a dumpster out of sight, probably thinking a little differently now about chasing an armed man, and anyway, he would never catch him.

He rounded another corner and ducked into the open passenger door of a waiting car. The vehicle pulled from the curb, merged into traffic, and sped away. He looked through the rear window. Nobody was following, they were safely away and the security guard would probably get a bonus for trying to stop an armed robber.

All in all, this was a win-win situation.

CHAPTER 29

Friday, September 2nd, 10:35 a.m.

JAKE WAS PACING THE living room floor expecting a call at any time, anxious to hear from the kidnapper who'd promised to phone this morning. He was uneasy about Mrs. Coleman's safety and wanted this to go off without a hitch.

He started when his cell phone rang, then pulled it from his pocket and looked at the caller ID. It was Coleman, not the kidnapper.

"Jake Lincoln."

"Jake, it's Walter Coleman. It appears I won't need your services after all." Coleman explained how he'd been accosted outside the bank and the money taken from him. He finished with, "The robber handed me a note before he ran."

"Read it to me."

"It says, 'Thank you from the Merchant of Life.'"

"Was it written on newsprint?"

"Yes."

The fact that a note written on newsprint had been left on the body of Mrs. Gould hadn't been released to the public. And now this note, also written on the same type of paper, seemed to prove this was the work of the same kidnapper. It couldn't be a copycat.

"Have you heard from your wife yet?" Jake asked.

"Not yet, and I'm concerned."

"We've kept our end of the bargain, Mr. Coleman. All we can do now is wait and pray for her safe return."

"Should I … should I call the police?"

Jake hesitated. "Not until your wife is home. We don't want to endanger her."

"Yes, yes, whatever you think is right, but there were witnesses. It happened right in front of the bank. I left right away because of my wife, but I'm sure they've called the police."

"Mr. Coleman, will you bring that note to me? Or I can pick it up, whatever you prefer. And try not to handle it too much; it might have fingerprints on it." Jake doubted there would be, but still, you never knew.

"I'll drop it over to you right away. I'm still on the road and not far from your place."

Jake terminated the call. He'd wandered into the kitchen during the phone call and sat down, setting his cell on the table. He was unsure what to do now. This was a messy situation and the police would need to be informed … eventually. But for now, Mrs. Coleman was the top priority.

His phone rang again. He scooped it up and looked at the caller ID. Unknown number.

"Jake Lincoln."

"Good morning, my friend. I'm sure you're aware by now a successful transaction has taken place?"

"I'm aware."

"The funds have been counted and the amount is correct."

"And Mrs. Coleman?"

"Ah, dear Mrs. Coleman. She's a feisty one."

Jake ignored the comment and waited.

"She tried to leave before our transaction was brought to a satisfactory conclusion. Needless to say, I wasn't happy."

"You have your money now. Have you let her go?"

"Not yet, Jake. I'm weighing the matter."

Jake's frowned. "What do you mean by that?"

"She was a party to the contract as well and she tried to break her side of the deal by prematurely terminating our acquaintance."

Jake jumped to his feet, glared at the phone and shouted, "We kept our end of the bargain. The police weren't called and you have the money."

"Calm down, my friend."

Jake took a deep breath and spoke firmly. "You must release her immediately."

"I would Jake, I would, but ..."

"Yes?"

"Unfortunately, during Mrs. Coleman's attempt at leaving us before the proceedings were concluded, she happened to catch a glimpse of my colleague. Fortunately, he was able to coax her to return and stay with us until such time as our deal could be concluded, but there's no guarantee she'll remain loyal to our bargain."

"I can assure you, she will."

"But you can't speak for her, Jake."

"Let her go ... please. I'm begging you."

A deep eerie laugh came over the line. "It doesn't become you to beg, Jake."

"Just let her go."

"I'll consider your request."

The line went dead.

~*~

ANNIE WAS UPSTAIRS and when she heard Jake shouting, she was curious. She dropped the load of laundry and hurried down to the kitchen.

Jake was sitting at the table, his head in his hands.

She stood beside him and placed her hand on his back. "What is it?"

Jake lifted his head and looked at her. He told her about Coleman's call and the robbery and then said, "The kidnapper just called. I ... I don't think he's going to let Mrs. Coleman go free."

Annie sat at the table and leaned forward. Jake's grief for innocent victims weighed him down and he was taking this personally.

"We'll get him," Annie said.

"Yes, but how many victims will he kill before we do?"

Annie sighed. There was no answer to that question.

When the doorbell rang, Jake stood. "That'll be Walter Coleman." Jake followed Annie into the foyer, where she let Coleman in and invited him in to the living room. Coleman took a seat at one end of the couch, Annie at the other, facing him, her hands in her lap. Jake settled into the armchair.

Annie saw the worry on Coleman's face and the sadness in his eyes. He reached into his shirt pocket and removed a piece of paper. "Here's the note," he said, leaning forward and handing it to Annie. She took it by one corner and dropped it on the coffee table, then used the tip of a pen to help unfold it, careful not to mar any fingerprints that might be on it.

Jake leaned forward and read the note out loud. "Thank you from the Merchant of Life."

Annie spoke. "It appears to me the kidnapper wasn't sure whether or not we'd called the police and he devised this foolproof plan to get the money in a way no one could anticipate."

"But where's my wife?" Coleman asked, his shoulders slumped.

Annie debated with herself. Should she tell Coleman about the kidnapper's call and that he might not let Mrs. Coleman go free, or should she remain quiet and hope for the best? She exchanged a glance with Jake, his eyes telling her he was unsure as well.

"We'll have to give it a bit of time," Jake said.

Coleman nodded. "I ... I guess that's all we can do."

"Mr. Coleman," Annie said. "The police have a few leads and they're working around the clock to find the kidnappers, so don't give up hope."

Coleman closed his eyes and took a deep breath. "You're right, of course, but if I don't hear from her in a couple of hours, I ... I think I'll call the police. The witnesses at the bank might be able to recognize the robber, but right now, the police have no reason to see it as anything other than a mugging."

"Whatever decision you make, we'll honor that," Jake said. "I'm hesitant to advise you either way, but the question is not if we notify the police, but when."

CHAPTER 30

Friday, September 2nd, 11:35 a.m.

ROSEMARY COLEMAN WAS a determined woman. Who wouldn't be, when faced with almost certain death?

Her captor was making no effort now to hide his face. That could only mean one thing. They were never going to let her out of here, at least not alive.

He'd been coming down to check on her more often now, careful in coming down the stairs in case she caught him unawares again, and he always wore a mocking grin when he saw her, still trussed up and helpless.

There could only be one reason they still held her and still kept her alive. Her husband hadn't paid the ransom yet. Their bank account was pretty healthy, but she had no idea how much they would ask, and once the money was rounded up and paid, she was doomed.

She had to get out of here.

The door at the top of the stairs rattled and she heard a footstep. Soon his legs appeared, then his head came into view, the evil grin again twisting his face.

"I'm glad to see you're still here," he said.

She didn't try to answer. She couldn't. The duct tape over

her mouth made it hard to breathe, impossible to talk. She showed her hatred through her eyes, determined never to let her fear take over.

He laughed and crouched in front of her. "I just wanted to let you know, your husband paid us."

She fought back the panic. Had he come to kill her now?

"The boss'll deal with you when he gets here. Don't worry, it won't be long now."

What did he mean?

Then he stood and ambled back up the stairs, humming to himself. The door slammed, a bolt lock slid, and she was alone again.

Sore from sitting so long on the hard concrete, she leaned back against the metal support column and adjusted her weight. She had little room to move. Her shoulders ached from her hands stretched behind her and tied around the pole with not one, but two cable ties. But at least her legs were free.

Though she sat now, off and on she had stood by pushing with her back against the pole, folding her legs underneath, then heaving up and sliding her bound wrists up the pole. It was uncomfortable to stand for long in that position, but it alleviated the discomfort from prolonged sitting.

She had slept sporadically throughout the night, but had spent as much time as possible working at the ties, rubbing them against the pole in an effort to wear them through, stretching with her wrists until raw and sore. She hadn't made much headway, though. Perhaps none.

But she had a few minutes before her captor came back and she had devised another plan.

The building was old and probably destined for demolition before long. She dug at the concrete with the heel of her runner. It didn't do much good, but it told her the concrete was starting to rot from age and ever-present dampness.

She glanced at the ceiling. It appeared solid near the walls, but then bowed down somewhat, and then back up at the center of the room where the pole supported the ceiling and the floor above.

It was a desperate and dangerous plan and might not work, but it was all she could think of.

She had noticed the base of the pole gave slightly when she forced her weight against it. Very slightly, but perhaps she could loosen the screws from the rotting concrete if she worked at it.

Struggling to her feet, she was glad she'd spent a lot of time jogging and working out. She'd built up her leg muscles that way and she was going to need all the strength she could muster.

While balancing on one leg, she kicked back with the other foot against the pole. Yes, it moved, almost an imperceptible amount, but it had moved. She kicked again and again and then worked her way around to the other side of the pole and kicked some more. After several minutes, she was getting somewhere. Her crazy plan just might work.

The door opened again, so she slid back down the pole and closed her eyes. She heard footsteps, then a chuckle, and he retreated back up.

She continued her work. Her right leg was strongest, but the bottom of her foot was getting sore. She switched legs and continued, until finally, the pole moved a couple of inches.

The ceiling creaked. She looked up into dust, released as the ceiling settled. The bottom of the pole was loosened and another heave or two would swing it free. The top of the pole was still fastened to the rotting beams, but the screws at one edge had begun to work loose.

It was now or never.

Her rubber soles increased the friction as she dug in her heels, bent her knees, took a deep breath, and heaved.

A scrape. A creak. She groaned. Then timber crackled and the pole broke free and dragged her to the floor, her arms still behind her back.

The ceiling had bowed and she heard the squeal of wood against wood as the floor above her settled.

She slipped her tied wrists down the pole and off the end and then crouched and swung her hands under her feet and in front of her. Her wrists were still tied, but she was otherwise free.

The ceiling groaned again.

Footsteps sounded above. Running. A shout.

She dove for the corner. The ceiling was coming down and that was the safest place.

Like Samson, she'd brought down the column where she'd been bound, but she hoped that unlike Samson, she wouldn't have sacrificed herself in the process.

She lay in a fetal position, her face to the wall, her hands protecting her head, as broken floorboards and what had once been a ceiling crashed and settled around her.

CHAPTER 31

Friday, September 2nd, 12:25 p.m.

JAKE STILL HADN'T heard back from Walter Coleman regarding the return of Rosemary. He feared the worst, sure now she wouldn't be returned alive. The fact she'd tried to escape and had seen the face of one of the kidnappers didn't bode well for her.

He gave Coleman a quick call to find out if he'd heard from his wife.

He hadn't.

"I was about to call the police," Coleman said. "I can't wait any longer."

"They'll want a statement from both of us," Jake said. "Why don't I swing by and pick you up and we'll run down to the station?"

Coleman agreed. Jake hadn't talked to Hank since the press conference the day before, so he called to see if Hank was available. The detective was on the road but would meet them at the precinct in fifteen minutes.

Jake poked his head into the office where Annie was going over some notes. He explained the situation to her. "Maybe you should come along," he said.

"I'll be there in one minute."

"And bring the kidnapper's note." Jake pointed toward the desk. "It's in the top drawer."

He grabbed his keys and went outside to warm up the Firebird. Annie joined him a minute later and they roared from the driveway.

Coleman was waiting at the curb when they arrived at his house. Jake climbed out to let Coleman into the backseat and in five minutes they arrived at the precinct.

Hank was at his desk, his head in some papers, and he glanced up when they approached.

"This is Walter Coleman," Jake said, motioning with his hand.

Hank half-rose from his seat, shook Coleman's hand, and waved toward a pair of chairs in front of his desk. "Have a seat."

Coleman and Annie sat while Jake found another stray chair, dragged it over, and plopped into it.

Hank closed the file folder, pushed it aside, and looked back and forth from Jake to Coleman. "What's this all about?"

"It's my wife," Coleman said. "She's been kidnapped."

Hank leaned forward and dropped his arms on the desk, a frown on his face. "Kidnapped?"

Between Jake and Coleman they managed to fill Hank in on the details.

"I was hesitant to come to the police," Coleman said. "But I'm afraid for her life."

"And you said there was a witness at the bank?"

Coleman nodded. "At least one. A security guard. Perhaps more."

Hank swung his chair and faced his computer monitor. He

tapped a few keys and whistled. "There was a report of a mugging in front of the Commerce Bank this morning. The call came in at ten twenty-eight. The victim and the assailant are both listed as unknown. Officers interviewed a loan officer, as well as a security guard who chased the suspect."

"I didn't stay around after I read the note. I didn't want the police involved until my wife returned home."

"And the note?"

Jake slipped a ziplock bag from his pocket and handed it to Hank. "We didn't touch it, so if there're any fingerprints on that, other than Mr. Coleman's, then—"

"I'll get it to the lab right away. In the meantime, I'll need a complete statement from all of you and don't spare the details." Hank turned to Jake. "I assume you recorded the calls?"

Jake nodded. "As always."

"I'll need those too."

~*~

AFTER COLEMAN AND the Lincolns left, Hank made a copy of everything that pertained to both kidnappings, tucked it all into a file folder, and tapped on Diego's open door. "Got a minute, Captain?"

Diego looked up and beckoned him in.

Hank sat in the guest chair. "We have another kidnapping," he said as he dropped the file in front of the captain. "It's all in there."

Diego sighed and flipped open the folder. "I hope we don't have another body."

"Not yet, but I'm afraid there might be."

Diego worked a crick out of his neck. "Then why're you hanging around here? Get on it."

"This might be time-sensitive and I need some more officers. The victim might have been kidnapped while out jogging yesterday morning. I need some guys to comb the area, interview the neighbors, etcetera."

"Whoever is not doing anything that's of dire importance you can have." Diego leaned forward. "Whatever it takes to catch these people, I'm behind you. We don't want any more victims. The press is raking us over the coals right now and the mayor is after my butt."

"Thanks, Captain," Hank said as he stood. "I'll get right on it."

Diego waved toward the door. "Go. Get out of here."

CHAPTER 32

Friday, September 2nd, 12:30 p.m.

ROSEMARY COLEMAN'S eyelids fluttered as she regained consciousness. At first, she didn't remember where she was and then the awful truth of her predicament hit her. She was still a captive.

She must have been knocked out when the ceiling gave way. The back of her head was aching and with her fingers, she felt a lump had risen. It wasn't bleeding but it was tender to the touch.

She didn't know how long she'd been lying there, perhaps a few minutes, perhaps longer, and when her senses finally returned, she rolled over carefully and inspected her situation. A part of the ceiling had fallen and barricaded her in behind the rotting boards. The dust still settled around the bits of broken timber that surrounded her.

She stopped breathing as she heard a sound, like the sound of footsteps on stairs. Whoever was up there was coming down, looking for her.

"Where are you, Mrs. Coleman?" The voice was mocking her.

She looked around frantically. A length of solid wood, a

couple of feet long, lay at her feet. It was difficult with her hands still tied, but she managed to twist her body around, stretch, and retrieve the sturdy board. She gripped it in both hands and hefted it. It weighed a few pounds and would do as a weapon. It had to do.

"I'm over here," she called. "Behind the floorboards. I'm trapped."

He laughed, still mocking. "I thought you might've been hurt. That would be a shame."

With barely room enough to maneuver, she crawled to her knees and held the weapon, waiting, afraid, and desperate.

"I can't move. Please help me."

She heard the creak of boards and the crunch of feet on debris as he drew closer. The wood forming the barricade moved as he worked it loose. She twisted around to shield the weapon from his view as he groaned and dragged a large chunk of the barricade aside.

"So, there you are," he said as he leaned over and his face appeared, glaring through the large space he'd managed to clear. His sickening grin was so close she smelled his foul breath.

She gripped the weapon, held her breath, adrenaline pumping, and drove the board like a battering ram. It connected with his forehead, knocking his head back. He let out a whoosh of air and fell sideways, stunned.

Still holding the weapon, she squirmed from the space and whacked him again before he could recover. She heard a sickening crunch and realized she might've broken his nose.

Her anger welled up inside. Anger from the hours, the days, of capture and fright she'd endured, all came out in a torrent as she continued to batter his face, over and over. She finally sank down, exhausted and panting, her emotion spent, and observed the results of her now depleted rage.

His face was a mess, blood flowing from his nose and forehead, but he was alive. He moved his head and groaned, his vacant eyes staring up at her. Then his head dropped to one side, and he closed his eyes and lay still, his breathing rasping and shallow.

He wasn't going to harm her anymore. She'd made sure of that.

And then it finally hit her: she was alive and relatively unharmed. And free.

She tossed her weapon aside, stumbled to her feet, and looked at her surroundings. A large portion of the center of the ceiling had collapsed, drawing garbage from upstairs and ceiling debris with it. The stairs against the far wall seemed to have escaped damage.

She took one last glance at her former captor and picked her way across the litter-strewn floor to the stairs to freedom. She tested the first step. It seemed to be solid, so she carefully made her way up and stepped onto what was left of the floor.

The room where she'd been held constituted only a portion of the entire basement. Most of the upper floor was intact, and to her left was the back door where she'd almost escaped before.

She skirted around the caved-in floor and made her way to the back of the room.

She wished she'd checked her attacker to see if he had a cell phone. Too late now. She wasn't about to go back down there. She would have to find a phone elsewhere.

She slid the bolt back on the metal door and ground it open. The fresh air welcomed her and she breathed it in, taking deep breaths. She was going to make it this time.

She hurried into the narrow alleyway and ran to the left,

circled around a blue van, past the rear of other boarded-up buildings, and finally stepped onto the sidewalk of a narrow side street. Except for the occasional well-used car parked along the curb, litter and waste rattling in the gutter, and someone on a bicycle pedaling the other direction, the street was empty.

The back of her head throbbed but she ignored the pain and hurried to the intersection. This street didn't look much different, no one in sight. She wasn't familiar with this part of the city, but there must be someone around somewhere.

Traffic hummed to her right so she ran that way, toward a main thoroughfare. A man shuffled her way, a cell phone jammed in his ear, intent on his conversation.

She approached him.

"Please, may I borrow your phone? This is an emergency."

The man slowed, eyed her filthy clothing, her matted hair, and her bruised face, and hurried past.

She glanced up the street. A taxi was coming, its vacant sign glowing. She stepped off the curb into the street and held up her hand. Tires squealed and the cab ground to a halt.

The cabbie jabbed his horn angrily, leaning out the window. "Get out of the way, you maniac."

She didn't move. The driver stepped halfway from the cab and glared at her, aggravated.

"Please, I need your help," she said. "I've been kidnapped. I need to call the police."

He frowned at her a moment and then his face softened and he nodded slowly. "All right," he said.

CHAPTER 33

Friday, September 2nd, 12:45 p.m.

HANK PARKED HIS CHEVY in front of the Commerce Bank and went through the revolving doors. He glanced around the main area. Tellers were busy trying to pare down a long line of fidgeting customers. Faint music sounded somewhere overhead. A security guard leaned against the wall near an office doorway, his arms folded above his ample belly, a bored look on his face. Everything seemed to be business as usual.

Hank approached the security guard and showed his badge. "I'm Detective Corning. Are you the guard who chased the robber this morning?"

The security guard bounced off the wall, stood straight, his arms still folded, and nodded. "Yup. Almost caught him, too, but he slipped away." He offered his hand. "I'm Zeke Chalker."

Hank shook the guard's hand and then slipped out a well-worn notepad and thumbed to an empty page. "Did you get a good look at him?"

Chalker shrugged. "Big bushy beard. Average height. Average weight. Didn't see him up close. He was already running away when I got there. I already told all this to the officers that came."

"I realize that," Hank said. "But I need to hear it firsthand."

"Of course. I know that. I was going to be a cop." He shrugged again. "Didn't make the cut. You know how it is."

Hank suspected he knew how it was. If you weren't willing to apply yourself and get in shape, there was no room for you in the academy.

The guard continued, "I chased him up the street and into the alleyway and then when he fired at me, I had to duck for cover. He barely missed me and I didn't want to take any chances. By the time I was able to give chase again, he was gone onto the next street and I couldn't catch him."

"Did you see him after that? Did you see which way he went?" Hank asked.

Chalker shook his head. "By the time I got there he was gone. Maybe had a car waiting or something, or ducked into a building, but that was the last I saw of him."

Hank scribbled in his pad and then asked, "Did you see what he was wearing?"

"Just blue jeans and a black t-shirt."

"Shoes?"

"Not sure. Maybe running shoes. I didn't get a good look."

Hank flipped his pad closed and tucked it in his pocket. He hadn't gotten anything helpful, but the description was pretty much the same as Coleman had given earlier.

"Any security cameras here?" Hank asked, glancing around.

"Sure. Lots inside, but nothing out there." He pointed toward opposite corners of the room. "Camera there, and there, but neither of them has a view of the outside. I already checked for that."

Hank pulled out his pad again and consulted a page. "There was another witness," he said. "Can you tell me where I might find—?"

Hank twisted around and looked over his shoulder as Chalker pointed to an office on the far side of the bank. "Right there. Mrs. Kato. She saw the robbery through her office window."

"Okay, thanks, Mr. Chalker."

"Zeke. Just call me Zeke."

"Thanks, Zeke," Hank said and turned away. He walked across the bank and tapped on the office door below a sign that said, "Marie Kato, Loan Officer."

A pleasant voice said, "Come in."

Hank pushed the door open. Mrs. Kato sat forward in a straight-backed chair, papers in front of her, a pen poised in one hand, her eyes on Hank as he entered. She was midthirties, perhaps. Asian, maybe Japanese, Hank couldn't tell. Thin and great looking, her long dark hair framing a face painted to perfection. Filled out her charcoal-gray business suit really nicely.

Hank showed his badge. "Mrs. Kato, I'm Detective Corning."

She motioned toward the guest chair.

Hank sat and leaned forward. "I understand you saw the mugging this morning?"

Mrs. Kato set her pen carefully on the desk. "Yes, I saw it." Her voice was precise. Not much of an accent. "However, it happened so quickly I didn't have much chance to respond."

She gave the description of the mugger and it pretty much

fit with what Zeke had said—the main thing being the big bushy beard.

"I didn't get a good look at the weapon," she explained. "I alerted the security guard as soon as I saw what was happening." She sat back and crossed her legs, her hands clasped together in her lap. "I believe that's all I can tell you, Detective. It was over in a few seconds."

"You've been a big help," Hank said as he stood. He removed a card from his pocket and handed it to her. "If you think of anything else, please contact me."

She took the card and stood. "I will, Detective."

Hank left the office. Zeke was back in his position by the door, arms crossed and vigilant, guarding the security of the bank's patrons. Hank nodded at Zeke and went out to the sidewalk through the swinging door.

He climbed in his vehicle and sat awhile, thinking. The information he'd gotten from Zeke, Mrs. Kato, and Walter Coleman, was basically the same, but was enough to form a good picture of what had happened here this morning.

The kidnapper was proactive and had struck unexpectedly. He'd gotten his money, avoided a possible showdown with police, and gotten away with barely a whimper. A smart move and unforeseen.

He was contemplating his next move when his cell rang. Hank looked at the caller ID. It was Jake.

"I've got good news," Jake said when Hank answered. "Mrs. Coleman is free."

"He let her go?"

"No, she escaped. She's at the hospital right now. She had a nasty bump on her head, but after she called 9-1-1, she called her husband and he called me."

"Escaped? How?"

"We don't know anything yet," Jake said. "It just happened a couple of minutes ago. Annie and I are about to go and see her at the request of Walter Coleman. Of course, I realize you'll want to interview her in depth, but we'd like to be there."

"I can meet you there," Hank said. "I'm just a few minutes away."

CHAPTER 34

Friday, September 2nd, 1:00 p.m.

JAKE PULLED INTO THE parking lot by the emergency entrance of Richmond Hill General Hospital. He hadn't been here for a while and was amazed at the price of parking. But he knew hospitals were vastly underfunded and he didn't begrudge the extra cost. Jake chuckled at a sign that read, "Emergency Department Valet Service." Just like a hotel.

Hank was already there, leaning against the front fender of his vehicle, pulled off to the side of the circular emergency driveway. The police sticker displayed on his dashboard ensured he wouldn't be tagged or towed.

Jake and Annie stepped from the Firebird and joined Hank.

"I called dispatch," Hank said. "Apparently Rosemary Coleman was being held in an abandoned store downtown. First responders have already shown up there and forensics is on their way now. That's all I know at the moment."

"This might be the break we need," Annie said.

"I hope so," Hank said, motioning toward the double doors leading into the hospital. "We'd better go in."

An ambulance siren blared far away, getting closer, while another was just pulling from the ambulance bay.

The waiting room inside the massive building was busy. People of all ages, in various stages of pain and suffering, sat, slouched, and stood, patiently waiting their turn for treatment. The room smelled lightly of disinfectant mixed with the scent of disease and healing. A sign boasted that the emergency department was open twenty-four hours a day, offering walk-in services for patients with emergencies. Jake wondered how much of an emergency it was if the patient could walk in.

Hank showed his badge to the receptionist, who squinted at it and then frowned at Jake and motioned toward a pair of double doors. Jake nodded, smiled at the receptionist, and followed Hank through the doors.

The large main room of the hospital's emergency department seemed well equipped to treat patients with serious medical conditions and injuries. Hank approached a nurse in a starched white uniform who seemed to be in charge, and showed his badge.

"I'm looking for Rosemary Coleman?"

The nurse motioned toward one of many private treatment rooms that lined the far wall. A uniformed officer was keeping watch outside one of the curtained-off rooms.

"We're keeping her for observation for a few hours," the nurse said. "The doctor has already examined her, so you can see her now." The nurse frowned. "But just two of you at a time."

Jake looked at Annie, and Annie looked back. "I'll wait out

here. You can fill me in later," Annie said as she turned and took a seat in a small waiting area.

Hank approached the room and nodded to the officer. He pulled back the curtain and he and Jake entered the small, dimly lit room. A woman was propped up in the hospital bed, her head to one side, her eyes closed.

"Rosemary Coleman?" Hank said softly.

The woman's eyes shot open. "Yes," she said.

"I'm Detective Corning." Hank motioned toward Jake. "And this is Jake Lincoln. Are you able to talk?"

She nodded.

Hank explained to Rosemary who Jake was and how he was involved. She seemed to be in a calm, composed mood despite her recent predicament.

"The place where you were held is being thoroughly examined now, but I have a few other questions."

She nodded again.

"Did you see the face of your captor?" Hank asked. "Would you be able to identify him?"

"There were two of them in the woods, but they wore masks and they took me to a cellar. I ... I almost escaped once and there was only one man there at the time and I saw his face, but he caught me again. He didn't hide his face after that, so I knew they were never going to let me out alive."

"Would you recognize him again?"

"Yes," she said. "I would know his face anywhere."

"As soon as you're able, we'll get a forensic artist to conduct an interview with you, then get you to look at some mug shots later," Hank said and made a note in his pad.

She nodded.

Hank looked up. "How did you escape?"

She smiled slightly. "I pulled the building down."

Hank tilted his head. "What do you mean?"

She explained how she'd freed herself, resulting in half the ceiling coming down, and how she'd beaten down her abductor with a piece of wood.

Jake grinned as he pictured the scene. She had a lot of spunk.

"It was the only choice I had," she added.

"You didn't kill him, did you?" Hank asked.

She laughed. "He was still breathing when I left."

"You did the right thing, Mrs. Coleman. Your husband paid the ransom demand, but we have reason to believe they had no intention of letting you go."

She nodded slowly and said quietly, "I was afraid of that."

Hank got more details from her as to when, where, and how she was abducted, and what had happened during the period she was held. She stopped and frowned. "I think there was a blue van parked behind the building." She closed her eyes a moment. "Yes, I'm sure there was."

Jake exchanged a look with Hank. They'd been looking for a white van all this time. Perhaps they'd been on the wrong track, or maybe there were two vans involved.

The curtains to the room slid aside and Walter Coleman stepped in. "Darling," he said. "I came as fast as I could."

The small hospital room was getting crowded as Jake stepped back to allow Coleman past. Coleman squeezed through, leaned over, and kissed his wife on the forehead. "Are you all right?"

"I'm okay," she said.

The nurse appeared in the doorway. "Gentlemen, I'm going to have to ask one of you to leave."

"It's okay. I believe we're done here," Hank told her, and then looked at Coleman. "I'll arrange for an officer to stay at your home once your wife is released. We have to take every precaution until these guys are captured."

"Thank you, Detective. Thanks, Jake," Coleman said as they turned to go. "I appreciate it."

Jake and Hank joined Annie in the waiting area. "Let's go to the abandoned store where Mrs. Coleman was held," Hank said. "Jake can fill you in on the way."

CHAPTER 35

Friday, September 2nd, 1:44 p.m.

ANNIE WAS VAGUELY familiar with the part of the city where the abandoned store was located. As they drew closer, she saw that many of the buildings in this area were run-down, vacant, and probably earmarked for demolition at some time in the near future.

Jake pulled the Firebird in behind Hank's Chevy where half a dozen police cars, along with the forensics van, sat in front of a boarded-up storefront. Onlookers had gathered across the street in groups of two or three. Officers hung about in front, keeping back the curious, with a pair of cops at the door of the building, barring access to the unauthorized.

The Lincolns climbed from the car and joined Hank, already striding toward the front of the store. The officer nodded at them and let them inside.

Annie wrinkled her nose as she was hit with a musty odor, the staleness of rotting wood and perhaps the faint smell of human waste. Garbage littered the floor, old newspapers and trash spread about, piled in corners and along the peeling walls. A pair of dusty showcases sat near the front. A fold-up chair and a cardboard box to serve as a table, strewn with empty coffee cups, were the only signs anyone had been here recently.

An investigator stood beside a gaping hole in the floor, staring into the basement below, his arms folded. Annie recognized him as the lead crime scene investigator, Rod Jameson.

Other investigators were at work. The entire contents of the store were being carted away to be studied, scrutinized, and examined thoroughly. The job would soon be done.

Annie stayed out of the way as she went to the back of the store. The door was open and she stepped outside. An officer leaned against the doorframe and Annie smiled at him.

"Hello, Yappy," she said.

Officer Spiegle was called Yappy by almost everyone. No one knew how he got the name, but he didn't mind it. He considered himself lucky to have this job and normally would've been passed over during the hiring phase, but his daddy had been a well-respected sergeant who'd been killed in the line of duty. Nobody disliked Yappy. He was pleasant enough, but his assignments never much more than menial.

"Hi, Annie. I heard you guys were on this one," Yappy said.

"Not by choice this time. It seems like we've been chosen."

"Yeah, I heard about that," Yappy said with a wide grin.

Annie looked up and down the alley. The blue van Mrs. Coleman had seen was gone and likely the abductor was gone with it.

She wandered down the access road. A big orange dumpster a few stores away, a rusty vehicle which looked abandoned, trash and litter everywhere, but no signs of life in this nearly forgotten street.

She nodded to Yappy and went back inside. Hank was talking to Jameson and Jake stood beside him. The bulk of the job was done, with most of the contents removed.

She wanted to see what was downstairs where Mrs. Coleman had been held. She caught Jake's eye and he came over to her.

"Let's go downstairs," she said.

"I think they're finished down there," Jake said as he headed for the steps. "It should be okay."

Annie followed Jake down the stairs. They stood at the bottom and looked around. The floor was a disarray of broken boards, wood chips, splinters and ... blood?

Annie stepped over to the wall. This must be where Mrs. Coleman had beaten back her abductor. She knelt and examined the floor. The porous concrete had soaked up most of a small pool of drying blood, and blood was sprayed across the broken boards. The kidnapper had survived and somehow picked his way up the stairs. He was likely the one who'd taken the van and would be long gone.

She stood and scanned the room. This was undoubtedly the same place the doctor's wife had been held and perhaps where she'd been murdered. She shuddered when she saw a broken chair and recognized it as the same chair both victims had been tied to when photographed.

Jake was examining the ceiling. "It's no wonder this all came down. The ceiling joists are almost completely deteriorated by dry rot. I'm surprised it lasted this long, and when Mrs. Coleman knocked out the support pole, the whole thing came tumbling down."

"But it's not that damp in here," Annie said.

"Dry rot doesn't need much moisture," Jake explained. "It's actually fungus that grows and it's hard to eradicate.

Eventually, the decay can cause instability and the entire structure can collapse. That's what happened here."

"Then it's fortunate for Rosemary Coleman they picked this place."

Jake nodded. "Yes, it is. And now, we'd better get out of here."

They went back upstairs and joined Hank. Jake explained his theory and added, "This place should've been torn down long ago."

Hank said, "It was boarded up but somehow they managed to get in. We'll soon know who owns this building and that might shed some light on our perps. Maybe."

Annie doubted it would.

Hank continued, "And now that we know exactly where Rosemary Coleman was abducted, officers are on their way there. Detective King'll be spearheading that and they'll go over the wooded area with a fine-toothed comb. They might find something."

Annie interrupted. "The blue van is gone."

Hank nodded. "I checked that as well and if it was the kidnapper's vehicle, he's gone with it, I presume."

"He left a lot of his blood downstairs, though," Jake said.

"The hospitals and clinics have been informed in case he shows up for medical aid," Hank said. "And I already have Callaway cross-checking the records for any registered blue vans."

Rod Jameson approached. "We're done here, Hank. It's too soon to tell what we have, but there are some fingerprints around. Some on the coffee cups, and we might get some DNA from them as well. And of course, the blood downstairs is going to help identify one of them."

"We have a physical description of the injured perp as

well," Hank said. "Mrs. Coleman was sure she could identify him and once we get him, we're well on our way."

"If he talks," Jake added.

"He'll talk," Hank said. "I don't think he was the brains behind this operation and if the crown offers him a lighter sentence ... he'll talk."

"Then we have to find him before someone else is hurt," Annie said.

CHAPTER 36

Friday, September 2nd, 2:15 p.m.

WHEN HANK STEPPED from the store he almost ran straight into Lisa Krunk. She seemed to have been trying to get some information from one of the officers guarding the door, but she spun around when she saw Hank and shoved the microphone at him.

Hank brushed it aside and moved to the front of the boarded-up windows, out of the way. Don's camera followed his moves and Lisa was right behind.

"Detective Corning," she said. "What can you tell me about the events taking place here?"

Hank paused. Lisa could be a royal pain, but if handled properly, she could be of some help. Besides, she owed him one. He disregarded his annoyance for her and spoke pleasantly for the watching camera.

"Good afternoon, Lisa. I received a call that a second kidnapping victim had been held in this building and fortunately, was able to escape. She's now under protection and we're well on our way to rounding up the perpetrators."

"Can you give us her name?" Lisa asked.

"Not at this time. Investigators are still studying the mountain of evidence and rest assured, there's lots of it."

"Detective, do you believe this is the work of the kidnapper who abducted and subsequently murdered Linda Gould three days ago?"

"We have reason to believe so, yes."

"And was a ransom paid this time as well?"

Hank hesitated and then said slowly, "A ransom was paid."

Lisa's mouth flapped. "If the ransom was paid, why would the victim be afraid for her safety?"

"The victim is able to identify her captor. Remember, she wasn't released, she escaped, so we're taking every precaution."

"Do you know who's responsible for the abductions?"

Hank looked directly at the camera. "We have a good idea who's responsible and if you're watching, we advise you to turn yourself in. We have your description and you can't get away. It's just a matter of time until you're caught."

Jake and Annie had stepped outside but were standing back. Lisa noticed them and motioned toward Don. He spun his camera their way as Lisa stepped over and confronted Jake.

"Jake Lincoln," she said. "You're becoming involved in a number of high-profile cases lately. Do you have any information on this case you could share with the public?"

Jake frowned and leaned into the mike. "We have no information the police don't already have and our investigation is parallel to theirs. As we have the same goal, any information we obtain is immediately turned over to them." He straightened up and crossed his arms. Hank knew Jake wasn't too happy with Lisa right now and he would have no more to say.

Lisa looked back and forth from Annie to Jake, obviously

hoping for another comment. None was forthcoming. She frowned at Annie. "Mrs. Lincoln, do you agree with that?"

"Absolutely," Annie said.

Hank motioned toward Lisa. "I'd like to add one more thing."

Lisa's eyes lit up and she eagerly swung the mike his way. The camera followed, its red light glowing.

Hank spoke, "The perpetrator we're looking for has sustained several wounds about his face and neck in an altercation with the victim. He's of medium build with dark hair. He also might be driving a blue van. I urge the members of the public to call our Crime Stoppers hotline if you see, or suspect, anyone with that description. He might or might not be in the company of others. Do not try to approach him as we have reason to believe he might be armed."

Lisa held the mike steady as Hank gave the phone number to call and then he paused a moment before adding, "I would also like to repeat my warning from yesterday's press conference. Please take precautions. Use common sense, be vigilant if in secluded places, lock your door at night and don't open it to anyone you don't know."

"Do you believe there is more than one kidnapper involved?" Lisa asked. "Is the Merchant of Death actually two people?"

"We believe there're two and that makes our job easier." Hank glared at the camera. "We'll hunt you down, so be afraid. We're coming for you."

"Is there anything else you can add, Detective?"

"That's all for now, Lisa. I've got a job to do, so let me get at it."

Lisa pulled the mike back and motioned toward Don to shut down the camera. "Can I get a shot inside the building?" she asked Hank.

"From the doorway. I can't let you go inside. It's still a crime scene and could be dangerous."

"Dangerous?"

Hank chuckled. "You'll see."

Lisa nodded. "Thanks, Detective." Don followed her to the doorway, the camera humming.

An officer was working on a roll of familiar yellow tape, about to lock the front door and seal it. He looked up when Lisa approached, then looked at Hank. Hank nodded an okay to him and the officer stepped back.

Hank turned to Jake. "Now that I have a better idea of what went on here, I want to have another talk with the Colemans as soon as Mrs. Coleman is released."

"Anything we can do?" Annie asked.

Hank shrugged. "I don't believe so. I have people looking into every aspect of this case and unless you can think of something else—"

Jake laughed and put his arm around Annie's shoulder. "Annie always comes up with ideas, but for now, I hope we can just take a break."

Annie looked up at Jake. "We'll take a break later, when Hank does, and the kidnappers are behind bars."

Jake shrugged and looked at Hank. "See what I mean?"

CHAPTER 37

Friday, September 2nd, 2:30 p.m.

JAKE POPPED THE CLUTCH and left a little rubber on the asphalt as he pulled away from the curb. He glanced over at Annie. She seemed to be deep in thought, her brow wrinkled, and she didn't seem to notice the squeal of the tires as the vehicle sprang ahead. After seventeen years of marriage, she was probably used to it by now.

Normally, he didn't like to park his baby in a neighborhood like this, but with all the police cars around, thieves would have to be pretty brazen to jack it up and swipe his Sportsman S/Rs wrapped around Boze brushed aluminum rims.

"We've been so busy lately," he said. "I haven't had time to look into that insurance scammer. The company is going to be after us to get something done."

Annie looked at him, his comment taking awhile to register, then said, "They'll wait. I told them it might be a few days before we get at it. They're used to that."

Jake yawned. "Hopefully, we'll get a rest tomorrow and I can take care of it then."

"That doesn't sound like a rest to me."

"It's a change anyway. Something different to do." He paused. "Don't get me wrong, I want to catch the kidnappers as much as anyone, but a change will give us time to think of a new approach. We've got little to go on right now anyway."

"I'm afraid you're right, but there's always something. I just haven't thought of it yet."

Jake laughed. "Oh, I'm sure you will. Your mind is always working overtime. Maybe you should've been a cop."

"I'm a bit small for that, don't you think?"

"Yeah, maybe." Jake glanced at her. "But you do look mean."

Annie giggled and slugged him on the shoulder. "I do not look mean."

Jake gave her a wink. "I meant it as a compliment. You're lean and mean in all the right places."

"Keep your eyes on the road. There's time for that later."

Jake roared with laughter. "I might take you up on that."

He was still laughing when his cell phone rang. He scooped it from his belt holder.

"Give me that," Annie demanded, holding out her hand. "You're driving."

Jake handed her the phone and she put it on speaker. "Annie Lincoln."

There was a pause on the line and then a deep voice said, "Hello, Annie Lincoln. It's nice to talk to you."

Jake frowned and reached for the phone but Annie held on. "Did you want to speak to Jake?" she asked.

"If he's busy I wouldn't want to interrupt him."

Annie motioned for Jake to pull over. He thought it was a good idea, considering the nature of the call.

"He's right here," Annie said. "Just a moment."

Jake pulled to the curb, shut down the vehicle, and took the phone from Annie. "This is Jake."

"Jake, my friend, it seems we've had a little mishap."

"Oh?"

"I noticed a commotion going on. Police officers everywhere, the media, you and Annie. It's a nasty, nasty situation. Very unfortunate indeed and an unexpected turn of events, wouldn't you say?"

"What did you expect? That the police not be called?"

A sigh on the line and then, "I expect people to play fair. Nobody seems to want to play by the rules anymore. It's a sad situation when you can't trust anyone."

Jake slammed his fist on the steering wheel. "You got your money. Isn't that enough?"

"I got my money, yes, but Mrs. Coleman neglected to hold up her end of the bargain. She couldn't wait until our little transaction was completed. Women are so impatient these days."

Jake glared at the phone and raised his voice. "You weren't going to let her go. I knew it, you knew it, and she knew it."

"I hadn't decided that, Jake. But now ... now, because of the current situation, somebody must pay." Another sigh, then, "I must decide who'll pay for this. I don't mean financially, of course. That's already been covered, but someone will pay."

Annie put her hand on Jake's arm and shook her head slowly, telling him to remain calm, but he found it hard. He took a breath and said, "You're the one who'll pay."

The caller laughed. It was a sinister sound, designed to mock. "I'm getting tired of being so repetitive, Jake. It's starting to grate on my nerves and I'd hoped you would know the rules by now. I implore you, for the good of everyone involved, please ensure complete compliance next time. Not just from yourself—you've actually been rather good about that—but from the others."

Jake dropped his head back and closed his eyes. Next time. Always a next time. He changed his mind about taking a rest the next day and vowed to never let up until this scumbag was flat on his back.

"Next time will be your last time," Jake said firmly. "You have my word."

"Perhaps it will be, Jake. Perhaps it will be." A pause. "And now, until we meet again, I must bid you goodbye and please, give my fondest regards to your lovely wife. You're a fortunate man, you know. A woman like her needs to be protected, guarded, defended with your life. It was such a pleasure to speak to her."

Jake gritted his teeth and glared at the phone. This guy knew just how to get to him and unfortunately, he was letting it happen.

"Until next time," the caller said and then the line went dead.

Jake sat a moment and stared quietly out the windshield. This was becoming an extremely stressful job, living every day surrounded with the knowledge of people's capacity for evil. But the desire to see that evil stopped dead kept him going. Rosemary Coleman might be safe, but Linda Gould was dead and the doctor would have to live with her death on a daily basis. It would never go away.

It had to stop now.

Annie spoke quietly. "We'd better get the recording of this call to Hank. They might be able to make something of it."

Jake nodded and looked at his watch. "We might not get home before Matty. Maybe you can call Chrissy and let her know to watch for him."

Annie sighed. "I think you're right. It seems we haven't seen much of him in the last few days."

Jake pushed in the clutch and turned the key, and the vehicle roared to life. "We'll make it up to him," Jake said. "He's a smart kid. He'll understand." He pulled from the curb, venting some of his anger by leaving behind another patch of rubber.

CHAPTER 38

Friday, September 2nd, 3:18 p.m.

HANK WAS AT HIS DESK filling out some paperwork when Jake and Annie arrived at the precinct. He forced a grin when he saw them, tossed his pen aside, and sat back.

"Have a seat," he said.

Jake and Annie sat in the guest chairs.

"So much paperwork," Hank said with a sigh. "If I didn't have to spend so much time at my desk I might be able to get this case wrapped up sooner."

Jake handed his cell phone to Hank. "I got another call."

Hank raised his brows and leaned forward. "Already? Not another kidnapping?" he asked as he took the phone from Jake.

"Not yet," Jake said. "Just a warning. And a threat."

Hank listened to the recording of the call. When it was finished, he said, "Someone'll pay? What could he mean by that?" He sat back and rubbed his chin. "We'd better keep Mrs. Coleman under twenty-four-hour guard until this is wrapped up."

"Perhaps he means the next victim or someone else entirely," Annie said.

Hank seemed to consider that a moment before spinning around in his chair. "Callaway," he called.

Callaway looked up from his monitor and Hank beckoned him over and handed him the phone. "Make a copy of this call. And see if you can find out where it came from."

"I'll get right on it, Hank."

"And did you find out who owns that store?"

"Not yet, but I'm working on it." Callaway hurried back to his desk.

Hank folded his arms. "The detail Detective King put together has finished canvassing the city looking for that white van." He shook his head. "No luck. That seems to be a dead end, but now I have them out looking for blue vans."

"At least that one's a solid lead," Annie said. "And there won't be as many of them."

"That's for sure," Hank said. "The list is rather short. I hope to hear something soon."

Jake spoke up, "And what about the woods where Mrs. Coleman was abducted? Anything there?"

Hank shrugged. "Nothing in the woods that looks promising, but officers are checking door-to-door to see if anyone saw anything in the area, specifically a blue van. I'm presuming she was taken away in the van Mrs. Coleman saw at the store."

"What about the sketch artist?" Annie asked.

"He should be at the hospital now. They won't let Mrs. Coleman leave for a while. Afraid she might have concussion, but she's safe there."

"I have to ask," Annie said. "I know everyone is a suspect, even Walter Coleman—"

"Coleman's alibi checked out. He was in King City all day yesterday doing a landscaping job. His workers vouched for that as well as the client. There's no way he could've been home before five p.m."

"So who does that leave us with?" Jake asked.

Hank sighed. "Nobody. Which makes it more important than ever we find that blue van and its driver."

Callaway approached Jake and handed him back his phone. "I'll dissect that recording," he said to Hank. "There might be something on it."

"Any luck tracing the call?"

Callaway shrugged. "It's almost impossible to trace a call after the fact. I'm afraid that's a dead end."

~*~

WHEN JAKE AND ANNIE got home, Jake went straight out to the back deck and sat down, propping his feet up on another chair. He could see Matty and Kyle next door, kicking around a soccer ball.

He stood and leaned over the railing and called to his son. "Matty, come here a minute, will you?"

Matty spun around, grinned when he saw his father, and sped up onto the deck. He bounced on the edge of a chair.

"What's up, Dad?" he asked.

Jake looked at his son with pride. He seemed to be growing bigger every day. "I just wanted to talk to you a minute."

"Sure."

"I realize your mother and I have been pretty busy lately, often in the evenings, and haven't been able to spend a lot of time with you."

"That's okay. I know what you and Mom do is important. And everybody at school knows who you guys are. That's all the kids are talking about these days and about the kidnappings and stuff."

Jake laughed and then asked, "How about you and I take a little fishing trip one of these days soon? Maybe go up to Grand River or Humber River for a couple of days and see if we can bring home a few trout."

"Yeah, that sounds cool, Dad. When can we go?"

"As soon as we get this case wrapped up." Jake sighed. "I hope it won't be long."

"Can Kyle come too?" Matty asked.

"Sure, why not. We'll make it a guy thing. Camping out. Black flies, mosquitoes, the whole shebang. It'll be great."

Matty jumped up. "Hey, Kyle," he shouted. "Get over here."

Kyle appeared a moment later, gasping for air. He looked expectantly at Matty.

"Wanna go fishing with us?" Matty asked.

Kyle frowned. "Right now?"

Matty giggled. "No, in a few days. Just you, me, and my dad."

"Sure," Kyle said. "Mom won't mind."

"Yeah, she'll probably be glad to get rid of you for a couple of days," Matty said dryly and then ducked as Kyle aimed a punch at his shoulder. The two boys charged back out to the yard and in a minute, were rolling around on the grass.

Annie stepped from the back door onto the deck. She'd fixed up a jug of ice-cold lemonade and she set it on the table along with four glasses, and filled two.

Jake told her of his plans to take the boys fishing.

"What about Hank?" Annie asked.

"Nah, not this time. He'll have so much paperwork to do after this case he'll still be doing it when we get back. He won't even notice we were gone."

CHAPTER 39

Friday, September 2nd, 4:18 p.m.

HANNAH MARTIN PULLED her SUV into the driveway. It'd been a long day and she was glad to be home. Once she got the groceries in the house and put away she would take a break and maybe enjoy a cup of tea.

She popped the trunk, stepped from the vehicle, and stopped short as a yellow van pulled into the driveway beside her. Perhaps it was the plumber. The kitchen sink was leaking and she'd been after Eli to get someone to fix it. Funny thing though, the van had no sign or other markings on it.

She waited until the passenger door opened and a man stepped around the front of the van. He wore a baseball cap, pulled low, but she saw he had a number of scabs, nicks, and healing wounds on his face, like he'd been in a car accident, or some kind of scuffle.

"Mrs. Martin?" he asked.

She answered cautiously. "Yes?"

"I have a delivery for you."

She watched curiously as he moved to the side of the van, ground the door open, and reached in. He turned around with some kind of a black cloth bag in his hand. Whatever could be in that bag?

With one deft move he slipped the bag over her head and drew the drawstring tight. She struggled and swung at him to no avail. Strong arms held her from behind, spun her around, and pushed her, kicking and trying to scream, into the side door of the van.

Then she was rolled onto her stomach, her hands wrenched behind her, and she felt him on top of her, weighing her down. A cable tie zipped and she was helpless. Through the cloth bag, she felt the cool metal of the truck bed on her face. The confines of the bag, along with a sudden panic which overtook her, made it hard to breathe.

His weight was removed from her back, the van door slammed, and, in a few moments, the engine roared as the vehicle backed from the driveway. She struggled against her bonds as the van braked to a stop, then leaped forward, picked up speed, and carried her away.

She'd heard about the kidnappings that had taken place lately. Was this the same man she'd heard about on the news? Was she now about to be treated like a piece of merchandise? Would her husband pay the ransom? Of course he would, but they weren't rich. She feared for her life and lay trembling and feeling very much alone.

After a few minutes, the van pulled to a stop and the engine died. The driver-side door creaked and then slammed. All was silent for several long minutes, seemed like hours, she couldn't tell. Too many thoughts in her head, too much terror.

She struggled to remove the bag but the drawstring was too tight, her hands helpless. She kicked against the door, but nobody came to help. Nobody heard her muffled screams and nobody knew where she was.

The van door slid open and rough hands grabbed her

from behind and half-dragged her from the vehicle. She tried to stand, stumbled, then was prodded forward, unable to see, and pushed through a doorway.

"Watch the steps."

While held from behind, she felt her way down a flight of stairs. She was greeted by a strong odor, something chemical, and an unknown taste assaulted her taste buds.

When her feet touched the hard floor, she was pushed to the right, a door creaked open, she was prodded again, and then the bag was loosened from around her throat and removed. She took a breath and gasped in the damp, clammy air.

When she turned around, her abductor had gone from the tiny room that now held her, slamming the door behind him. She heard a bolt slide and she was alone—alone in a small, dark room, the only light seeping from under the sealed door, her hands still tied.

As her eyes grew accustomed to the dark, the tiny ray of light revealed the tomblike space. Concrete floor, concrete walls, cool and damp.

She slumped down against the cold, hard wall and cried.

~*~

A CALL CAME IN to 9-1-1 at 16:30 hours and RHPD dispatch was notified immediately. A neighbor had witnessed a kidnapping at 96 Westwind Drive. The astute eyewitness had gotten the license plate number of a yellow Chevrolet van that was used to abduct her neighbor, a Mrs. Hannah Martin. First responders were on their way.

Hank was apprised of the situation. The kidnapper had warned there would be another abduction. Hank was expecting it, but not so soon. But at least there was a witness this time.

Hank jumped from his chair, raced across the precinct floor, and dropped a sticky note on Callaway's desk. "Looks like we might've caught a break," he said. "A yellow van, license number MHW 396. What can you get me on that ASAP?" Hank sat opposite him and waited.

Callaway swung into action, faced his monitor, and tapped rapidly on the keyboard. In a moment, he recited, "MHW 396. MTO has it listed as a red 2014 Hyundai. Registered to a Meyer Summerdale, here in the city."

Hank tilted his head and frowned. "A 2014 Hyundai? It should be a yellow Chevy van. That's what the neighbor saw."

"Are you sure she got the right number?" Callaway asked.

"She seemed positive. Said she wrote it down right away. Given the accuracy of everything else she said—"

"Just a minute." Callaway was glaring at the screen again. "A Meyer Summerdale reported his license plates stolen. MHW 396. His vehicle was parked along the curb in front of his house and this morning he noticed them missing."

Hank slumped back in his chair. He just couldn't catch a break. He would have a look at the statement the responding officers took and check out Meyer Summerdale, but he doubted it would lead him anywhere.

CHAPTER 40

Friday, September 2nd, 5:18 p.m.

JAKE WAS IN THE BACKYARD with Matty and Kyle
when his cell phone rang. He looked at the caller ID, gave the
soccer ball one last kick to Matty and answered the call.

"Jake Lincoln."

"Mr. Lincoln, my name is Eli Martin. It ... it's my wife.
She's been kidnapped and I just got a call from the kidnapper.
He ... he said I must call you if I ever want to see her again."

Jake took a deep breath and stepped onto the deck. *Here
we go again.*

"Tell me what happened, Mr. Martin."

"A ... a neighbor saw my wife being abducted this
afternoon and called the police. It ... it happened right in the
driveway of our house. I've already given a statement and
they said a detective would want to talk to me as well. And
then ... I received a call from the kidnapper."

"Did he have a deep voice?" Jake asked. "Like a
camouflaged voice?"

"Yes, and he wants fifty thousand dollars. He wants you to deliver it."

Jake sat on a deck chair and leaned forward. If someone witnessed the abduction, hopefully the police could finally stop this guy before someone else died.

"He said he would call you," Martin continued.

"I'll do everything I can to help, Mr. Martin, and to get your wife home safely."

"He sent me a picture of her," Martin said. "To my phone. I ... I can't tell where she is. In a room somewhere. A concrete room."

"Mr. Martin, I know it's hard, but try to relax. I'm sure the police are on this even as we speak. Let them do their job and I'll be in touch with them as well. I'll let you know as soon as the kidnapper calls me."

"I'll pay the ransom, Mr. Lincoln. I just want my wife back safely."

"This is not the first kidnapping," Jake said. "He doesn't allow a lot of time to get the money together. He might want it tomorrow. Is that a problem?"

"No, no problem. I have enough here in my safe, but ... he said he knows the police are already aware of this and I'm not to talk to them. I ... I don't know what to do."

The police were already involved and nothing could be done about that. But right now, he wanted to be sure Mrs. Martin didn't end up dead. "The police will keep it discreet," he said. "But first, I have to wait for the kidnapper to call, then we'll know how to proceed."

"I ... guess all I can do is leave it in your hands," Martin said. "And the police."

Jake sighed. His hands weren't all that capable right now,

but there didn't seem to be any choice. "I'll be in touch," he said.

~*~

TEN MINUTES LATER Jake's phone rang again. He looked at the caller ID. Unknown number. He was pretty sure he knew who was calling.

Jake pushed back from the kitchen table. "I think it's him," he said to Annie as she dropped her book on the table and sat back.

He put the phone on speaker. "Jake Lincoln."

"Good evening, Jake."

It was him.

The deep voice continued, "I'm sure you've heard the good news?"

Jake took the bait. "What good news?" he asked.

"We have another transaction to take care of. What could be better news than that?"

"I could think of a few things. Perhaps seeing you behind bars might be better news."

A laugh came over the line. "Now, Jake, let's not be bitter, shall we?"

Jake stood, paced the floor, and said nothing.

"I assume you received a call from Mr. Eli Martin?" the caller asked.

"I did."

"And did he tell you the amount of the purchase? I think fifty thousand dollars is reasonable, don't you?"

"He can get the money."

"I didn't doubt it for a minute."

Jake raised his voice. "But we don't want any harm to

come to Mrs. Martin. He's willing to do as you ask, but please, you must release her."

"All in good time, my friend."

Jake looked at Annie. She'd been listening intently to the call and was frowning at the phone.

The kidnapper continued, "As you know, Jake, I'm not all that fond of the police. I'm well aware they know about this current transaction, but you must keep them from further involvement, or … just let me say, things might get messy."

"I can't stop them from doing their job," Jake said. "They're already involved, thanks to your sloppy work."

"You must not tell them my delivery instructions. We can do this discreetly."

"That would be up to Mr. Martin," Jake said.

An unnatural laugh and then the caller said, "I do hope he makes the right choice."

"I'll advise him to do what you ask, but it's his choice."

"Excellent, Jake. I'll be in touch with you again soon to let you know the further terms of our contract and how the transaction is to take place. I've already informed Mr. Martin to have the funds ready as soon as possible, but I'm relying on you to impress upon him the urgency of this matter."

"I will," Jake said and then the line went dead.

"Did you record that?" Annie asked.

Jake nodded, a deep frown on his face. "I don't know what the witness saw," he said. "I have to talk to Hank, but hopefully it was enough to nail this guy."

Jake dialed Hank's number and the call was answered on the first ring. He told the cop about the calls he'd received.

"I'm just finishing up something here," Hank said. "And then I'll go and interview Eli Martin. I'll pick you up on the way there."

CHAPTER 41

Friday, September 2nd, 6:02 p.m.

HANNAH MARTIN SAT HUDDLED against the wall of her cell. She didn't know for sure how long she'd been here and how long she would have to remain. She was terrified for what her future held, shivering with fear and cold.

Her abductor had returned once to snap her picture, and then left without a word.

She knew he was outside the door, in the next room. She heard him moving around from time to time and her banging on the door to attract his attention had gone unheeded.

She didn't know where or what this building was and had screamed as loud as possible, over and over, trying to attract someone's attention. Her screams seemed to have gone unnoticed, or more likely, unheard by anyone except her jailer prowling around in the next room. Once he'd yelled at her, "Shut up in there," and then seemed to pay no mind to her after that.

Her voice had gone hoarse and she'd finally given up hope of being heard.

She was hungry and thirsty and the thin shirt she was wearing did little to protect her from the cold. But most of all, she was fearful for her life. She never expected to be a kidnap victim, and wondered if these were the same kidnappers she'd heard about.

She had heeded the news warnings and been careful not to go out at night, especially alone, and to keep her doors locked at all times. But to be abducted in front of her own house in broad daylight was beyond anything she could've imagined.

The lock on the door rattled and the door grated open.

"I got some food for you."

She strained to see his face against the brightness of the room behind him.

"You better eat," he said as he crouched down and tossed a bag toward her. "It's a burger."

She saw his face now. It was the same man—the one who'd forced her into the van and brought her here.

"I'm thirsty," she said.

He pointed to the bag as he straightened up. "There's a drink in there too." He pulled a knife from his pocket. "Stand up and turn around."

She stood and turned slowly, and he cut the ties holding her wrists.

"Okay, you can eat now," he said.

She turned back and picked up the bag as he stood in the doorway, watching her, his arms folded.

"Why are you holding me?" she asked.

He shrugged. "You'll find out, I guess."

"Are you going to let me go soon?"

"Can't say when. I guess we'll let you go, but I have to do what the boss tells me. It ain't up to me."

She examined his face carefully. Despite the wounds, he didn't appear to be a cold-blooded killer. But then, if what he said was true and he was following orders, then who knew what he would do?

"If you let me go," she said, "I can make it worth your while."

"I doubt that. I'm getting paid pretty good for this job."

"I can pay you more."

He laughed. "I don't see how that would work. You have no money on you and if I let you go get it, then you wouldn't keep your word. I'm no dummy. I know better than that."

"I'm not necessarily talking about money," she said, forcing a seductive smile.

He laughed again and leaned against the doorframe. "If I wanted that from you, well, I could just take it, couldn't I?"

"But you wouldn't. You're not that type of man."

He chuckled. "And how would you know that?"

"Because if you were, you would've done it by now."

"Yeah, that's true," he said in a thoughtful voice, and then a little gruffer, "But I still can, you know."

"You won't."

He studied her face a moment and then looked her up and down. Finally, he said, "Yeah, you're right, I wouldn't. I might be many things. Probably not the best man you'll ever meet, but I gotta draw the line somewhere I guess." He looked at her defiantly. "And I ain't never killed nobody either."

She believed he was sincere and that gave her a ray of hope. She understood it wasn't him she needed to be afraid of, but whoever he worked for. But he was the gatekeeper standing in the way of her freedom and she had to do something. It didn't look like she would be able to bribe him, either with money or the promise of sex.

One last try. She took a step toward him and smiled again. "Can we make a deal?"

He shook his head. "Nope. I guess not."

"Don't you find me attractive?" she asked, pretending to be disappointed.

"Uh, of course I do, but you know, I just can't do that. The boss would kill me for sure and all for what? A couple minutes of fun?"

She took another slow step forward, now just three or four feet away from him.

He bounced off the wall, stood upright, and pointed to the bag on the floor. "Eat your food. I'll be back again." He turned his head sideways and reached for the doorknob.

It was now or never.

She leaped forward, knocking against his shoulder as she scrambled past him, through the doorway into the other room.

"Come back here," he shouted.

She looked around for a weapon, anything at all she could use to ward him off while she got her bearings. Shelving, containing rows and rows of boxes, lined the walls. She spun around. Something that looked like a short piece of garden hose lay near the wall close by. It wasn't much, but she dove for it, gained her footing, and swung it wildly in the air as he approached.

He stood back out of the way of the swinging weapon. "Drop that," he said. "You can't get away."

She disregarded him and looked toward the stairs leading up. They were on the other side of her abductor and she needed to get to them, the only way from this wretched dungeon.

He followed her gaze. "You'll never make it," he said. "That hose ain't gonna protect you much."

She moved toward the stairs, whipping the hose round and round. It sang as it spun through the air.

He glared at her, raised his arms to protect his face, and dove, straight for her legs. She was knocked off balance. The hose spun away and he pinned her to the floor, his hands holding her arms firmly against the concrete.

He grinned down at her. "Told you it wouldn't work."

She gritted her teeth. "Let me go."

"Can't do that."

"Please," she begged.

He rose to his feet, still holding her by one arm, forced her up, and glared at her. "You almost had me fooled," he said. "But no more." He spun her around, wrenched her arm behind her and prodded her back toward the small room.

With a final thrust he pushed her through the doorway. She fell forward onto her knees as the door slammed shut behind her and once again she was alone, all hope gone, and terrified.

CHAPTER 42

Friday, September 2nd, 6:16 p.m.

HANK PULLED HIS CHEVY into the driveway behind Annie's car and stepped out. He squinted up at the lowering sun. It'd been a great day, weatherwise, and he'd much rather be spending the coming evening relaxing, but the dark cloud of fear which hung over the city would be his first priority—his only priority—until this thing was solved.

He strode up the pathway and tapped on the front door.

Annie opened it immediately. "Come on in, Hank."

Hank stepped inside. "I'm just here to pick Jake up. Can't stay long."

"I'm ready." Jake popped out of the kitchen. "Let's go." He looked at his wife. "You coming, Annie?"

"Not this time. I have a few things to do. Besides, I don't want to overwhelm Eli Martin with too many people around. You can fill me in later."

Jake followed Hank from the house and they climbed in Hank's car.

"What's Detective King up to?" Jake asked, turning to Hank.

Hank started the engine. "He's checking out all the yellow vans registered within ten miles of the city."

"These guys use a different van every time," Jake said. "What about the blue van? The one they used to abduct Mrs. Coleman?"

Hank shook his head. "No luck with that." He backed from the driveway, dropped the shifter into drive, and sped away. "I have a feeling this yellow van is going to be a dead end as well."

"What about the witness?" Jake asked.

Hank glanced over at Jake and shrugged. "She got the plate number. Unless she got the number wrong, it appears they used stolen plates."

"Did she see the driver?"

"Sure, but not clearly. He was wearing a baseball cap and she couldn't make out his face."

"It strikes me as being rather brazen," Jake said. "Kidnapping her in front of her own home like that."

"And with the stolen plates," Hank added. "It almost seems like they wanted to be seen."

"It sure does. The doctor's wife, what's her name … Linda Gould, was taken from the underground parking, a secluded spot, and Rosemary Coleman was taken in a secluded spot as well, out jogging in the woods."

"Maybe they're just getting braver."

"Or careless."

"I hope you're right," Hank said. "I sure hope you're right."

"But you know what worries me?" Jake asked.

"What's that?"

"If the kidnapper didn't wear a mask, or hide his face this time, then that means Mrs. Martin can identify him."

Hank frowned. "Which means they aren't going to let her go."

There was silence a few moments, then Jake said flatly, "We need to catch these guys. And soon."

Hank pulled to the curb behind a bright red pickup truck. "This is it."

They climbed out and surveyed the small house. The dwelling appeared to be well kept, could use a bit of paint maybe, but overall seemed pleasant enough. The property was separated from its neighbors on each side by a row of manicured hedges.

Jake followed Hank past a black SUV parked in the driveway, strode up a stone walkway to the front door, and rang the bell.

Eli Martin looked like the average working guy. A buzzed-off haircut, a roundish face underneath three days' growth, perhaps a bit overweight, but with some obvious strain showing in his dark brown eyes.

Hank introduced them and showed his badge. Martin glanced at it, ushered them into the front room, and waved toward the couch. He sat in a matching chair as Jake and the cop settled into their seats.

"I was at work when the police contacted me and told me what had happened," Martin explained. "I came right home. The officers were still here, checking out my wife's vehicle, taking pictures, etcetera. They asked me a few questions but I'm afraid I wasn't much help."

Hank had a notepad out, thumbing through the pages. He found a blank one and asked, "Where do you work, Mr. Martin?"

"Please, call me Eli." He took a breath and continued, "I run an auto repair shop off Main Street. Martin Auto. I've been doing that for a lot of years."

Hank scribbled in his pad. "And you were there when the police called you?"

"Yes. I have a mechanic helping me full-time and I was in my office when they called."

Hank would have to check that out, to be thorough, but he was more interested right now in getting some information that might help them in their search for the killers.

"When you got home, Eli, was your house locked up? Was there any signs of entry, legal or otherwise?"

Eli shook his head. "Everything was still locked up securely and the alarm set. Apparently, my wife had just gotten home from doing some shopping when she was ..." He reached to a stand beside his chair and retrieved a cell phone. "The ... kidnapper called me a few minutes later." He motioned toward Jake. "He advised me to call Mr. Lincoln, which I did."

"That was about five fifteen or five twenty," Jake said. "And then a few minutes later, the kidnapper called me."

Eli handed his phone to Hank. "They sent me this photo," he said, his voice trembling.

Jake took the phone and looked at the photo on the screen. A woman, presumably Mrs. Martin, was huddled on the floor, her arms behind her back. She was looking at the camera, terror in her eyes.

"I'll need to keep this for now," Hank said.

Eli nodded.

Hank dropped the phone into his jacket pocket. "Do you have a photo of your wife?" He paused. "Other than this one?"

Eli stood, went to a bookcase, and leafed through an album. He returned a moment later and handed Hank a photo. "Here's a recent one. A couple of weeks ago."

Hank took the photo and glanced at it. It was a full-length shot of Mrs. Martin, standing on the front lawn, her arm around a young girl.

"That's her niece," Eli explained. "Her sister's daughter."

Jake tucked the photo into his notebook. "Where does your wife work, Eli?"

"She has a part-time job at a beauty salon. Just keeping track of appointments and so on. It gives her something to do and gets her out of the house awhile." Eli smiled faintly. "We have no kids, so her life is rather boring sometimes."

"Did she work yesterday?" Hank asked.

"I don't believe so. She works Tuesdays and Thursdays. Unless she was called in for something, but I don't think so."

Eli gave him the name and address of her work and Hank made a notation in his pad. He would check at her job, but that was unlikely to yield any results.

"Eli, would you like me to send an officer here to stay with you … just in case?" Hank asked.

"I don't think that'll be necessary, Detective. I doubt if I'm in any danger. If they want a ransom for my wife, then they wouldn't harm me."

"Makes sense," Hank said.

Eli looked at Jake. "Did they give you any delivery instructions yet?"

"Not yet. He said he would call back."

Eli shook his head thoughtfully. "I have the funds ready," he said. "But there's one problem."

"What's that?" Hank asked.

Eli hesitated a moment. "He warned me strictly the police weren't to be involved during the delivery of the money. I… I don't know what the best thing is to do."

Hank took a deep breath and observed Eli before

speaking. "I must advise you to let me know the details," he said slowly. "I would be remiss to suggest otherwise."

"In other words," Jake said, "it's up to you, but Detective Corning can't tell you that."

Eli shook his head slowly. "My wife's safety is my only concern."

"Mine too," Hank said.

"Then ... please, Detective," Eli said. "Please bring my wife home safely. But be careful, I can't afford for anything to go wrong."

CHAPTER 43

Friday, September 2nd, 6:45 p.m.

JAKE BUCKLED HIS SEAT belt as Hank pulled from the curb. "Do you know what bothers me?" he asked. "This is the third kidnapping and we're beating our heads against a wall."

"We have a few things," Hank said. "We have the vans, the phone recordings, and the eyewitness."

Jake turned, dropped his arm on the back of the seat and faced Hank. "And how far has that gotten us?"

Hank shrugged. "Not so far yet, but give it time."

"We don't have time, Hank. We don't want another body on our hands."

Hank glanced at Jake. "We'll get them. They won't get away this time."

Jake's phone rang. He looked at the caller ID. "This might be him," he said. "Unknown number."

"Put it on speaker. Wait a second, I'll pull over," Hank said as he touched the brakes and pulled to the side of the street. He shut down the engine and nodded at Jake.

Jake touched the screen, put the call on speaker and said, "Jake Lincoln."

"Hello, Jake. How nice to hear your voice again."

Hank had turned in his seat and was listening intently to the disguised voice.

"I can't say the same," Jake said.

"I understand. I realize it's hard for you when you don't hear my real voice. It kind of puts a barrier between us and makes it less personal. I apologize for that inconvenience, but I'm afraid I have no choice in the matter."

"Can we get down to business?" Jake said. "Eli Martin has the money ready."

"That's good news indeed. That was rather quick, I might add. I haven't prepared our little rendezvous until tomorrow, so he has indeed been expedient. I'm rather pleased, Jake."

Jake closed his eyes and shook his head in disgust.

"Are you still there, Jake?"

"I'm here."

"Excellent. Now, let me fill you in on your instructions—"

Jake interrupted. "We want a guarantee Mrs. Martin will be released safely."

"I can only give you my word, Jake. You know I'm a man of honor and you disappoint me if you're suggesting otherwise."

"You've given me no reason to trust you," Jake said. "Your record speaks for itself. Now, what guarantee can you give me?"

A deep sigh came over the line. "I'm afraid I'll have to call your bluff, Jake. You know Mrs. Martin's future is in my hands and you're in no position to dictate terms."

Hank was drumming his fingers on the steering wheel, his brow creased in thought. He turned toward Jake and whispered, "We have no choice."

Jake nodded, hesitated a moment and then spoke into the phone, "What are your terms?"

"That's better, Jake. I knew we could work that out." A pause and then, "The most important detail is our good friends at RHPD. I realize they're already aware of the current situation. That's unfortunate and was beyond my control, but this is as far as their involvement can go."

Jake glanced at Hank. "We'll keep them out of it."

"Excellent. I'll personally give Hannah Martin the good news. She'll be pleased to hear it. She's been in a little discomfort lately, in somewhat cramped quarters. Unfortunately, our prior establishment had sustained a good deal of damage and it couldn't be used." A mock sigh came over the line and then, "I'm afraid her current accommodations are somewhat less than ideal and the best that could be obtained on such short notice."

Jake rolled his eyes and said nothing.

"Do you have my remuneration ready, Jake?"

"The money is safe," Jake said. "Just tell me when and where and I'll be there."

"Let's do this thing sometime tomorrow morning, shall we? Does that fit into your schedule? I wouldn't want to inconvenience you in any way."

"Tomorrow morning is fine with me."

"Excellent. Let's say around eleven a.m. That should give you enough time to prepare."

"Eleven it is. When and where?"

"You'll get the funds together, take Annie's car, and drive to Midtown Plaza. Park the vehicle at the far north end of the lot and wait. I'll meet you there at eleven a.m. sharp." A pause. "Did you get that?"

"I got it," Jake said.

"And remember, you must come alone, and if the police are anywhere around, it might not go so well. I have a great deal of respect for our officers of the law, but in this current situation, I'd rather not see them."

"I understand." Jake glanced at Hank. "You won't see them."

"Don't twist my words, Jake. I hope my meaning is clear. The police are not to be near, hidden or otherwise. And don't underestimate me. If the police are hidden, I'll know."

Jake raised his voice. "They won't be around."

A deep laugh came over the line. "Then I can anticipate a smooth transaction and a subsequent happy reunion."

"Just keep your word and we'll keep ours."

"You can count on it, Jake."

The line went dead.

Jake hung up and turned to Hank. "We can't trust this guy."

Hank nodded. "I realize that and I'm going to make sure we do everything possible to nail him before he gets away."

"He's not going to meet me there," Jake said. "He's going to call, like last time, and lead me off somewhere."

"Don't worry, we'll have that covered as well. We won't leave anything to chance this time."

Hank started the vehicle and pulled away from the curb. "Just do your part and leave the rest to me."

CHAPTER 44

ANNIE WAS IN THE OFFICE when she heard the guys come in. She overheard Matty greet them at the door with his usual, "Hey, Uncle Hank."

She pushed back her keyboard and stifled a yawn. As of late, her workload was wearing her out and she could use a bit of extra rest one of these days. Hopefully soon.

She put her iMac to sleep, then stood and wandered into the kitchen. Hank had set his briefcase on the floor and he and Jake were taking a seat at opposite sides of the table. Matty plopped down at one end and dropped his arms on the table. He looked expectantly back and forth between Hank and his father.

"How did the interview with Eli Martin go?" Annie asked as she settled into the remaining chair.

"It went well," Hank said. "Naturally, he's concerned about his wife."

"He has the funds already," Jake said. "He has enough in his safe. Guess he doesn't trust banks."

Hank glanced at Jake. "Jake got the call he was waiting for."

"Oh, he called?" Annie looked at Matty. He seemed to be losing interest, which was just as well. He was aware of what they did for a living and seemed to take it all in stride. She usually allowed him to listen in on their conversations unless things got particularly gruesome. She watched him slip from his chair.

"I'll be watching TV," Matty said as he wandered toward the living room. He called back over his shoulder, "Let me know if you need any advice."

Jake watched him go with a grin before turning to Annie. "The delivery is in the morning. At Midtown Plaza."

"I hope you put the pistol and vest away carefully?" Hank asked.

"The pistol and the ammunition are locked in the office desk," Annie said. "And the vest isn't going to hurt anyone."

Hank nodded. "You're going to need them again."

"I have to take your car," Jake said to Annie.

"Oh?"

Jake shrugged. "That's what he said, but I don't know why."

"Callaway'll be here early in the morning," Hank said to Jake. "He'll install a tracker on the car and one on you as well."

"What about putting a tracker with the money?" Annie asked.

Hank shook his head. "We can't chance that. You know how strict he is about keeping the rules. If it were discovered—one slip-up and it might not go well for Mrs. Martin."

"Of course," Annie said. "Our main concern is to get her home."

"I do have some good news though." Hank said. "Mrs.

Coleman was released from the hospital. The police sketch, in combination with some mug shots, helped us identify one of the kidnappers."

Annie leaned forward. Finally, a lead.

"The one she IDed was the guy whose face she took a board to. He's a small-time punk with a long record." Hank pulled his notepad from his pocket and thumbed through it. "His name is Antony Miflan, better known as Mouse. Been in and out of prison a few times in his life."

"Any luck in tracking him down?" Annie asked.

"Not yet. We've checked with his known associates. Seems like nobody's seen him for a while. He's been behind bars for the best part of the last five years and was just released about three months ago. We've got our feelers out there, but so far, no luck."

"What was he in for?"

"Burglary, car theft, petty crimes."

"Murder?"

"Nope. Never anything violent as far as we know," Hank said. "I don't think he's our killer. He's just a hired punk. According to Mrs. Coleman's statement, he claimed never to have killed anyone. He said he leaves that up to the boss and he just cleans up."

"If that's so," Jake said, "then that still makes him an accomplice to murder."

"Yup. And the same as if he'd done it himself. That's why it's so important we find him. Judging by his record, he'll talk to save his own skin and lighten his sentence." Hank reached down and retrieved his briefcase and snapped it open. He produced a photo and handed it to Jake. "Here's the most recent shot we have of him."

Jake took the photo and Annie leaned over to take a look.

The name "Mouse" befit the face she saw. He looked timid in the mug shot, but with gray eyes like steel, cold and hard.

Hank grinned. "He looks a little different now, I suspect. Mrs. Coleman did a number on his face. He might have a few telltale marks."

"Did you find out who owns that run-down store where she was held?" Annie asked.

Hank leafed through his pad. "That whole block of buildings was acquired by a development group, Ramsey Development, a few years ago. Seems they have plans to eventually tear the whole block down and put up condos."

Annie frowned. "Those buildings are dangerous."

"After this, I'm sure the city will force them to make the buildings more secure until they're torn down."

"How's Doctor Gould doing?" Jake asked.

Hank took a deep breath and shook his head slowly. "Not too good, understandably. He's immersed himself back in his job, working overtime, but unfortunately, he'll have to live with his wife's death for the rest of his life."

"And the fact she was murdered must be twice as hard," Annie said. "It's going to be a long time before he gets to the point where he can handle the pain."

Hank sighed. "And that's why we've placed a twenty-four-hour guard over the Coleman house. She was fortunate to have escaped, but she still might be a target. An officer will be camped out at her house until this is over. We're up against a cold-blooded killer, or two, and have to take every precaution."

"Any luck with the recordings?" Jake asked.

Hank shook his head. "Callaway has been trying to do something with voice recognition equipment, but he says not to be optimistic about that. We have a forensic psychologist going over the recordings to see if he can come up with a profile, but as you know, forensic psychology isn't an exact science."

"Without a psychology degree," Jake put in, "I can tell you this guy is a raving lunatic and unpredictable."

"Without a doubt," Hank said with a yawn. "And now, I've got to get some rest, or at least try to." He picked up his briefcase and stood. "I'll be on this bright and early tomorrow morning. We have some planning to do."

CHAPTER 45

Saturday, September 3rd, 7:11 a.m.

HANK FELT LIKE HE'D barely caught more than a few moments sleep since the day this case had come his way. But last night he'd managed to get in a good seven hours and he felt refreshed and ready to tackle his demanding job once again.

The kitchen table was strewn with files and photos, papers, reports, and notes. He'd been up later than planned last night, attempting to make some sense of this difficult case. He brushed them aside and sat down to a quick breakfast, a couple of eggs over easy, a slab of ham, and a piece of dark toast.

He flicked on the television as he ate. This case was all over the news and even now, a commentator was discussing it on an early morning news show with a couple of other talking heads. They all had their own opinions and they seemed to like the "Merchant of Life" title the kidnapper had given himself. It all made for great news but served little good.

The photo of Antony Miflan flashed on the screen, asking people to call if they saw him or knew where he was. Hank realized that "Mouse" might be the key to unraveling this whole mess.

He finished his meal, dumped his dishes in the sink and then scooped up the paperwork and stuffed it all into his briefcase. He checked his service weapon, grabbed his keys, and went out the door, heading for work.

When he reached the parking lot behind the precinct, Callaway had just arrived. He was carrying a satchel over his shoulder. Hank stepped from his vehicle and joined him.

"Morning, Callaway."

"Good morning, Hank. I see you brought some great weather with you."

Hank eyed the satchel. "What's in the bag?"

"I just came from the Lincolns. Jake is all set up with a tracking device and I put one on Annie's car as well. We'll know where he is every minute."

"Great. Let's hope that does the trick." Hank looked at his watch. Still some time to go. The drop was at 11:00 so they had almost three hours to make final preparations.

As they came through the precinct doors, Detective King stopped them. "Diego's waiting for you."

Hank tapped on the frame of Diego's open door, went in, and sat in the guest chair. King followed him in and plunked down on the corner of Diego's desk. Callaway stood in the doorway.

The captain looked up and gave King a backhanded wave. "Get off the desk."

King slipped off the desk, leaned up against a filing cabinet, and crossed his arms. Diego sat back and gave him a disapproving look. "Don't you ever change your clothes?"

"This is my uniform," King said. "I keep my good stuff for weddings and funerals."

Diego gave him the once-over, shrugged, and looked at Hank. "Are we all ready to go?"

Hank looked at King.

King said, "I have a detail put together and we'll cover that plaza like mud on a hog." He chuckled, then added, "Don't worry, they'll be out of sight."

Callaway spoke up, "I got the trackers installed."

Diego stroked his bristly mustache and looked at Callaway. "Did you have any luck with the latest photo? With that metadata whatever?"

Callaway laughed. "The Exif metadata. The location setting was turned off and the ID number showed the photo was sent from a throwaway phone. That's all I got on that."

"And the photo itself?"

"Didn't tell me anything except Mrs. Martin is being held in a concrete-walled room."

Diego turned to King. "And the vans?"

"No luck," King said.

Diego sat forward, his brow wrinkled. "Hank, what about that punk you're looking for?"

"His picture is all over the news, Captain. We hope to hear something soon."

"So what you guys are telling me is you have nothing at all." Diego shook his head and sat back again. "You'd better produce some results today. I don't want another dead woman."

"We're on it, boss," King said.

"Does Lincoln still have that gun?" Diego asked Hank.

"Yes. And the vest."

"See to it they're returned after this. The gun, at least. God forbid he ever had to use it. There could be some headaches."

"Right, Captain. I'll see to it."

Diego glanced at King, then Hank, then Callaway. "Anything else I need to know?"

"That's it. We're good to go," Hank said.

Diego dismissed them with a wave. "Then get on it. And keep me posted."

~*~

HANNAH MARTIN SAT up from the fetal position she'd been lying in most of the night. She didn't know what time it was, and wasn't even sure if it was morning, but she'd heard her captor rustling around in the room outside her cell and assumed the sun was up.

All she could do in this place was sleep, and though she had dozed off and on throughout the night, her discomfort in this cool room hadn't allowed for a peaceful rest.

She stroked a hand through her hair. It was a mess, stringy, grimy. She felt dirty all over.

The lock rattled and the door swung open. Her abductor stood in the doorway, one hand on his hip, the other holding a paper bag, scrutinizing her. She looked up at him, hoping he'd come to free her, but knowing he hadn't.

He tossed the bag her way. "Breakfast time."

She opened the bag and peered inside. Looked like a sandwich of some kind. She was hungry but in no mood to eat. She set the bag in her lap and looked up at him. "When ... when will you let me go?"

He laughed. "It'll soon be over. Not too long now."

Had her husband paid the ransom? She knew he had the money and she hoped he would pay soon. She just wanted to go home.

"Has the ransom been paid?" she asked.

He shrugged. "I expect it'll be paid today. At least, that's what the plans are."

Her voice became hopeful. "And then you'll let me go home?"

"I expect so. It's up to the boss when you get out of here. He makes all the decisions; I just do what he asks and get paid. That's all I care about."

With that he spun around and left. The door slammed shut and the lock rattled in the darkness.

CHAPTER 46

Saturday, September 3rd, 10:30 a.m.

JAKE ADJUSTED THE bulletproof vest. He didn't think he could ever get used to wearing this thing. It hampered his freedom of movement so much he'd considered leaving it behind. But Annie had insisted, so that was that.

He fastened the shoulder holster in place and then removed the Smith & Wesson from the drawer and snapped the magazine in, making sure the safety was on. It felt good in his hand, comfortable, like it was designed especially for him.

He put the weapon in its holster, adjusted the vest again, and put on a button-down shirt, leaving it unbuttoned, concealing the weapon at his side.

He picked up his cell phone and hit speed dial. Hank answered on the first ring.

"All ready at your end?" Jake asked.

"All set. Everyone's in place and we're watching every move. Nothing's going to happen in that plaza without us knowing it."

"I'm just about to leave," Jake said. "First I have to swing by Eli Martin's and pick up the money. I'll be there before eleven."

He hung up the phone and went into the kitchen, where Annie was sitting at the table with Matty, helping him with his homework—some kind of math problem. She looked up when he entered.

"You have the vest on?" she asked.

Jake pounded a fist on his chest. "It's under here."

Annie glanced at Matty and then back at Jake. "And the ... other thing?"

Jake grinned. "It's under here too."

She swung around on her chair, stood up, and put her arms around him, looking into his eyes. "Be careful," she said, a hint of worry on her face.

"Always." He gave her a quick kiss and caressed her cheek. "And now, I have to go."

Matty looked up, twirling a pencil in his hand. "Where you going, Dad?"

"Just have to make a quick delivery. I should be home soon."

Matty turned back to his homework, satisfied.

Jake picked Annie's car keys from a wicker basket on the counter and grabbed a couple bottles of water from the fridge. He headed out to Annie's Ford Escort, parked in the driveway, jumped inside, and pushed the seat all the way back. Callaway had installed a tracker somewhere inside and they would painstakingly follow his route.

In ten minutes, he pulled up in front of Eli Martin's house. He'd called earlier to be sure the money was ready. It was, and Martin met him at the door and handed him a cloth bag, tightened by a drawstring and knotted.

"Mr. Lincoln," Martin said. "Fifty thousand is a small price to pay for my wife's safety, but ..." He paused a moment and his lower lip trembled. He drew a deep breath. "Please make sure nothing goes wrong."

"I hate to say this, Mr. Martin, but it's out of my hands. I'll do all I can and leave the rest up to the police."

Martin nodded slowly and Jake went back to the car. He climbed in, tossed the bag of money onto the passenger seat, and glanced at the house. Martin was standing in the doorway, watching him, an anxious look on his face.

Next stop, Midtown Plaza.

The large plaza on Main Street was buzzing at this time of day. Most of the shoppers seemed to be favoring the Walmart store looming at the near end; however, the row of smaller shops and services were also getting their regular Saturday morning business, with people jockeying for parking spots as close to the storefronts as possible.

The north end of the parking lot was furthest from the action and there were several available spots along the row bordering the sidewalk. Jake picked a slot empty on either side, backed the Escort in, and shut down the engine.

He glanced around the lot. He knew the police were here somewhere, probably hiding in plain sight, but among the many shoppers coming and going, he couldn't pick out who they might be. A sniper might be on the roof of one of the shops. Maybe other officers waited in unmarked cars close by. Or perhaps some were across the street, waiting to follow anyone who came to pick up the money.

Wherever they were, they had it completely under control.

Jake looked at the clock on the dash. It was 10:54. Almost time. He watched the digital numbers click over several times and then his phone rang.

"Jake Lincoln."

"Hello, Jake. It's a lovely day."

"Yes, it's a lovely day, now where are you? I'm sure you already know, I'm waiting for you in the plaza."

The caller laughed. "You didn't actually think I was going to show up there, did you?"

"I was hoping."

"With all the police watching? Sorry to disappoint you, my friend, but that wouldn't be expedient of me, now would it?"

Jake was hoping the kidnapper would show up in person, or at least send someone else, but he didn't expect it. And now he was going to get the runaround. "I have the money," he said.

"Excellent. Now please start the car, Jake."

Jake sighed, felt for the pistol at his side, and started the engine. *Here we go.*

"As you know, Jake, it's not safe to be talking on a cell phone while driving. Someone could get hurt, so please be careful."

"That's the least of my worries. I'm waiting for your instructions."

There was an unearthly chuckle on the line. "We must go now. Hannah Martin is waiting and I'm sure Eli is anxious. Please exit the plaza onto Main Street and turn north."

Jake pulled the shifter into gear, eased from the spot, took a last look around the plaza for telltale signs of undercover cops, and pulled onto Main Street. He didn't know if any unmarked cars might be following him, but he knew Callaway would be aware of his every movement.

"Are you heading north, Jake?"

"I am."

"Excellent. Keep driving and when you come to the last set of lights north of town, let me know."

Traffic was light, the morning rush of workers now past, and in a couple of minutes he saw a set of traffic lights ahead.

Cherry Street. The lights were green and he zoomed on through.

"I'm past the lights," he said.

"Wonderful. Keep the speedometer at fifty."

Jake touched the gas slightly and increased the speed of the vehicle. There was silence on the line for several minutes and then the kidnapper spoke. "You should be approaching County Road 12, Jake. I assume you know where that is?"

"I do. It's just ahead."

"Turn left when you reach it."

Jake slowed the vehicle and made a left turn. Soon, he was crawling along County Road 12, the Escort bumping over potholes and old pavement.

The disguised voice came from the phone, "Do you know where the old Spencer residence is?"

Jake was familiar with that place. "I do," he said.

"About a quarter mile past there, but on your right, you'll see a small lane. Let me know when you reach it."

Jake drove carefully down the seldom-used road. He glanced to his left as the Spencer house came into view. It was now empty and boarded up, the old barn set away from the house, unused and likely to stay that way for a long time to come.

He slowed the vehicle as he approached the lane to the right, almost hidden behind a row of trees.

"I'm at the lane," Jake said.

"Pull to the side of the road and stop."

Jake did.

"Get out of the vehicle."

Jake felt under his shirt for his weapon and then grabbed the bag of money and climbed from the vehicle. "What's next?" he asked.

"Walk down the lane."

Jake stepped ahead a few feet, stopped, and gazed down the lane that led into a darkened forest. It was little more than a trail, a few weeds struggling through the hardened soil, a rut or two caused by the occasional vehicle, tangled shrubs and wild berries bordering the pathway.

He switched the bag of money to his left hand and reached under his shirt with his right. He worked the pistol from its holster but kept the weapon hidden beneath his shirt, ready, just in case.

He walked slowly down the lane, listening intently, hearing nothing but the rustle of leaves overhead as a breeze rippled through the trees. The chattering of squirrels at play sounded somewhere far away, a chorus of birds chirping off to his right.

The bright sky disappeared under a canopy of trees as he entered the edge of the darkened forest. The phone was silent except for a faint breathing on the line that told him the kidnapper was still there.

He kept walking and in a minute, a small clearing appeared, rays of light leaking through the treetops, a rare patch of grass flourishing, a slight rise in the terrain, over a knoll, and then—

Jake fell to his knees as the phone went silent and the caller was gone. He dropped his head into his hands and took a deep breath before finally raising his head and looking at the cold, lifeless body of Hannah Martin.

CHAPTER 47

Saturday, September 3rd, 11:35 a.m.

POLICE CARS AND emergency vehicles lined both shoulders of the narrow country road. Officers leaned against their cruisers talking in groups of two or three. An ambulance had parked near the spot where the lane touched the road, waiting for its burden. The forensics van was parked just ahead.

Hank pulled over at the end of the line, stepped from his car, and made his way forward.

Jake was leaned against the hood of his car watching the proceedings. He turned, shaking his head as Hank approached. "He said someone would pay, but I never expected this."

"Nor I," Hank said and noticed the bag of money lying on the hood of the car. "I take it you had no instructions to deliver the ransom?"

Jake shook his head. "It appears the only purpose of this trip was to lead me to the body. I don't think he had any intention to pick up the money."

"I'd better take a look," Hank said. "And you'd better lock that money up."

Jake grabbed the money bag, tossed it onto the passenger seat, and locked the car doors.

He joined Hank and they followed the path back to the scene. Tape was stretched from tree to tree, cordoning off the area. Rod Jameson and the forensics crew had finished documenting every aspect of the scene, taking pictures, making detailed notes, and gathering trace evidence. They were packing up their equipment. Physical examinations, laboratory tests, and a complete diagnosis would come later.

As they stepped to the top of the knoll they saw the body of Mrs. Martin. It was twisted halfway onto its side, mostly on its back, the legs bent underneath the body like a rag doll tossed aside. By the position of the body, it appeared it had been rolled down the grade and left where it landed.

Jameson stood to one side talking with an investigator. Hank approached him and interrupted. "Anything I should know about?" he asked.

Jameson looked at Hank and shook his head. "Nothing stands out. Once we process everything we have, I'll let you know, but right now ..." Jameson shrugged. "There's nothing blatantly obvious about who did this one."

"Thanks, Rod," Hank said. "But put a rush on this, will you? This guy moves fast and we want this to be his last victim."

"Will do, Hank," Rod said and turned back to the investigator.

Nancy Pietek had finished her preliminary inspection of the body and was crouched over, making some notes, when Hank and Jake came down the knoll and approached.

"Hello, Nancy," Hank said as he bent over and took a

closer look. He saw the marks on Mrs. Martin's neck, the same marks he had seen just days ago on the body of another victim.

"Hi, Hank," Nancy said. "This looks like the work of the same killer." She pointed to the wounds. "Same marks, the only visible signs of injury, presumably caused by a garrote. Perhaps the same one. No signs of defensive wounds at this point."

"Time of death?" Hank asked.

"Likely two to three hours ago. No way to tell where she was killed, but certainly not here."

"Check under her tongue," Hank said, pointing.

Nancy reached over and eased the victim's mouth open. She reached in with a gloved finger and worked out a folded piece of paper. She unfolded the newsprint carefully and held it so Hank could read it.

Handwritten in block letters, the message read, "I SAID NO POLICE."

Hank studied it thoughtfully and then nodded. Nancy tucked the note into an evidence bag and labeled it.

Hank stood and glanced at Jake, standing back a few feet, gazing at the body, his face grim, his eyes smoldering. He was taking this one personally, no doubt about it.

The detective went over to Jake and put his hand on his arm. "You okay?"

Jake looked at him and nodded.

"You're not responsible for this, you know," Hank said.

Jake was silent.

"There's nothing you could've done to prevent this. None of us saw it coming."

Jake moved his eyes back to the body of Mrs. Martin. "I know," he said quietly, almost in a whisper, as they turned and climbed back up the knoll.

They stopped as they saw Detective King coming down the lane toward them. The scruffy detective wandered over to where Hank and Jake stood.

"Caught this on the radio," King said. "I assume the vic is Hannah Martin?"

Hank nodded. "Yes, and she's going to be the last victim."

King cocked his head. "How can you be sure of that?"

"Because I'm not going to sleep until this scumbag is caught." Hank narrowed his eyes and glared at King. "And neither are you."

"Yeah, we'll get him," King agreed. He glanced around the scene and then stepped over to the edge of the knoll and looked down at the corpse for a few seconds before turning back to Hank. "Sure is a shame," he said and then added, "Want me to tell her husband?"

Hank shook his head adamantly. He didn't want the insensitive King involved in such a sensitive task. "I'll do it," he said.

King shrugged. "Whatever. I got other stuff to do anyway."

"Find anything out yet?" Hank asked.

"Not yet. I'm working on it," King said as he turned away.

"Keep me posted." Hank turned to Jake. "I expect you'll be getting a phone call soon."

CHAPTER 48

Saturday, September 3rd, 12:18 p.m.

LISA KRUNK WAS ON the other side of the city and when the report came over her police scanner regarding the body which had been discovered, she dropped what she was doing, hustled Don into the Channel 7 Action News van, and hurried to the spot along County Road 12.

As Don pulled the van up behind the last cruiser, she saw they had arrived late. The forensics van was just pulling away and the doors to the ambulance were being closed.

They jumped from their van and she hurried over to where the center of activity seemed to be. Don followed behind, his camera ready at a moment's notice. Whatever had happened here seemed to be down a lane off the main road.

An officer stopped her short when she attempted to access the pathway. "You can't go down there," he said.

She poked the microphone at him. "What happened here, officer?"

"You'll have to speak to someone else about that. I'm not at liberty to say anything."

Lisa glanced down the lane. At a distance, she could barely

see the telltale yellow of crime scene tape and the movement of several officers in the area.

She was certain this was connected to the recent abductions and was disappointed she hadn't gotten another call from the kidnapper. She was convinced her name was on the lips of everyone in the city, heralding her as the greatest journalist this crappy little town had ever seen. Maybe the greatest in the country, but if not, that title would soon be hers.

Someone in plain clothes was coming her way from down the lane. "Get ready, Don." As the figure drew closer, she recognized him as the recent arrival to the force, Detective King. She made it her business to know names. Her livelihood depended on it.

As King drew closer, she took a couple of steps his way but stopped when the officer gave her a warning look. She held the mike ready and in a moment, King had reached the spot where she stood.

"Detective King," she said. "It's good to see you again."

He nodded at her as the camera rolled.

"Detective," Lisa said. "Can you tell me what happened here?"

King scratched his head. "I can't tell you a whole lot. A body has been discovered here and we're in the middle of investigating."

"Who's the victim?"

"I can't tell you that."

"Is this another of the kidnap victims?"

"Yeah, I'm afraid so."

"Do you have any leads yet as to who the perpetrators are?"

King glanced down the lane and then back at Lisa. "I'm working on it. We expect to make an arrest shortly."

"Detective King, was Jake Lincoln involved in this incident as well?"

King shrugged. "Yes, he was. For some reason, he's been chosen by the kidnappers to deliver the ransom."

"So, the ransom was paid?"

"I'm afraid not," King said as Hank and Jake approached.

Lisa swung the mike over to Hank. "Detective Corning, can you give me the name of the victim?"

Hank frowned. "You know better than that, Lisa."

Lisa smiled, her wide mouth threatening to split her face. "What can you tell me?"

"Very little, I'm afraid."

She turned to Jake, poking the mike under his nose. "Jake Lincoln, were you the one who discovered the body?"

"I was," Jake said as he turned away. He didn't appear to be in a good mood and Lisa watched him thoughtfully as he made his way down the shoulder of the road. She'd hoped to get a little more from him, but she could always try later.

She turned back to the detectives and continued to pepper them with more questions, trying to squeeze some information from them, but was unsuccessful and eventually turned away, disappointed, and headed back to the van, Don dutifully following.

They were on their way back to the city and she was contemplating her next move when her cell phone rang. It was an unknown number and she answered it.

"Hello, Lisa. I want to thank you for broadcasting my message on Thursday. It has been a great help in my endeavor."

The deep voice coming over the phone was a dead giveaway. She put the phone on speaker, pulled out her digital audio recorder, switched it on, and held the phone close to the microphone.

"I did it in the interest of news," Lisa said into the phone. "I don't owe you any favors." She motioned frantically for Don to pull over and stop the van.

"Of course you don't, Lisa, but I wanted to call and give you advance notice of my next production. It'll take place tomorrow, so I'm depending on you to warn the public to be careful."

"Are you talking about another kidnapping?"

"That's one way to put it. As the Merchant of Life, I prefer to call it a business arrangement."

Lisa was perplexed. "What kind of business arrangement is it when you kill the victims and don't collect the money?"

"Certain rules were broken, Lisa. It seems all too many do not heed my message. And that's why I need you."

"I ... I'm afraid I can't help you this time."

"Oh, but you must."

"And why is that?"

"For the safety of the public. You can treat it as a public service announcement."

Lisa hesitated. She struggled with her sense of morality versus her future career. Finally, she said, "I'll consider it, but I can't make any promises."

"That's all I ask, Lisa. That's all I ask. And now, I hope you have a fine day and a wonderful tomorrow."

The line went dead.

She hung up and sat still, gazing out the front window of the van. Detective Corning had practically promised her first crack at this story once everything was wrapped up. She didn't want to jeopardize that now by keeping this new information from him. Besides, an obstruction of justice charge was not something she wanted to face. It might not be good for her career.

She made up her mind and glanced to Don. "Turn the van around. I need to get this recording to Detective Corning."

CHAPTER 49

Saturday, September 3rd, 12:26 p.m.

JAKE SAT IN HIS vehicle for several minutes before finally pulling the car from the shoulder, spinning it around, and heading back to the city.

Hank would be dropping by the house later to get Jake's complete statement and he could talk more with Hank at that time, but for now he just wanted to get away from this place.

He glanced at the bag of money on the seat beside him. He would have to get it back to Eli Martin, but the money would be the last of Martin's worries right now. And he didn't envy Hank's uncomfortable task of telling the new widower about the murder of his wife.

He'd taken off the gun and vest and tossed the vest in the backseat. The weapon lay in its holster beside the unused ransom money. He was glad he hadn't needed to use the pistol, but at the same time he wished the kidnapper was around. He wouldn't have hesitated to use it then.

Or would he? He wasn't sure.

On second thought he decided he wouldn't lower his standards to those of the kidnapper, no matter how deserved it might be.

Maybe he would just shoot him in the leg.

As he spun off the old road and onto the main highway back to the city, he bore down on the gas pedal in an attempt to work off some frustration, covering a few miles in no time flat. Annie's car wasn't made for the kind of speed he liked, so he let up on the pedal and the vehicle eased back to a normal cruising speed. But he felt a little better.

He resolved to echo Hank's determination not to rest until these lowlifes were behind bars. Whatever it took.

As he neared the outskirts of the city his cell phone rang. He looked at the caller ID. Unknown number. He touched the brakes and pulled to the side of the road, the wheels grinding to a stop in the soft gravel. He threw the car in park, took a couple of deep breaths and answered the call.

"Jake Lincoln."

"Such a lovely day for a walk in the forest, don't you think?"

Jake felt a sudden resurgence of anger. He leaned back in the seat, dropped his head back, and closed his eyes. He had to remain calm. Then, in a flat, unemotional voice he asked, "Why did you kill Hannah Martin?"

"I'm sorry, Jake, but it was necessary. These punitive measures pain me to no end. It would be lax of me not to take some form of corrective action."

"Is it necessary for that corrective action to involve murdering innocent victims?"

"No one is innocent, Jake. We all cause harm and offense to others from time to time."

"I've never murdered anyone," Jake said flatly.

"Oh, but you'd like to, wouldn't you, my friend? I'm fairly certain you'd like to murder me, isn't that right, Jake?"

Jake was quiet a moment before saying, "Hannah Martin

caused you no harm. Was her death necessary?"

"Jake, Jake, always the same questions and by now, you should know the answers." A sigh came over the line. "The noncompliance of those involved necessitated extreme action."

Jake gritted his teeth. "You're the one who got the police involved. You abducted Mrs. Martin in front of her house in broad daylight."

"Ah, yes, but it could've stopped there. There was no need for either you or Mr. Martin to involve the police further. Jake, you have such an uncooperative attitude, it's astounding."

Jake took another deep breath. "I've cooperated with you and your demands every time. You've always gotten the money and this time didn't need to be any different. I'm sure you could've found a way."

"Certainly I could've, but that wouldn't be operating in the spirit of good faith. You see, Jake, I'm a dealmaker, but it takes two to make a deal. And though we had a bargain, your insubordination and disregard for our bargain speaks otherwise. That cannot and will not be allowed."

Jake raised his voice. "You can't put this on me. You're the one who's murdering innocent victims."

"I'm an entrepreneur, Jake."

"An entrepreneur? Is that what you call yourself?"

"What would you call it? Never mind. We've been over this enough and I can anticipate your answer." A pause, breathing on the line. "I've already had the pleasure of conversing with our mutual friend, Lisa Krunk, and she has agreed to oblige me once more."

"In what way?"

"She'll warn the public to be careful, but if an unfortunate circumstance should befall them, they should not be defiant. Follow the rules and everyone's happy."

"When will this stop?" Jake shouted.

"Calm down, my friend. I can't say when it'll stop. Perhaps soon. Perhaps never. I'm having too good a time to put an end to it now. Aren't you having fun, Jake?"

Jake pounded the steering wheel with his fist and said nothing. He knew there was no sense in arguing any further with this psychopath.

"We'll try again tomorrow, Jake. I'm hoping this time we'll have more favorable circumstances. And next time, please try to adhere to the rules of our contract and urge others to do likewise."

Jake sighed. "I'll do my part and do my best to convince them, but they must make up their own minds."

"Thank you, Jake. Please see to it you do. And now, I must bid you a good day and may the rest of your weekend be as pleasant as today."

The line went dead. Jake tossed the phone onto the seat and sat still awhile. He renewed his vow not to sleep until this was over. He owed that much to all the victims and their families.

He started the engine and pulled carefully back onto the road, heading for home.

CHAPTER 50

Saturday, September 3rd, 1:44 p.m.

JAKE HAD TOLD ANNIE about the morning's events and as she mulled it all over in her mind, she was struck with the callousness with which the kidnappers treated human life. It seemed they looked for any excuse to kill and the money was only secondary.

She set her thoughts aside as she heard Jake come in the front door. In a moment, he appeared in the living room where Annie was settled in a comfortable chair, her legs tucked underneath herself.

Jake dropped the vest, holster, and what appeared to be a money bag on the floor beside the couch. He went to Annie, leaned over, and gave her a hug before dropping onto the sofa. He looked somewhat dejected and weary.

"Hank'll be here shortly," Jake said. "He has to go by Eli Martin's first and give him the news. I don't envy him that task."

"You must be hungry," Annie said.

Jake nodded and stretched out on the couch. "I could use something."

Annie went into the kitchen to fix him a sandwich. It

seemed to her this business of being private investigators sure wasn't like a nine-to-five job. But it was challenging. There was no doubt about that. Probably not like being a cop. Cops don't get to pick and choose their cases, but it gave her a better idea of what Hank was up against on a daily basis.

She brought Jake's lunch into the living room and set it on the coffee table. He sat up and devoured the meal in silence. He needed to be alone with his thoughts and she didn't interrupt.

When the doorbell rang, she went to the front door. It was Hank. She swung the door open and led him into the front room. He sat his briefcase on the floor and set on the other end of the couch, laying his arm across the back.

Jake had finished his meal. He pushed back the plate and faced Hank. "I guess you want my statement."

Hank nodded, picked up his briefcase, and snapped it open. He removed a large pad and pen and set it on his lap.

"Start at the beginning," Hank said.

Jake relayed the events that had transpired since he'd left the house that morning, including the call he'd received on the way home. Hank wrote it all down, stopping occasionally to ask a question or to get clarity on a certain point. When he'd finished, he motioned toward the money bag on the floor.

"Do you want me to return that?"

"I'll do it," Jake said. "I'm responsible for it. Besides, I need to talk to Mr. Martin."

Hank nodded. "And the gun?"

"I'll lock it up. Don't worry. It appears I might need it again."

"How's Eli Martin?" Annie asked.

Hank shrugged. "As best as he can be, considering the

circumstances. He broke down and wept for a few minutes." He paused and gave a sigh. "It was pretty hard to watch, and something I'll never get used to."

"I've been thinking about the victims," Annie said, "and what they have in common. I didn't come up with much. They're all women, and though Rosemary Coleman survived, I believe she would've been killed as well."

"I believe so too," Hank said. "And that's why we're keeping a close guard on her."

"The relatively small amount of ransom money strikes me as odd," Jake said. "Like it's just an afterthought and not important."

Hank agreed. "And that raises the question, is this for sport? It doesn't seem to be for money. Certainly it's not a get-rich-quick scheme."

"He called himself an entrepreneur," Jake added. "But why are they killing? And how do they pick their victims?"

"Officers have been pounding the streets asking questions," Hank said. "King has contacted all of his CIs, but still no sign of Mouse. It appears he's not known among the criminal elements in this town. And he's keeping well out of sight."

Jake turned to Hank. "How do you think they would have known about the police involvement?"

"They might have just assumed we were involved. However, with the first victim, Linda Gould, had they been watching the house they would've seen the police there. That would be a dead giveaway. With Rosemary Coleman, it's uncertain if they actually knew."

"And with Hannah Martin," Annie added, "they must've known because it seemed like they purposely wanted a witness, which leads me to believe, they're nothing but killers."

She believed that might be the key to the whole thing. It didn't appear to be about the money, but it wasn't just the killing either. If they wanted to kill to satisfy their deranged craving for victims, then why stage a kidnapping?

Maybe it was all about show. About making an unforgettable spectacle. Or did someone have a vendetta against the police and a desire to make them a laughingstock?

Maybe someone had it in for Lincoln Investigations. But who? And why?

Hank had stood and was pacing the floor. He stopped and turned to Jake. "They're being rather bold about their intentions. They've promised another abduction tomorrow and there'll always be some who won't heed our warnings. When you're determined, victims aren't hard to find."

Hank stopped talking abruptly and grabbed his briefcase. "I need to get down to the precinct. I want to have a chat with Callaway and run a few thoughts past him. Maybe he can come up with something." He headed for the door. "I'll talk to you guys later. In the meantime, let me know if you come up with any ideas. We're running out of time."

CHAPTER 51

ANNIE WAS IN THE office going over what they knew so far about the kidnappers and it wasn't much. She'd been concerned about Dr. Gould and had given him a call. He was hanging in there, but she could sense an emptiness in his voice, a feeling of being beaten down, and she had no good news for him regarding their progress.

The whereabouts of Antony Miflan, otherwise known as Mouse, were bothering her. If he was just a hired punk and a loose end, then perhaps his body was lying somewhere waiting to be discovered. If not, then he was hiding out in an unknown location. All attempts by the police to roust him out had been unsuccessful. He was nowhere to be found.

But one thing concerned her most of all: why were they killing the victims? It was bad for business and not at all necessary.

She sat back in her chair as Jake came into the office, lugging the vest, the holster, and the bag of money. He dropped them on the desk.

"We'd better lock this weapon up again," he said, "and I'll get this money back to Eli Martin as soon as possible."

Annie slid open the bottom drawer of the desk and slipped the gun and holster inside. She shut the drawer, turned the key, and removed it, dropping it into the wide top drawer of the desk.

Jake tossed the vest onto an unused chair. "No need to lock that up."

Annie looked at the cloth bag on the desk in front of her. "I'm still trying to figure out why they didn't want that. It would've been easy to have you throw it from the vehicle at some location, just like the first time." She frowned. "It's fifty thousand dollars."

Jake shrugged. "I assume it is. I never counted it. Actually, I never even looked in the bag."

He fiddled with the knot, got it loose, and tugged the bag open. He whistled. "It sure looks like fifty thou, all bundled up nice and neat."

He pushed it across the desk to Annie and she leaned forward and peeked inside at the stacks of fifties, each wrapped in a paper band and stamped by the bank. She looked at Jake. "Eli Martin had this in his safe, right?"

"That's what he said."

She peeked in the bag again, her brow crinkled in thought. "That's funny," she said. "When people keep cash at home in a private safe, it's usually money they're trying to hide. Cash they've picked up somewhere—a job done under the table, perhaps. Why is this money bundled up so neatly and stamped by the bank?"

"He must've withdrawn it at some point."

Annie shook her head. "Not likely." She dropped her elbows on the desk, cupped her hands under her chin and stared at the bag. After a few moments, she asked, "Are you sure you never opened the bag before?"

He shook his head adamantly. "Never. It was tied up when I got it from Martin and I just left it the way it was."

Suddenly she jumped to her feet and grabbed the bag. "Come with me," she said as she hurried into the kitchen.

Jake followed her. "What's up?"

She tossed the bag onto the table. "Sit down for a second. I'll be right back."

She hurried upstairs to the bedroom, opened a box on the vanity and selected a soft makeup brush. She ran it across the palm of her hand. That should do fine.

She ran back downstairs and dropped the brush on the table. Jake looked at her with bewilderment as she scurried into the office. She found an ink pad in the desk drawer along with a magnifying glass and a sheet of white paper.

Returning to the kitchen, she dropped everything on the table, sat down, and reached inside the bag of money. She carefully removed three stacks, holding them by the edges. She lined them up in front of her. "I forgot something," she said.

She went to the cupboard and returned with a jar of dry cocoa and a small plate.

"Is this some kind of experiment?" Jake asked, a perplexed look on his face.

She laughed. "Something like that."

Jake watched her curiously as she twisted the lid off the cocoa, dumped a small amount onto the plate and then dabbed the brush into the cocoa. She ran the brush lightly across the bands of the three stacks. When she was done, she gently blew off the cocoa and peered closely at her handiwork.

There, on the middle stack, was a fingerprint. Not too clear, but unmistakable.

A light dawned in Jake's eyes and he chuckled. "I get it," he said.

She flipped open the ink pad, grabbed one of his big hands, and pressed his thumb down onto the pad and then onto the paper. She smiled with satisfaction.

"A perfect thumbprint," she said.

She picked up the magnifying glass and peered through it, studying the prints. "I'm no expert," she said. "But I think they're a perfect match."

"Let me see that," Jake said as he grabbed the magnifying glass. He studied the print and whistled. "Son of a gun. You're right. They're exactly the same."

"So you know what that means?" Annie asked.

"I sure do. The money Eli Martin gave me is the same money Dr. Gould and I picked up at the bank. That's where my prints got on them." He leaned in and looked closely at the stamp on the band. "The Commerce Bank. It's the same bank."

Jake and Annie stared at each other a moment, not speaking. Jake's eyes grew wide and his mouth dropped open.

"There's only one way Eli Martin could have gotten that money," Annie said. "He's the kidnapper."

CHAPTER 52

Saturday, September 3rd, 2:42 p.m.

JAKE STARED AT THE stacks of money on the table, then at the bag holding the rest of the fifty thousand dollars. He could hardly believe Eli Martin was the kidnapper. But as far as he was concerned, the proof was there in front of them.

Annie was pacing the floor. She stopped and said, "We should call Hank."

Jake nodded, reached for his cell phone, and then paused. "Maybe we should wait. This is evidence, but it's just circumstantial and not enough to get a conviction. It might be enough to get a warrant, but that would only put Martin on guard and I'm sure they won't find anything in a search of his house. He's too smart for that."

"What're you suggesting?" Annie asked.

"Let's wait a couple of hours. I have an idea and if I don't find out anything, then we'll call Hank. The worst that can happen is they bring Martin in for questioning and at least put a stop, or a delay, on Martin's plans for tomorrow."

"What's this big idea of yours?"

Jake shrugged. "Not so big. I'm just going to find Martin

and see what he's up to. I'll follow him around if I have to."

Annie sat, leaned forward, and looked thoughtfully at Jake. Finally, she said, "Okay, give it a try. In the meantime, I'll do a little research and see if I can come up with something on Eli Martin online."

"Sounds good."

Jake knew if Martin was the kidnapper, then he would stop at nothing to finish what he accomplished. He'd even killed his own wife and that was the confusing part. Why go to all this trouble to get rid of his wife? He was beginning to doubt their whole theory, but yet—

He looked at the stacks of bills again. How else could his fingerprints have gotten on those bills? He had to find out what was going on.

Jake grabbed his iPhone and dialed a number.

"This is Jeremiah."

"Geekly. Jake here. I need some advice."

"Hello, old friend. Anything I can do to help would be my utmost pleasure."

Jake laughed. "I need to track someone. More specifically, a vehicle. Do you have anything to help me?"

"I've never been involved in anything like that, but I'll tell you what you need. Get yourself on over to Techmart and tell them you want a GPS tracking device."

Jake wrote down the info. "Thanks, Geekly. I gotta go now. I'm under a time crunch, but I'll talk to you soon."

He hung up, sprang from his chair, and grabbed his car keys from the counter.

"Do you think you should take the pistol with you?" Annie asked.

Jake hesitated. "I'd better not. Could get in a pile of trouble for that. I'm only authorized to carry it when I'm delivering a ransom." He left the kitchen, heading for the front door.

"Wait," Annie called. "Do you have Martin's address?"

Jake slunk back into the kitchen, a crooked grin on his face. "Guess I need that, don't I?"

Annie went to the office and returned with a notepad. She copied down Martin's home address and the address of his car repair shop and handed it to Jake. "I want you to wear the vest," she said.

Jake nodded. She was probably right. He retrieved the vest from the office, struggled with it awhile, and finally got it in place.

"You can go now," she said.

Jake leaped for the front door.

"And be careful," Annie called from the kitchen.

Wasn't he always careful? Well, not exactly.

He raced down the sidewalk, jumped in the Firebird, and spun from the driveway. Ten minutes later he pulled into the parking lot of Techmart, a store that dealt in everything electronic, including a wide range of security and surveillance equipment. Jake had been there several times; in fact, it was one of his favorite places to browse. But he had no time to browse today and in another ten minutes, he'd returned from the shop with a small package.

He spent a few minutes and skimmed over the directions. It was easy enough to use. The device was in a small waterproof magnetic case. It was motion-activated and only had to be switched on, and its movements could be tracked in real-time from his cell phone.

Now to find Martin.

Jake assumed his quarry would either be at home or at the shop. Probably at the shop, but since Martin's residence was almost on the way, he would swing by there first.

It turned out Martin was at home. At least, his black SUV was parked in the driveway. Jake idled by the house and pulled over around a small curve in the street. He grabbed the tracker, slipped it into his side pocket, and stepped from the vehicle.

It wouldn't do to be seen, so he crossed the street, walked past the house, then crossed back over and approached the SUV from a position where the vehicle would block anyone inside the house from seeing him.

He looked up and down the street, his hand gripping the tracker in his pocket. Nothing. No one in sight.

He stepped boldly up to the side of the vehicle, still hidden from view of the house, slipped the tracker from his pocket, flicked the tiny switch on the side of the case, and reached under the bumper.

It wouldn't stick. Plastic bumpers. Everything was plastic these days. He knelt down, peered under the vehicle, and found the metal frame. He heard a satisfying click as the magnetic case snapped into place. He wiggled it to be sure. It should hold.

He hurried back, crossed the street, and made his way to his vehicle. He jumped in and switched on his cell phone. The satellite map was web-based and the tracker wasn't emitting any signal, but if it moved, Jake would know.

He didn't have to wait long, maybe half an hour, and his cell phone beeped.

Eli Martin was on the move.

The little red dot on the map showed Martin was heading the other way, so Jake started the Firebird, swung around, and eased ahead. He propped the phone on his dash so he could keep an eye on it while driving. He watched the dot take a couple of turns and finally start moving up Main Street. It looked like Martin might be heading for the shop.

His assumption was proven right when the dot stopped beeping. Jake recognized the address on the screen, down a side street just off Main, as that of Martin Auto.

He should have brought Annie's car. It would fit in invisibly anywhere, not like the Firebird. It stuck out like a sore thumb, so he parked on Main Street a half a block from the shop, rummaged in the glove compartment for a small pair of binoculars, grabbed his cell phone, crossed the street, and walked up Main until he was opposite the shop.

Martin Auto was located on a quarter acre of property. The main building was set back from the street, with a small parking area out front. There was a larger vehicle parking lot behind the shop, but it couldn't be seen from where Jake stood. The SUV occupied one of the customer slots in front.

Jake stepped back into a doorway, leaned against the wall, and trained the glasses on the front window of Martin Auto. There was a girl sitting behind a counter. Probably a receptionist. Beyond, he saw what appeared to be an office, with Martin standing in the doorway, turned sideways. He was carrying on a conversation with someone unseen.

He would give anything right now to hear that conversation. Maybe it was nothing, but then again …

Jake moved the glasses over until he had a view of the roll-up door. It was closed, but he could make out a car on a hoist, a mechanic doing something underneath. He was hoping to see a van inside—the van the abductors used to ply their awful trade. Maybe it was around behind the shop. He would have to get back there and see.

Too late. Martin was coming this way. He stopped to talk

to the receptionist a moment and then left the building, heading for the SUV.

No time to look for the van. He would get to that later, but right now, he had to find out where Martin was going.

He gave Annie a quick call to inform her of his whereabouts and that he would be following Martin and then hurried back to the Firebird and got in, propped the cell phone on the dashboard, and waited for the little red dot to move.

CHAPTER 53

Saturday, September 3rd, 3:51 p.m.

ELI MARTIN HAD THE plan firmly set in his mind. There was no way he could allow it to fail. It had better not, or he would be in deep trouble.

He climbed into his SUV, started the engine, and backed from the parking spot. He checked the bulge under his shirt as he pulled onto Main Street. It was still there, waiting and ready.

The death of Rosemary Coleman was going to be a learning experience. She should never have been allowed to escape in the first place, but soon ... soon that would be rectified.

He'd been there several times, watching, spying from across the street, and he knew the cop rarely budged from his seat in the living room. Rosemary probably felt uncomfortable with him around all the time because she was often elsewhere, sometimes in the garden out back, or in the kitchen, and as far as he could tell, she rarely entered the front room during the day.

His plan hinged on that.

He chuckled to himself. One of the perks of owning a car

repair shop, there was always a customer's car he could borrow awhile and never have to use the same vehicle twice during his trips down that street.

But this time he would be taking a slightly different route.

He made it to the outskirts of town in a few minutes and stopped his vehicle on the shoulder of a gravel road. Soon the city would extend along here, but right now, this area was nothing but trees and For Sale signs. He stepped out and glanced up a knoll to the trees beyond. He knew this spot well. After all, this was where they'd abducted Rosemary Coleman, and the Coleman residence was just through those trees, less than a quarter mile away.

~*~

ANNIE WAS HOPING Jake would call her again to inform her of his progress. She'd called his number and got a message he was unavailable and although she wasn't surprised he hadn't called her, she was anxious to make some headway on this difficult case. Tomorrow was coming and with it there might be another kidnapping. They were running out of time.

Matty was next door at Kyle's most of the day, coming home long enough for a quick lunch and then leaving again. Annie gave Chrissy a call to let her know she would be going out awhile and ask if she could please watch Matty for her. Of course, Chrissy was always more than willing.

She went into the office, unlocked the bottom drawer of the desk, and found a small canister of pepper spray. She looked at the pistol resting comfortably in its holster. It wasn't legal for her to carry it, but she had half a mind to anyway. They were up against some very nasty people.

She left it where it was, closed and locked the drawer,

went into the kitchen, grabbed her handbag and keys, and made her way outside. A few darkened clouds hung overhead, threatening rain. Not what she wanted right now; she had some business to attend to. Maybe they would blow over.

She climbed into her car and made the trip to Martin Auto in a few minutes. It wasn't an industrious part of the city, but an area not known for a lot of money, with struggling businesses and folks just getting by.

She parked along the side street, a minute's walk from the shop, grabbed her handbag, walked up the sidewalk to the entrance, and boldly went inside.

No one was in the store area but some banging came from the adjoining garage, probably a mechanic fixing a customer's vehicle, left alone to tend the business. The smell of old oil and hand cleaner hung in the air. A soft-drink machine sat sweating in the corner, begging for change. Cigarettes and chocolate bars were displayed alongside cans of oil and window washer, all offered for sale behind the counter. There was a bell beside the cash register. A cardboard sign taped to the register asked her to ring for service. She didn't bother.

Behind the counter she saw an office, its door wide open. She glanced toward the garage and then stepped behind the counter and peered through the door. A battered desk filled one corner of the small room, a filing cabinet and some metal shelving almost filling the rest. A coatrack held greasy overalls and a well-used cap. The floor could use a sweeping. The banging continued. She slipped open the top desk drawer. A stapler, paper clips, pens, other office stuff. A dirty ashtray lay on the desk holding down some papers like a paperweight. Looked like invoices.

The banging stopped and she held her breath. More banging and she pulled open a side drawer of the desk. Just papers, invoices, receipts, soiled by greasy smudges and stains.

She closed the drawer and glanced around. Nothing of interest on the shelves. It looked like she wasn't going to find anything in here. She left the office, went through the store, and stepped back outside. She squinted at the sky. The sun had reappeared, the showers held off for another day.

She took the sidewalk along the side of the building, past a window covered with gunk, to the rear of the property. A private parking lot behind the shop had spaces for several vehicles. A chain-link fence cordoned off the lot, with a double-width gate forbidding entrance. A chain hung on the clasp, a padlock swinging free. She opened the gate far enough to slip through.

A big blue dumpster bulging with green bags and cardboard boxes sat near a metal door in the back of the building. A similar door had a sign: "Service Entrance." It probably led into the rear of the shop, the first door, perhaps down to the basement. Another greasy window, one pane boarded up, was located in the wall beside the door.

She glanced around the lot. This didn't look like the kind of place one would take their Mercedes, Porsche, or Jaguar. Instead, the lot held beat-up autos, some with fenders coated with rust-proof paint, waiting for a final coat. A dusty Ford sat in the corner, jacked up on blocks, useless now with no wheels and a broken windshield. Another car was smashed in the front; its driver might not have escaped alive. An unsteady stack of used tires tilted along the rear fence.

A black van in the corner stood out among its companions—all shiny and sparkling in the sun, almost like brand new and out of place among the rest of these clunkers.

Her footsteps crunched on the gravel as she crept to the

window in the back of the building. She couldn't see inside so she rubbed at a spot in an attempt to remove some of the grime. It helped a bit, just enough to make out a vehicle on a hoist, straight ahead. A man stood under the vehicle, his hands up in the bowels of the underbody. She heard the faint sounds of an air wrench and the running compressor that powered the tool.

The walls and shelves were lined with auto parts, belts, hoses, and boxes. She rubbed at the window again to see better. This was more than an auto repair shop. It was a body shop as well. Over to the side hung a plastic sheet, floor to ceiling, separating a large area from the rest of the garage. The sheet was pulled back revealing a rainbow of paint splashes and splatters. Reds, blues, yellows, white, and black. This was where vehicles were painted after scratches were repaired, body parts replaced, and dings pounded out and smoothed over.

Annie turned her attention to the black van. She'd been formulating a theory over the last couple of days and now she could test it out.

She took a look around. The sidewalk was deserted and even if someone had walked by, it wasn't likely she would be seen. There were no windows in the side of the van, so she stood on the running board and peeked inside the driver-side window. A couple of empty coffee cups were in the console, litter and another cup on the floor. The cloth seat covers were stained. One had a rip. It looked like a well-used vehicle inside, brand new outside.

She stepped down and went to the rear of the van, stood on her tiptoes, and peered inside. It was empty except for a grocery bag bulging with something. She went to the side of the vehicle and crouched down by the rear tire. She reached into her handbag and removed a small flashlight and her key ring. The light flicked on and then carefully, so it wouldn't be noticeable, she scratched at the paint just inside the wheel well with a key.

Her assumption was correct. Underneath the fresh black paint was a hint of yellow. She scratched some more. Blue, and then white, and then bare metal.

This was the vehicle the kidnappers had used, covered with a fresh coat of paint each time. She suspected it was unregistered as well and that's why Callaway hadn't been able to track it down. It might've been rescued from a wrecking yard at some point and fixed up.

She had to get inside.

Digging in her handbag, she removed a small leather case and flipped it open. It wasn't the first time she'd used her lock-picking tools. They'd come in handy before and she'd practiced since. It took a few minutes to spring the lock and she pulled the door handle up and climbed in.

She went straight for the bag and looked inside. It was hair; no, wait, it was a beard, a fake one. She suspected it was the one Mouse had worn when he'd robbed Walter Coleman outside the bank.

She decided not to search the rest of the vehicle. If she was correct, she didn't want to mess up any evidence. She would let Jake know. His phone rang several times before he answered.

"Hi, honey," he said. "I can't talk now. I'm using the GPS tracker and following Martin."

She told him what she'd found. He whistled and then said, "Martin has stopped somewhere. I'll call Hank as soon as I get there." He paused, then added, "I hope you're being careful?"

"Of course."

"Good work, honey," Jake said. "We're gonna get this guy."

"And you be careful too," Annie said.

Jake chuckled. "Always."

She hung up. There was no doubt in her mind now they had the right guy. She just had to check one more thing.

CHAPTER 54

Saturday, September 3rd, 4:29 p.m.

ELI MARTIN REACHED under his jacket and fingered his weapon of choice. It was deadly, silent, and all he would need. That and his wits.

Of course, if anyone was around, it wouldn't do to be recognized, so he opened the glove compartment and removed a black ski mask. He stuffed it into his side jacket pocket and got out of the SUV.

He took a glance up and down the road before climbing through the ditch and making his way up the incline to the forest's edge. Soon, all these trees would be cut down to make room for the exploding population, but for today, they would serve their purpose.

The darkened woods kept him hidden as he crept through the trees and stopped at the tree line bordering the rear of the Coleman house, only fifty feet from where he stood. He crouched down beside a bush and put on the ski mask. It would cover his features should anyone other than Rosemary come along while he was doing his task.

He waited.

He knew she wouldn't be going on her daily jog. She

hadn't done that for a while, too afraid now to venture so far from her home. The cop was likely in the front room and didn't concern him in the least. He only had to be patient until Rosemary came into the backyard. And she would.

And she did.

Eli Martin watched as the back door slid open. She had some garden tools in her hand, ready to do some gardening. Perfect. He smiled grimly, adjusted the ski mask, and rose to his feet. He waited patiently until she came a little closer and bent down by the flowerbed, close to a towering maple that occupied the center of the backyard. She held a small hand shovel, another tool in her other hand, and she began to dig in the flowerbed. She was only thirty feet away from him now.

He moved silently to the right. The maple tree was hiding her from his view, but better still, it hid him from her.

Just as planned.

He stepped out and crept forward. The cushy grass under his feet allowed for a silent approach. Just a few more feet and he stopped behind the maple. Rosemary was humming to herself. She sounded contented, obviously unaware she was about to die.

He reached under his jacket and removed the garrote. The wire was thin, like piano wire, strong, and deadly. The wooden handle at either end assured he would have a firm grip, a deadly grip, as Rosemary's breath was cut off and she quietly died of asphyxiation.

He was going to enjoy that part.

He licked his lips and gripped the weapon.

One last glance around and then he stepped out.

Was it the faint sound of his footsteps on the grass? Was it intuition? Or was it by chance? She turned her head just as he raised the weapon. He leaped forward and flipped the garrote. It was around her neck, but by instinct she'd brought her hands up, the small shovel still held tightly in her fist, keeping his weapon from finding her throat.

She gasped and tried to scream but no sound came out.

As she struggled and broke free, he swung his fist. It connected viciously with the side of her head, knocking her to her back. She was stunned, but as he leaped on her she rolled to the side, swinging the shovel in one hand like a knife, a small rake in the other. It nicked the side of his head and he felt a stinging in his ear.

He dove again and this time he was on her. He wrapped his hands around her neck and squeezed. As his grip tightened about her windpipe, in desperation she swung the tool again. He ducked out of its way and had to let go of her throat to avoid another painful blow.

She stabbed at him with the shovel, again and again. This crazy chick was tougher than he'd expected. But he couldn't fail. Never. Never.

He should've brought a knife with him, just in case. He cursed his luck. He had a small pistol in his vehicle but didn't dare use it. He'd wanted this to be a silent kill.

But things weren't working out exactly as planned.

She swung again, connected again, and he was dazed for a few seconds. Just long enough for her to struggle free, and by the time he'd recovered, she'd stumbled to her feet and was getting away. She was a good five yards from him before she wobbled, fell to one knee, rose again, and turned around.

He'd made it to his feet and stood between her and the house, the wooded area behind her. She glanced toward the house, hoping to make it to safety, but he stood his ground. They panted and glared at each other.

She was feisty, he'd give her that, but she couldn't get away now. She'd dropped the garden tools in her escape and was helpless. He still clung to the garrote by one end, the other dangling at his side.

He dove for her but she spun and headed for the trees. But she could never outrun him.

Or could she?

He chased her as she tore madly through the bush. He ducked low hanging branches that swung back at him as she thrust them aside. He was getting closer. He could touch her now. He grasped her shoulder but his foot caught a root and he fell heavily against a tree.

Then she tripped, landed on all fours, and sprang up again as he caught the back of her shirt. It ripped loose, leaving most of her right sleeve in his hand. He tossed it aside and cursed her.

They were getting close to the other edge of the wooded area now. He had to catch her before she got to the road. He'd found out the hard way she was fast and agile, probably due to her daily habit of jogging. Once they got to the road she would outrun him. Why hadn't he brought his pistol with him?

She was circling around now, heading for the road at an angle, calling for help. Where's she going?

And then he saw what she saw.

A car had backed into a small lane by the road and she headed straight for it. He could make out a figure in the driver seat.

Eli Martin spun to a stop, stepped behind a tree, and

peered around the trunk. He watched helplessly as Rosemary ran frantically toward the bright red vehicle.

He cursed to himself. Even that fool Mouse couldn't have bungled this any worse than he had. Now all he could do was get back to his vehicle, get out of here, and try again later.

Next time he would bring a rifle.

CHAPTER 55

Saturday, September 3rd, 4:55 p.m.

JAKE HAD BACKED his vehicle into a small lane leading off the main road. Martin's SUV was parked on the shoulder, some ways back. He didn't know what Martin was up to, but whatever it was, it wasn't good. He knew the Coleman residence was just through those trees and he feared the worst.

Annie had found enough evidence to prove Martin's involvement, so it was time to call the police. But until they arrived and put a stop Martin's plans, he would have to take matters into his own hands.

He picked his phone up off the dashboard and closed the browser. He stopped, his finger poised above the dial button. What was that?

From somewhere close by he'd heard a call for help. It was a woman's voice, urgent, almost pleading.

He squinted through the window and peered up the grade leading into the woods. Through the darkness of the trees he saw a woman running his way, stumbling as she raced toward him.

He tossed the phone onto the dash and jumped from the

vehicle. As the woman drew closer he recognized her. It was Rosemary Coleman. He didn't see her pursuer but suspected it was Eli Martin. But where was he?

He sprinted up the grade and she fell into his arms as he reached the top. She was out of breath, panting, and she clung to him, her voice a hoarse whisper. "Thank God. Please help me. He's trying to kill me."

Jake pushed her back by the shoulders and stared into her frantic eyes. "Who?"

"I ... I don't know."

He scanned the woods for signs of Martin but saw nothing.

Rosemary's legs gave way and she crumpled to the ground. Jake leaned down and picked her up. She couldn't have weighed much more than a hundred pounds and was barely a hindrance to him as he spun around and climbed back down the grade.

He set her on her feet at the passenger side of the vehicle, steadying her with one hand while he opened the door with the other. He helped her inside the car.

Now what should he do?

An engine came to life a hundred yards away. It was Martin. He was on the move again. He had to follow him.

He ran around, jumped into the driver-side door, and grabbed his phone off the dash. He got the tracer working. But the red dot was moving this way. Instead of going back the way he came, Martin was heading out of town. The black SUV breezed past, heading north.

Jake glanced over at Rosemary. She'd finally caught her breath, calmed down, and was watching him.

"There he goes," Jake said, pointing to the vehicle speeding away. "Do you know who was chasing you?"

She shook her head and watched the vehicle disappear from view. "He was wearing a ski mask. I couldn't see his face."

"It was Eli Martin," Jake said. "Do you know him?"

She frowned. "I've never heard the name. Is he one of the kidnappers?"

"I'm afraid so, and it looks like he came back to finish the job."

She looked at him anxiously. "We should call the police."

"We will," he said, holding the phone up as he talked. "But I need to follow him and I can't use the tracker at the same time."

Rosemary squinted at the phone. "Your battery is almost dead. It's down to one percent."

He spun the phone around and glared at it. He hadn't charged it up the night before and the continuous use of the tracker had drained its remaining power. Now what? He'd better use the last of the battery and call the police. He would have to follow Martin manually. He'd better get moving.

He handed Rosemary the phone. "Call the police. I have to concentrate on following that guy."

Rosemary took the phone from him and Jake dropped the shifter into gear and spun ahead, tossing up dust and gravel as the tires bit in. The vehicle swung onto the road and he rammed the gas pedal to the floor.

Rosemary held up the phone. "The battery's dead."

Jake glanced at her, frowned, and made a quick decision. He couldn't let Martin get away. He might be a mile or so up the road, and who knew where he would end up? Jake had no choice but to follow. The speedometer climbed higher. He kept the pedal to the floor as the road wound around gentle curves and over hills.

"Why was he trying to kill me?" Rosemary asked.

Jake glanced at her. "That's what I don't know. I assume it's because you can identify his partner, and if he's found, he'll probably turn on Martin."

They roared over a knoll, his stomach dropped, and the front tires left the road for a brief moment. The performance shocks cushioned the landing, the rear springs doing their job well as Rosemary clung to the dashboard.

"But I already identified him," Rosemary said. "Apparently, they know exactly who his partner is. A guy named Antony Miflan."

Jake nodded. "Better known as Mouse. But Mouse hasn't been found and Martin might've gotten rid of him already."

"You mean ... killed his partner?"

Jake shrugged. "Why not?"

They reached a long stretch of straight road and saw the SUV ahead. A long ways off, but they were gaining. He didn't have a plan as to what he would do when he caught up to Martin. He would have to decide that when the time came.

"Does he have a gun?" Jake asked.

"I don't think so. If he did, he would've used it on me."

"So he had no weapon? Not even a knife?"

"He had one of those wire things, with handles on the end. He tried to choke me with it."

"A garrote."

She nodded.

"That's what he used on the other victims," Jake said.

She shuddered. "And he almost used it on me." She paused. "Do you have a gun?"

"Nope. Not allowed to carry one."

He checked the gas gauge. Lots of gas. He had topped it up yesterday. It didn't matter how far Martin went, he couldn't get away this time. The Firebird was tuned to perfection and its sixteen-gallon tank should outlast the SUV unless Martin had a full tank, and that wasn't likely.

He felt her gaze on him and he moved his eyes from the road for a second and glanced at her.

"Aren't you afraid?" she asked.

Jake thought a moment. "Not really," he said. "I'm more angry than afraid."

"You don't look it."

He grinned. "You'll have to trust me on that one."

Yes, he was angry, but he was trying to keep a cool head. He glanced at her again. "What about you?"

The SUV rounded a curve, out of sight, and the Firebird followed.

She shrugged. "I've been through a lot the last few days." She gave a nervous laugh. "I think I'm more angry than afraid now too." She paused. "Besides, I'm with you, and you look pretty capable."

She had broken the tension and he chuckled. "So far, I've been lucky I guess."

"I hope your luck holds for another day."

The vehicle came out of the curve and Jake's mouth dropped open. "He's gone."

Rosemary peered through the window. "He must've pulled off somewhere."

Jake touched the brake and pulled to the shoulder. He looked in the rearview mirror. "He couldn't have gone far."

Rosemary twisted around in the seat. "I saw a lane just back there," she said. "Perhaps that's where he pulled off."

"Let's find out," Jake said.

CHAPTER 56

Saturday, September 3rd, 4:29 p.m.

AFTER ANNIE HAD called Jake, she was still confused about Eli Martin's involvement in the murder of his own wife, what part he had in it, and the possible whereabouts of the man named Mouse.

She stepped over to the back of the building and peered into the window. The mechanic was still under the vehicle, concentrating on the repairs. She retrieved her lock-picking tools again and went to work on the door she suspected led down into the bowels of the building. In a moment, the door swung open and she peeked inside.

A set of wooden steps led down into a brightly lit basement. She listened a moment and then tugged the door open and stepped over the threshold onto the first step.

What was she looking for? She wasn't sure, but she carefully took each step until she landed at the foot of the stairs. She looked around. It appeared this room was used for storage of parts and equipment.

She checked in a cardboard box on the shelf and flipped through old business records, receipts, and bills covering the last couple of years. Other boxes held clamps, bolts, and a variety of fasteners.

A chair sat near one wall, beside a makeshift table covered with magazines, an ashtray, and empty coffee cups. Someone had spent some time down here.

Across the room, another set of steps led up, likely into the main part of the building. A door on the wall to the right was closed, probably leading into another room. She went closer to the door and examined it. There was a sliding bolt lock on it, pulled back. She twisted the knob and gently pushed the door open.

The small room was dark so she found her flashlight, flicked it on, and shone it around. The walls of the empty chamber were concrete like the rest of the basement. There was no window in the room and the ceiling was solid with heavy beams.

She shone the light on the floor, frowned, and crouched down. A dark patch had caught her eye. It was dried blood, now soaked into the concrete and staining the porous floor a reddish-brown shade.

Annie shuddered. Was this the place where Hannah Martin had been held? Judging by the stains on the floor, perhaps she'd been murdered in this very spot.

She'd seen enough.

As she backed into the main room and closed the door behind her, she heard the outside door at the top of the steps open. She spun around, darted to the far side of the room and ducked down behind a wooden barrel.

Footsteps clomped on the stairs, one at a time, until the newcomer reached the floor. She held her breath. Hopefully, he wouldn't stay.

What had she gotten herself into?

She searched in her handbag, removed the container of pepper spray, put her finger on the nozzle and waited.

Annie heard him moving across the floor and then a sigh as he dropped into the chair. A magazine rustled, a lighter flicked, and the distinct smell of cigarette smoke filled the air.

It appeared he was here to stay and she couldn't hide for long.

She took a deep breath and stepped out from behind the barrel. She stood six feet from Mouse, between him and the steps, and held the container of spray at arm's length in front of her.

Mouse's eyes widened, his mouth dropped open, and the magazine fluttered to the floor.

"Stay still or I'll spray you."

"Who … who're you?" he demanded as he recovered from the surprise and leaned forward in the chair.

She threatened him by swinging the container to the side as she tapped the nozzle lightly. A fine mist shot out. "Don't move. This is pepper spray and you'll be sorry if I use it on you."

He frowned and sat back. "What do you want?"

"I want to know who killed Hannah Martin."

His eyes narrowed. "Who's Hannah Martin?"

"I think you know."

He glared at her a moment, then at the can of spray. "I don't know who killed her."

Annie waved the spray and repeated, "Who killed Hannah Martin?"

"Who're you?" he asked.

"I'm Annie Lincoln. Now talk or I spray."

His mouth dropped open again. "Are you Jake Lincoln's wife?"

"Yes."

"Then you're not a cop and you have no reason to be here."

"It doesn't matter." Annie pointed to the container and tightened her finger on the nozzle. "I don't need a reason."

Mouse held up his hands. "I'll tell you if you let me go. It ... it wasn't me. I didn't kill nobody."

"Then who did?"

He hesitated, then said, "It was Eli Martin. He does all the killing. I just do as I'm told and don't ask no questions."

"And who dumped her body in the forest?"

He shrugged. "I did. But she was already dead. I swear, I didn't kill her."

"And what about Mrs. Gould?"

"Same thing. Eli Martin killed her and I just dumped her body by the road."

Annie pointed up the stairs. "And is that the van out there you used?"

He nodded.

"Where's Eli Martin now?"

"I ... I don't know. He doesn't tell me where he goes. He just goes. I don't ask."

Annie glared at Mouse, the pepper spray never wavering in her hand. "We know you were the one who robbed Walter Coleman at the bank."

He glared. "I just did what I was told."

Annie waved the spray. "Stand up," she ordered.

"Why?"

She raised her voice. "Stand up?"

He stood and she motioned toward the room. "In there."

He shook his head and said nothing.

"Now. Get in there or I spray."

He moved reluctantly toward the room, glancing at her over his shoulder. He stopped at the door and turned around. "Can I have my cigarettes?"

"You don't need them."

"Please?"

She hesitated and then waved the can at him. "Go inside the room and I'll get them."

He turned, opened the door, and stepped inside. "It's dark in here."

"That didn't seem to matter to you when Hannah Martin was in there."

No answer.

She shut the door, stepped back to the chair, and picked up the package of cigarettes and lighter. She returned, opened the door, tossed them inside, and shut the door again, securing the bolt in place.

That would hold him until the police arrived.

She put the can of spray back into her handbag and climbed the stairs to the outside. She shut the door behind her, made sure it was left unlocked, and left the lot through the gate. She stepped onto the sidewalk and sat on the grass under a tree.

Retrieving her cell phone, she called Jake's number. A voice said the caller was unavailable.

That's strange. Why would he turn his phone off?

The police should've been here by now and she wondered if Jake had called Hank yet. She decided to call Hank herself. The van was enough evidence for a warrant to search the building, and when they found Mouse, he would surely live up to his name and tell them all he knew.

CHAPTER 57

Saturday, September 3rd, 5:22 p.m.

JAKE WASN'T SURE exactly where Eli Martin had pulled off, but the lane they'd just passed seemed like the most likely spot.

He spun the Firebird around and eased back the way they'd come. He pulled the vehicle to the shoulder a hundred yards from the lane, shut down the engine, and turned to Rosemary. "You'd better stay here. I'll go take a look."

She shook her head adamantly. "No way. I'm going with you."

Jake watched her a moment, thinking. For someone who'd been through what she had, she had a lot of spunk. But it could be risky and he didn't want to put her in additional danger.

She interrupted his thoughts by opening the car door and climbing out. She leaned down and looked at him through the open door. "Are you coming?"

It looked like he had no choice. She was coming with him whether he liked it or not.

"Shut your door quietly," he said and he climbed from the vehicle and eased his door shut.

273

They walked up the side of the road to the lane. Set back from the road, perhaps five hundred feet, a small house—more like a cabin—could be seen. Martin's SUV was nowhere in sight.

"Stay behind me," he said as he turned and headed up the lane.

She paid no mind and stepped up beside him, striding to keep up with his pace.

He frowned down at her, held her by the arm, and stopped. "Look, I just want to see what Martin's up to. With both of us, there's more chance of being seen."

"I'll be careful. You don't have to worry." She pulled her arm loose, gave him a quick smile, and continued up the lane.

He sighed and took a couple of long steps to catch up. She was one of the victims and if she was determined to come along, then so be it.

As they drew closer to the cabin, Jake could see the building had known better days. The front yard was overgrown with weeds. A couple of windows were broken, the paint was peeling, and the closed door sagged on its hinges.

Rosemary followed Jake's lead as he circled around to the far side of the building. If Martin was inside, it was unlikely he could see them from there. They ducked under a single window and continued to the back corner. Jake peered around. From that vantage point they could see that Martin's SUV was there, but Martin was nowhere to be seen.

"He must be inside," Rosemary whispered.

Jake nodded. "I'll take a look." He crept back and took a quick glance through the dusty window. There were no lights on and Jake doubted if there was any electricity coming to the building. Martin couldn't be seen in the main room. There were a couple of adjoining rooms but their doors were closed.

He ducked back down. "I don't think he's in there."

"That's because I'm right here."

Jake spun around and Rosemary gasped. Eli Martin stood ten feet away, a pistol in his hand, a forced smile curling his mouth.

"Jake, my friend, do you think I'm stupid?"

Jake didn't answer as he put his arm in front of Rosemary, nudged her back, and stood between her and the gunman.

"I was well aware you were following me. I'd recognize that beautiful car of yours anywhere. It is a magnificent machine, Jake."

Jake glanced at the pistol. He didn't see any chance of disarming Martin and he didn't want to take a chance with Rosemary there. It would be too dangerous for both of them.

"You can't get away with this, Martin," Jake said. "The police know who you are and they're on their way now."

"Oh, is that so? Then why didn't you wait until they got here before you came barging in?"

Martin had a point.

The kidnapper continued, "No, Jake. Nobody knows you're here, and now it's just you, me, and dear Rosemary."

Jake looked around desperately trying to come up with an idea, some way to get the better of Martin. He knew he could make a dive for the killer and hope for the best. If he was shot at and the shot missed, he could disarm him. If the shot didn't miss, the vest would stop the bullet, but he would be knocked flat on his back. And then Rosemary would be in more danger.

The best bet would be to bide his time and wait for a better chance. He was glad Annie had insisted he wear the vest.

Martin seemed to sense Jake's thoughts and waved the pistol for effect. "You can't get away, Jake. You must face it."

Rosemary eased out from behind Jake and took one step toward Martin. "Why were you trying to kill me?"

The pistol moved toward Rosemary. "My dear, dear woman. Surely you must know."

She shook her head. "I have no idea."

Martin laughed. "Perhaps you'll find out why before you die."

Rosemary jutted her chin. "Go ahead. Shoot me."

Jake put a hand on her shoulder. "Rosemary, please relax." He moved in front of her again.

"Well done, Jake. Well done." Martin chuckled. "Now, please turn around, both of you."

Jake met Martin's gaze and glared at him a moment before turning around, careful to keep himself between Martin and Rosemary.

"Walk to my vehicle."

Martin stayed back a few feet as they moved toward the SUV.

"Now, get down on the ground, both of you, and lay face down."

Jake turned and scowled at Martin before doing as he was told and then watched as Martin opened the rear door of the SUV, rummaged around, and removed a yellow nylon rope. The killer slipped a knife from under his jacket and cut the rope in two. While holding the pistol in one hand, he tied Jake's hands and feet securely. The knot was pulled tight and Jake was helpless.

Rosemary was next and she put up more of a struggle, but Martin managed to tie her as well. He stepped back and a smile appeared on his face. "This is so much fun," he said.

The smile turned into a laugh as he tucked the pistol under his belt. He leaned down and rolled Jake onto his back, and then Rosemary.

They lay side by side, helpless.

"Why don't you kill us?" Jake asked.

"In due time, Jake. Please be patient. I have much better plans."

Martin went to the SUV and returned with a cell phone in his hand. "Smile for the camera," he said and the camera clicked. He turned the phone around. "Ah, an excellent shot. You make a great couple. Annie will be delighted to see you two so nice and cozy."

"Leave her out of this," Jake roared. "You don't need her. You have me."

"But she's already involved, Jake. I couldn't leave her out if I wanted to. Besides, that wouldn't be fair, would it?"

CHAPTER 58

Saturday, September 3rd, 5:36 p.m.

ANNIE LEANED AGAINST the tree, her phone in her hand. She'd been unable to get a hold of Jake and she was anxious to inform Hank of what she'd discovered. Before she had a chance to make the call, her cell rang. She looked at the caller ID. Unknown number.

She answered, "Annie Lincoln."

"Annie Lincoln, I'm so delighted we finally get to talk," a deep voice said.

It was him. It was Eli Martin.

Why would he be calling now and why would he be calling her? Annie said nothing, her mind in a whirl, as breathing came over the line.

"Are you still there, Annie?"

"I'm here."

"You'll be happy to hear your husband is safe."

Whatever did that mean? What was he talking about?

Martin continued, "He and the lovely Rosemary are a little busy at the moment. Perhaps you'd like to see what they're up to. Wait, I know. I can send you a photo. I happen to have a lovely shot of just the two of them."

She gasped as an image appeared on her screen: Jake and Rosemary, tied and helpless.

"I've always wanted to be a photographer," Martin said. "I think it's in my blood." Silence. "Did you receive my latest masterpiece, Annie?"

"I see it," Annie said, almost a whisper.

"I've no intention of hurting your husband." More silence, then, "Do you believe in love, Annie?"

"Of course."

"Your husband thinks a lot of you. He actually offered himself up if I would spare you."

Annie listened quietly, fearfully.

"Would you do the same for him?"

"Yes."

"Would you like that chance? A chance to prove your undying love?"

Whatever was he driving at?

"Please forgive me," Martin said. "I'm a hopeless romantic."

His low laugh sent a chill up Annie's spine as she waited.

"It's your choice, Annie. I'll spare Jake and take you in exchange. Would you consider that?"

Of course she would, but that wasn't going to be necessary. At least … she hoped it wasn't. "I would do that," she answered softly.

A chuckle came over the line, then, "Excellent. So, shall we put it to the test?"

What choice did she have? "Yes," she answered.

"There's one condition, Annie. You must come alone. Otherwise, it'll be impossible for me to keep my end of the bargain, and I'm afraid that would result in a horrendous outcome."

"I'll come alone," Annie said.

"Marvelous. It'll be amazing to finally get to meet you. I've heard so much about you and your marvelous escapades, and now." He sighed, then said, "I have to admit, Annie, I'm a fan."

"Just tell me where you want me to go and I'll be there."

"Well, well, aren't we just a little bit impatient?" Martin paused. "Very well, then. Do you know where Hamlin Road is?"

"I do."

"Such a lovely neighborhood. Pleasant and quiet. No nosy people to disturb you. However, once you get out of the suburbs, it's even more peaceful. One could shout—even scream—as loud as they wanted and would never be heard."

Silence.

"And that's where we can meet up, Annie. Hamlin Road soon turns into a long, lonely highway, and just five miles east of the city you'll go around a rather large curve and then … then you'll be close. Keep your eye on the right-hand side for a delightful little lane. It's a long lane, beautiful really, all lined with wildflowers and colorful shrubs, but it'll take you right into our meeting place."

"I have the directions," Annie said. "I'll be there."

"Wonderful. And please hurry. I'll be waiting and so will Jake."

"What about Rosemary Coleman? Will you release her as well?"

He hesitated. "Yes, I will—if you come alone. You have exactly one hour to get here. Otherwise I can't be responsible for the consequences."

"I'm downtown," Annie said. "I need a bit longer to get there."

"Very well. You have one hour and fifteen minutes. Not a second more. Drive carefully now."

The line went dead.

Annie dropped her phone in her lap, lay back against the tree and closed her eyes. She realized at that moment she would give her life to save Jake, but even if that were the only answer, Eli Martin could never be trusted to keep his word. Never.

She had to come up with a plan and quickly.

She stood and hurried to her car, wondering if she should call Hank. She decided against it. Martin likely expected her to and would be ready. He was stringent with the rules he'd set and she wasn't going to take any chances. Lives were at stake. Her husband's life was at stake.

She climbed in her car and sat still, hatching a plan—a daring plan—but it just might work. It had to work. She would only have one shot at this.

Annie thought about Rosemary Coleman and about Walter Coleman. Should she let him know what was going on? He had every right to know since his wife was in mortal danger.

She drove faster than usual through town, hoping she wouldn't get pulled over for speeding and in a few minutes arrived home. She ran into the house and straight to the office.

The iMac came to life when she touched the space bar. She spent a few minutes on Google Maps, made a printout, folded the paper, and tucked it into her back pocket.

When she unlocked the side drawer of the desk and gazed at the Smith & Wesson, she wished Jake had taken it with him. But he hadn't, and so now, she would make good use of it. Jake was in danger and nothing else mattered.

The harness had to be adjusted to fit her, and when she slipped the gun into the holster, it felt heavy. She adjusted the harness again and popped the magazine in, thankful Jake had taken the time to show her that much. She knew how to load it, but wasn't sure how well she could shoot. She hadn't had much occasion to practice in the past, but was certain it couldn't be that hard.

Just aim and pull the trigger.

Binoculars. She pulled a pair off the shelf and tucked them into her handbag. A knife. A kitchen knife would have to do. What else? A jacket. Dark green. It was Jake's and rather large on her, but it would be fine. And a cap. Also Jake's.

She was ready.

Ready and determined.

She looked at her watch. One last thing to do. Walter Coleman would just be on his way home from work. She picked up the office phone and called his cell number. He answered right away.

She told him who she was and said, "I have some disturbing news for you, Mr. Coleman."

"Yes?"

Annie explained all she knew, who the kidnapper was and what he was demanding of her.

"You shouldn't go alone," he said, concern in his voice. Concern for Annie, but primarily for his wife. "Let me come with you."

"I must go alone," Annie said.

"What about the police?"

"No. I can't chance it."

"Then at least tell me where Rosemary is. I need to know." He was pleading.

Annie felt deep sympathy for Walter Coleman. Because of

this dangerous situation, she could almost feel what it would be like to lose Jake. It would be no different for Coleman.

"They're about five miles east of the city along Hamlin Road," she said. "There's a cabin there where I'm supposed to meet them. But stay away, Mr. Coleman. Rosemary isn't in any danger at the moment."

"I can help you."

"No. There would be twice as much danger with you there and I don't want to chance it."

"Then please, call me as soon as possible. As soon as you know anything."

"I will," Annie promised.

CHAPTER 59

Saturday, September 3rd, 5:57 p.m.

ELI MARTIN STOOD twenty feet away from where Jake and Rosemary lay on the ground. Jake had turned his head to the side, watching him. While Martin had made a phone call, Jake struggled against his bonds. It was no use. They wouldn't budge.

Martin put the phone away and came over to them. "On your feet," he said, brandishing his pistol. "We're going inside the cabin."

Jake managed to get to a sitting position. It wasn't an easy task to get to his feet with his hands tied behind his back but Martin grabbed him by the arm and Jake finally stood upright. His bound feet only allowed him to move forward a few inches at a time.

Martin helped Rosemary to her feet and stepped back. "Let's go. We have a date with a pretty lady."

He had called Annie. Jake was sure of it. What was Martin up to?

Jake twisted his head around and glared at his abductor. "You'll never get away with this. Annie's too smart for you."

Martin laughed. "Not this time, she's not."

"If you harm me, my husband will hunt you down," Rosemary said.

Martin laughed again and pointed to the cabin. "Go."

It took a few minutes to get to the cabin door. Martin swung it open and prodded them inside. He pointed to a chair by a massive wooden table and said to Jake, "Over there and sit down."

Jake did as he was told while Martin shoved Rosemary toward another chair. He pushed her and she fell backwards, landing in a sitting position. She scowled up at him, fire in her eyes. "I might just kill you myself," she said.

"Not if I get to him first," Jake said.

Martin returned to Jake and adjusted his bonds, tied him snugly to the chair, and wrapped the end around the table leg, making a secure knot. He tied Rosemary the same way and then stood back and observed his handiwork. "That should hold."

He sat in another chair and leaned forward, a wide smile on his face. "Jake, my friend, you'll be happy to hear your lovely wife has offered to give herself up in exchange for you." He sighed and sat back. "It must be such a wonderful thing to experience such undying love."

"Is that what your problem is?" Jake asked. "You feel so unloved? Is that why you have the desire to kill the way you do?"

"Oh, no. It goes much deeper than that. Much deeper."

Rosemary had relaxed and she spoke in a calm voice. "If you let me go, let us go, I'm sure my husband will pay any ransom you want."

Martin chuckled. "And then you'll go straight to the police. I don't think that's a viable option." He shook his head. "No, I'm afraid I won't be in the position to let anyone go."

"What about Mouse?" Jake asked.

"I'll take care of Mouse soon enough and that'll just about wrap everything up. And did I mention dear Mrs. Lincoln? Of course, she'll have to be dealt with as well." He looked at his watch. "I'm expecting her to be in attendance before long."

"Annie'll call the police and they'll come down on this place like a swarm," Jake said. "You'll see."

"Oh no, I'm sure she won't." Martin stood, gave a quick bow and continued, "And now, if you'll excuse me, I have to get ready for our company." He spun around and headed for the door. "Don't worry, I'll be back," he called over his shoulder and then left the cabin, pulling the door shut behind him.

Jake struggled against his bonds, flexing his powerful muscles, but the sturdy cord wouldn't give. He had little room to move and the nylon rope bit into his wrists. He tugged at the table but it was too heavy. He glanced down. The table legs were bolted to the floor, secured firmly, impossible to move.

He glanced at Rosemary and again admired her spunk. She was more angry than afraid, but now with the both of them helpless, they could only depend on Annie, but she was walking into a trap.

For the first time, Jake felt desperation and total hopelessness.

CHAPTER 60

Saturday, September 3rd, 5:57 p.m.

THE LAST THING ANNIE wanted to do—could afford to do—was underestimate the cunning of Eli Martin. He would know Annie wouldn't merely walk in there and give herself up without a fight. Rather, he would calculate her intentions and devise his plans accordingly.

He might be a ruthless killer, but he wasn't stupid.

But then, neither was Annie.

From the printed map using satellite view, she knew the precise layout of the land surrounding the cabin, all the roads leading in and out of the area, and the exact approach she would take.

The cabin was set back from the road about a quarter mile, which meant, by her best estimate, it was three-quarters of a mile from a parallel road. The trek from that road to the cabin would be mostly through bush and overgrown terrain. If she hurried, the hike would take her thirty minutes, bringing her to her destination before Martin's deadline.

But she had to get moving if her plan was to have any chance of success.

She took a quick stock of what she needed, decided she had everything necessary and raced out the door. The drive to

Highway 23 took her almost fifteen minutes. Still enough time.

She parked on the shoulder of the road and waited until a tractor-trailer zipped by before stepping out. She put her cell phone on vibrate, tucked it into her side pocket, then consulted the map briefly and headed up the embankment, climbing over a wire fence. The first leg of her journey was across an open field, overgrown with weeds, but no other obstacles other than an occasional knoll and dip in the terrain.

She estimated she was halfway to her destination as she entered a thick forest. She looked at her watch. A half mile to go and still plenty of time.

She dodged fallen trees and low-hanging branches as she weaved her way and before long stumbled across a footpath. It was overgrown and rarely used, but a footpath, no doubt. She assumed it would lead her close to the area occupied by the cabin.

She stayed on the path until she sensed she was getting close to her goal. Topping a small knoll, she could finally make out the roof of the building through the foliage. She crouched down and listened. The breeze whistled through the treetops, high above. The occasional flutter of wings, distant sounds of animals at hunt or at play.

Martin would be watching for her, no doubt. She was unsure of where he would be stationed but she knew one thing for sure: he wouldn't be inside the cabin waiting. It was more likely he would be watching for her to drive up and would be somewhere between the cabin and the road he expected her to take.

She stood and pulled the binoculars from her bag and carefully scanned the area in front of her and at both sides.

Nothing moved and no one was around. She advanced a few more feet, went down the knoll, and repeated the process. Again and again. She wasn't taking any chances.

The trees ended and she crouched down beside a bush, the cabin in full view now as she swept the entire area again with the binoculars.

All clear. She glanced at her watch, stepped boldly into the clearing, then stopped and listened. Nothing.

The back of the cabin facing her had no windows. She wanted to see inside. There must be a window somewhere. She dipped back into the trees and skirted around, taking time to stop and listen, until she could see the side of the cabin. There was a window, just about eye level.

She used the binoculars again and that's when she saw him through the dusty window. Jake, tied to a chair. Rosemary must be there too, but Annie couldn't see her.

But where was Martin?

She crawled to the edge of the tree line and scanned the area again, taking a little more time, just in case. Nothing. She dashed to the window and peered inside. She saw Jake through the grimy pane, he and Rosemary tied to chairs.

She was lucky; the window wasn't locked. It made a low squeal as she raised it slightly. She raised it more and the screech of wood on wood sounded like thunder. She glanced around before looking inside.

"Annie." It was Jake. His face showed a mixture of apprehension and pleasure. He recovered his surprise and added, "He's not here."

Just what she needed to hear.

The window gave a final shriek as she lifted it all the way. She crawled inside and fell into a heap on the floor. Safe. For now.

She looked up. Jake was grinning, ear to ear. Rosemary's mouth had dropped open, her eyes wide.

"I knew you'd come," Jake said.

"I had no choice," she said as she dashed over to Jake, digging the kitchen knife from her bag.

"Martin is out there somewhere," Jake said. "He's watching for you. How'd you get past him?"

"I took another route." Annie pointed toward the back of the room. "Through the forest." She sawed at the ropes binding Jake's hands and feet, got them free, and then turned to Rosemary and cut her bonds.

Rosemary rubbed her wrists to restore the circulation. "Annie," she said. "He'll be back soon. We'd better hurry."

Annie looked at her watch. Her deadline had passed and in a few minutes she would know if her daring plan would work or fail.

Her cell phone vibrated. She pulled it from her pocket and looked at the display. Unknown number.

"Where are you, Annie?"

Annie took a deep breath. "I ... I've decided I can't meet you," she said. "I thought I could do it, but ..." Her voice trailed off.

"You know what that means, don't you?"

"Please ... don't hurt them." Annie was pleading.

"You've left me no choice."

The line went dead.

Annie turned to Jake. "Stay in the chair," she said. "Put your hands behind your back as if you're still tied. We'll wait for Martin and in the meantime, I'll call the police."

Too late.

The door rattled as Jake and Rosemary resumed their positions. Annie dove to the side, ducked behind a battered sofa, and slipped the pistol from its holster. She flicked off the safety of the already loaded weapon, gripped it with both hands, then held her breath and waited.

The door banged open.

Martin was back. "It seems like your beloved wife had a change of heart," the killer said.

Annie could tell by his voice Martin's back was to her. She rose up slowly. Martin had the pistol in one hand, pointed at Jake. She caught Jake's eye and they exchanged a knowing look. A plan.

With a blur, Jake's right hand came up and caught Martin by surprise. The huge fist pounded Martin's gun hand and the pistol spun through the air, hit the floor, and slid under the table.

At the same time, Annie stepped out to the side, in full view of Martin, her weapon raised and pointed at his head. "Don't move."

Martin turned slowly to face her. "I should've known you'd come," he said, his eyes narrowed.

Annie stepped back to a safer distance, her weapon never wavering. "I wouldn't miss it for the world," she said.

CHAPTER 61

Saturday, September 3rd, 6:36 p.m.

JAKE LET OUT HIS breath in relief. Annie's plan had worked to perfection, they'd caught the kidnapper, and Rosemary Coleman was safe. He turned to Eli Martin and pointed toward the couch. "Sit down."

Martin glared at Jake, then at Annie, and finally at the weapon she held. He gave her a black look and then turned slowly and sat where Jake had indicated.

Rosemary had risen from her chair. She took one step toward Martin and stopped, her hands on her hips. "Why'd you try to kill me?" she demanded.

Martin scowled and leaned forward in his seat, murder in his eyes.

Jake took a step toward Martin. "Sit back."

Martin sat back reluctantly and continued to glare at Rosemary. Jake sat on the other end of the couch to keep an eye on him.

The door rattled. It opened a few inches and the anxious face of Walter Coleman appeared. He looked at Rosemary and a relieved look crossed his face. The door opened and then slammed shut behind Coleman as he stepped into the room. He glanced at Annie, then at the weapon she held, and then he approached his wife.

"Are you okay?" he asked as he put an arm around her shoulder.

Rosemary smiled up at him. "I'm fine now."

Coleman turned to Annie. "I had to come."

"How did you find the place?" Annie asked.

Coleman shrugged. "You told me the general location, and then when I saw Jake's car parked on the road, I knew this was it."

"We'd better call the police now," Jake said.

Annie nodded and reached for her cell. She juggled the phone in one hand, the gun in the other, struggling to dial.

Coleman stepped over to Annie. "Let me hold the gun," he said, holding out his hand.

Annie handed the weapon to Coleman, who took it and stepped back a few steps, raised the weapon, and pointed it.

Straight at Annie's head.

"Drop the phone," Coleman said.

Annie's mouth fell open. Jake sat forward, Rosemary gasped, and Eli Martin chuckled.

Coleman waved the gun at Jake. "Stay there."

Annie took a couple of steps back and glared across the room at Coleman.

"Walter, what are you doing?" Rosemary asked, about to approach her husband. She stopped short as the weapon turned her way.

Eli Martin rose to his feet and approached Coleman. His grin dissolved into laughter and filled the room, then disappeared as suddenly as it had started. "This was too easy," he said as he took the pistol from his partner and turned to face his captives.

Jake was stunned. Coleman and Martin in league together? The truth dawned on him.

"And now look at what we have here," Martin said. "The last three witnesses."

Rosemary's hands were on her hips, her brow furrowed in confusion, and she spoke in an almost pleading voice. "Walter. Why?"

Her husband didn't answer.

Martin laughed again and spoke up, "Just our little way of dissolving our marriages."

Annie was furious. "And so you killed your wife and tried to kill Rosemary as well. But why'd you kill Linda Gould?"

Martin shrugged. "To throw suspicion away from ourselves." He laughed and slapped Coleman on the back with his free hand. "And everything went off smoothly. He kidnapped my wife, and I kidnapped his. Thankfully, mine is no longer with us and soon, Walter's dear wife will join her."

Jake spoke up, "Why'd you want me to deliver the ransom money for you?"

"Because we knew you'd do exactly what we told you to. You had no choice." Martin chuckled. "And we wanted to prove we're miles smarter than you and your wife put together." He paused, a grin twisting his mouth. "And of course, your word is beyond reproach. The perfect witness and the perfect patsy."

"But that's changed now," Coleman added. "But our plan will still come out perfectly." He turned to his wife. "Darling, do you remember that time you dinged up your little Honda? Well, I was fortunate enough to take it to Martin Auto to have it repaired. That's where I ran into Eli." He grinned. "We shared a few drinks on many occasions. One thing led to another and eventually, we found out we were in the same boat and soon came up with a foolproof plan."

Jake leaned forward and took Annie's hand, afraid she might make a harsh move. Though he fought against his own anger, he knew they had to stay calm.

Annie glanced at Jake, took a deep breath, and turned back to Coleman. "So your real intent was to kill your own wives."

"And it worked, too," Coleman said. "Nobody suspected a thing. Everyone was looking for a single killer, a kidnapper."

"And now all we have to do is finish the job," Martin added and sighed. "And I was having so much fun. I was really beginning to enjoy this and had plans to carry our little game on much, much longer." He sighed again. "But alas, it must end here. Unfortunately, there'll be some collateral damage, but it can't be helped."

Jake turned as a low growl came from Rosemary. She charged at Martin but Coleman stepped forward and swung his fist, dealing his wife a sharp blow to the side of her head. Rosemary staggered and lost her balance, falling heavily against the solid table leg. She groaned, turned over, and lay still, her back toward them.

Martin turned to face the Lincolns and waved the gun at Jake. "Stand up."

Jake stood reluctantly and put his arm around his wife.

Martin pointed the gun at Annie. "And now, we'll start with you."

"No," Jake roared as he stepped between his wife and the gunman.

The weapon exploded and the shot caught Jake full in the chest. He went down. Annie screamed and dropped to her knees beside him.

"Put the gun down."

They spun their heads toward Rosemary Coleman. She

gripped Martin's pistol, retrieved from under the table. She held her finger firmly on the trigger, the gun unwavering in her fist.

Martin's expression froze a moment before turning the weapon toward Rosemary. His finger tightened.

A shot exploded in the small room and Eli Martin's eyes widened. He staggered backwards, blood spurting from the hole in his chest, his weapon slipping from his fingers as he crumpled to the floor.

Jake groaned and tried to sit up. The vest had saved his life, but he felt like he'd been hit with a sledgehammer.

Walter Coleman froze a moment, staring at his partner, dying on the floor. He spun around and stopped with his hand on the doorknob as a second shot buried itself into the door near his head. He turned back, his arms out to the side. "You won't shoot me, Rosemary," he said.

There was fire in her eyes, a burning anger. "If you move, I will," she said and Jake knew she meant it.

EPILOGUE

Saturday, September 3rd, 7:32 p.m.

THE OFFICER SNAPPED the cuffs on Walter Coleman's wrists and tightened them. Rosemary paid no mind as they led her husband out to the waiting cruiser. For the first time, she broke down, her head bowed, the tears flowing as Annie sat beside her, an arm around her shoulder.

The body of Eli Martin still lay on the floor, the pooled blood beginning to turn a darker hue as it soaked into the wooden floor of the cabin.

Hank had arrived and was talking with Jake across the room. The ME was on her way and soon the area would be taped off. There would be a lot of questions they all had to answer, but Annie was certain Martin's death would be a clear case of self-defense.

Rosemary looked up as Hank approached. She dabbed at her eyes, cleared her throat, and smiled through her tears.

"We'd better go outside," Hank said. "This place will soon be overrun."

Annie helped Rosemary up and they skirted around the body and followed Hank and Jake outside. The forensics van rattled up the lane and investigators would soon start the necessary formality of gathering evidence and taking photos.

Annie turned to Hank. "We didn't have a chance to call you earlier. You can stop looking for Mouse. I have him locked up in the basement of Martin's shop."

Hank grinned. "You kidnapped him?"

Annie managed a faint smile. "Sort of."

"And you had illegal possession of a firearm?" Hank continued.

"Yup."

The detective laughed. "Well, I guess we won't be pressing charges."

"You'd better not," Jake put in. "I don't think we're going to get paid for this job. One client is dead and the other one is going to prison."

"Rosemary, did you have any idea this was possible?" Annie asked.

Rosemary shook her head. "It had been a little rough between Walter and me lately, but I thought we'd patched it up and I had no idea he would try to …" Her voice trailed off and she took a deep breath.

Annie put her arm around the shaken woman. "We'll help you through this. If there's anything you need, just ask."

Rosemary nodded as a small sob escaped her lips. "Thanks," she whispered.

Jake turned to Hank. "What happened to the officer at the Coleman house?"

"After a while he went to see where Rosemary was and when he couldn't find her, he called it in. Officers have been patrolling the neighborhood streets ever since, looking for her." Hank turned to Rosemary. "I'm glad you're safe."

Rosemary didn't seem to hear as she watched the police

cruiser carry her husband away. Annie felt deeply for her, but she knew Rosemary would find the strength to move on.

"Let me get you out of here, Rosemary," Hank said, offering his arm.

Rosemary smiled weakly and let Hank lead her away.

Jake put his arm around Annie and drew her close. They stood quietly and watched them go.

It had been a harrowing week for all of them and Annie was glad it was over. Maybe now they could get some long-overdue rest.

###

Made in the USA
San Bernardino, CA
19 September 2016